THE JUDAS SAINTS

A Novel of Political Intrigue

Keith M. Spence

Midnight Cipher Publications

Chapter 1

Magdalena Rodriguez had seen dead bodies before. Hundreds of them. Twenty-four years in Masaya, watching innocent people slaughtered in the streets. Men, women, children.

But nothing like the man in the bathtub of Room 157.

Dead. She knew death when she saw it. She remembered his face from two days ago during check-in. Handsome. Kind smile. Yesterday morning he left five dollars on the television. American money, the paper kind. No coins.

Today, no money.

Now she understood.

At least he was whole. One piece. Her father and brother had not been so lucky.

Blood covered everything. Floor, walls, the white sink, the toilet. The bathtub had spilled over. Water up to her ankles, soaking through her *zapatos*. Warm. Sticky. A wine bottle sat on the toilet tank, half empty. Two towels on the floor, stained dark.

The police would ask questions.

Magdalena had no answers to give.

The gruesome sight meant only one thing: more work. Extra cleaning after the police finished. Her *jefe* was too cheap to pay for special cleaners. But she could work the extra hours. She needed the money. Her mother was not getting younger, and the airplane from Managua cost more than two months of rent.

Without the blood, maybe she would think he died peaceful. His yellow hair floated in the red water. His chest rose above the surface, not moving. His face looked soft. Like a baby angel in the church paintings.

He was naked below the waist. White kneecaps sticking out of the water.

In Nicaragua, she had seen worse. Much worse. Her father and twelve-year-old brother, taken by the Dirección de Auxilio Judicial. Interrogated as *subversivos*. Dumped in the *callejón* two days later. *Quemados. Decapitados. Castrados*. Punishment for going to a rally. Just a rally for the opposition.

Sometimes, bodies piled in the streets. Left for the black *zopilotes*. Warnings to anyone who dared speak against the government. Families came to collect what remained. The mutilated bodies lay for days, sometimes weeks. Some families could not identify their own dead. Some took any body, just to have something to bury.

The smell had been beyond imagination.

Worse than the metal smell in this bathroom. Either the body was fresh, or the bloody water hid the odor. Either way, no hurry. The man was dead. Nothing to do for him now.

She finished cleaning what she could, then left the bathroom. Her *zapatos* left red footprints on the carpet.

Outside, July wind moved her hair. Hot, but clean. She thought of her father and brother before walking to find Belinda Chatwyn, the manager for weekends.

This was America. Belinda would know what to do.

***

"She the one who found the stiff?"

The voice came from the door. Magdalena looked up.

A large man filled the doorway. Very large. The uniform was brown, like chocolate, with a star on the chest. Sheriff, Belinda had said. Like the police in Nicaragua, but different. More power here.

The man was *gordo*. Very fat. The uniform looked tight, like it wanted to split open. His face was red and wet with sweat, even with the cold air blowing from the machine on the wall. A scar covered half his face, from the hair down to the jaw.

He pointed at her with a thick finger.

"Sheriff Helm, please." Belinda stepped between them. "She's new here. Cut her some slack."

"Ah. No green card." The man's eyes moved down Magdalena's body, slow, then back up. Not hiding it. He shook his head. "You know I'm always gentle with the pretty ones."

Magdalena sat still in the wooden chair. When the first police came, she put herself here, between the cold-air machine and the bed. She stayed while they looked through the dead man's things, spreading them on the floor and bed.

Forty minutes ago. This sheriff took his time coming.

Another officer tried to talk to her, but the sheriff waved him away. Said he would do it himself.

Now Magdalena understood why.

The bed made noise when the sheriff sat down beside her chair. Metal springs crying. Close. Too close. His knee almost touched hers.

"How'd I miss a looker like you?"

Magdalena kept her hands in her lap. Belinda had warned her about this man. But the words were not enough. This man reminded her of the officers in Masaya. The ones who came to take people away. The ones who smiled while they hurt you.

"I only work here one month."

"Maybe you can get to know me." The sheriff smiled. Yellow teeth, like old corn. "I'll give you English lessons."

He put his tongue out of his mouth.

"Or maybe you're better at French."

The scar pulled his face when he smiled. Magdalena recognized scars like that. From *El Chipote*, the torture place. Burns. Cuts.

But this man had not been tortured. This man was the torturer.

"I have *novio* in Nicaragua," Magdalena said. She kept her voice empty. "He come to America soon. We get married."

The smile disappeared. The sheriff's face became dark, red climbing up his neck like fire.

"Yeah, well, only if I don't ship you out first." He moved closer. Magdalena smelled *cebollas* on his breath. Old coffee. "That's what the government's 287(g) program is all about. People like you."

He pulled a small notebook from his shirt. A pen. Opened to an empty page.

"So what do you know about the dead guy?"

"Nothing." Magdalena looked at him. Straight. Like she had looked at the police in Masaya. "I come to clean room. I knock but nobody answer. I go in, he's in bathtub. Blood everywhere."

"Yeah, yeah." The sheriff moved his hand like he was brushing away a fly. "So you don't know anything."

Not a question.

"The man's name was Davy Clough."

Belinda's voice. Magdalena turned. The manager stood near the dresser, holding a paper. She looked *cansada*. Tired. Worn.

"He checked in two days ago. Supposed to check out tomorrow morning." Belinda read from the paper. "Says here he's from Arlington, Virginia. Drives a red Lincoln Navigator."

"Navigator?" The young officer looked up. Short, thin, with hair falling in his face. "Big city rich boy. Long way from home."

"Probably a drug dealer." The older officer stood near the bath-room door. Tall, with less hair. "Selling that newfangled smurf dope. Got what he deserved."

"You saying he deserved to kill himself, Alfred?"

The older officer stood straight. "This ain't no suicide, Sheriff. All that blood? Looks like somebody tried to clean it up with those towels. I do believe someone wasted Mr. Davy Clough."

"Maybe he was a neat freak."

The sheriff's laugh was wrong. High and sharp. Like a pig being killed. The older officer's face turned red, but he said nothing. Just went back to searching.

Magdalena understood. She had seen this before. Men who knew better than to argue with power.

"Sorry, Alfred, but we ain't had a murder in Kendall County in over a year." The sheriff pushed himself off the bed. The springs made noise again, relieved. "Ain't about to have one now. Did you see the slice marks on his wrists? No drug dealers killed Davy Clough. Neither did a jealous lover or some foreign government."

He walked to the bathroom. Looked inside.

"I do believe Mr. Davy Clough done killed himself."

The older officer didn't argue. Just kept looking through the dead man's clothes. His face said everything. The same face Magdalena had seen in Masaya. The face of someone who knows the truth doesn't matter.

The sheriff turned back to her.

"You can go. But don't leave town. I might have more questions."

Magdalena stood. Her legs were stiff.

"I live here. I work here. Where I go?"

The sheriff smiled again. Those yellow teeth.

"That's what I like to hear."

Magdalena walked past him, past Belinda, past the two officers. She did not look at the bathroom door. She did not want to see the blood again.

Outside, the hot air felt clean. She stood on the concrete, letting the wind dry the sweat on her face.

Behind her, through the open door, voices.

"Think I found the mother lode! Hey, Sheriff, come look at this."

The young officer.

Then the sheriff: "Billy, let me see that."

Silence.

Then the sheriff reading, slow: "TO ALL THOSE I LOVE. PLEASE FORGIVE ME. I AM WITH GOD NOW AND ALL IS WELL."

"Suicide note."

Magdalena closed her eyes. She did not need to see to know what would happen. The sheriff would take the note. Put it in his pocket. Say it was evidence. The investigation would end before it started.

Just like in Nicaragua.

The dead man had left five dollars yesterday morning. He smiled at her, said *gracias* in bad Spanish.

Now he was dead, and these men decided it did not matter.

Magdalena opened her eyes and walked toward the front desk. She had rooms to clean. Work to finish. A mother to bring from Nicaragua.

The dead could not help her with any of those things.

***

Dr. Samantha Burton had seen plenty of blood in four years as a medical examiner.

Nothing like this.

A private practice GP and the county's appointed ME since old Dr. Bailey stepped in front of a cement mixer. She dealt with death daily. Typically, older adults in the final stages of cancer or Alzheimer's.

Three murders during her tenure as ME. All gunshot victims, domestic disturbances. The worst had been Willis Drake, shot five times in the groin by his estranged wife Dorothy. Clear overkill, but Willis had been caught molesting Dorothy's nine-year-old daughter.

Who could blame her?

Samantha had no reason to suspect murder in Davy Clough's case. Still, the drained tub made her frown. The EMTs had let the water out, obliterating whatever trace evidence might have floated there. Beneath the body she found a Michelob bottle, a paper coaster, and most telling, a single-edged razor blade. The type used to scrape windows.

The first responders had discovered two plastic garbage bags in the bloody water, shoelaces wrapped around Clough's neck. Samantha suspected he'd planned to asphyxiate himself by pulling the bags over his head. At some point, he'd changed his mind. Opted to slit his wrists instead.

The wrist wounds didn't support murder. Eight distinct cuts on the right wrist, four on the left. Deep, but self-inflicted. She couldn't explain the blood spatter throughout the bathroom. Perhaps Clough had panicked during the act. Common when people attempt to slash their wrists, overwhelmed by pain and blood loss.

Deputy Rhodes might hope for a murder investigation to liven his routine, but Samantha found no scientific reason to indulge him.

"So what do you think, Sammy?" Sheriff Helm slapped her back. "We got a serial killer on the loose like Alfred says?"

She saw him glaring through the bathroom door at Rhodes.

"Keep your hands to yourself." Samantha didn't look up. "I'll let you know when I've finished."

Unlike most people in Kendall County, Samantha didn't fear the sheriff. Her husband Ken chaired the County Board of Commissioners. One of the wealthiest men in the state, software fortune, considerable political power.

Ken believed in Sheriff Helm. Crude methods aside, Helm had reduced the county's violent crime rate to near zero. He also protected Burton's business interests. Both the legal ones and the others.

Every four years, Ken used his wealth to keep Helm in office.

Samantha knew about the arrangement. Not every detail, but enough. Their relationship didn't concern her. Her silence made her complicit, but she'd made peace with that.

She'd stopped loving Ken for anything beyond his money years ago.

"Think I found the mother lode!" A voice from the outer room. "Hey, Sheriff, come look at this."

The younger deputy, Billy, appeared in the doorway. He held a crumpled piece of paper.

"Billy, let me see that." Helm snatched the paper. Slowly, he read aloud the words written in large block letters.

TO ALL THOSE I LOVE. PLEASE FORGIVE ME. I AM WITH GOD NOW AND ALL IS WELL.

"Suicide note."

Billy offered an evidence bag. Helm shook his head and slid the note into his shirt pocket.

Tampering with evidence. As usual.

"So now what do you think, Sammy?"

Samantha rubbed her chin. The note, the razor blade, the pattern of wounds. All pointed to the same conclusion.

"The medical examiner of Kendall County officially declares the cause of death as blood loss due to multiple self-inflicted injuries. Call Whitmore's Mortuary. Have them retrieve the deceased. I'll locate the next of kin in the morning."

Chapter 2

Mac Whitmore couldn't believe he'd been called in to work at 6:00 p.m. on a Friday. This was supposed to be his first weekend off in nearly two months, and the medical examiner had the audacity to request that he pick up a body at the Kendall County Country Inn on State Road 35.

He should have told the ME to go to hell and left the body at the motel to rot, but Samantha and Ken Burton steered considerable business toward Whitmore's Mortuary. He couldn't afford to offend his biggest clients. Besides, The Old Man would have flayed him alive for turning away money.

Whitmore couldn't help but think of The Old Man as he applied moisturizing cream to the naked cadaver lying on the stainless-steel embalming table in the preparation room. He'd already washed the body, disinfected the nasal and oral cavities with germicide, and wired the jaw shut.

Rigor mortis was so severe that he had to cut several tendons to return the arms to their natural position. Then, he injected the formaldehyde-based embalming fluid into the right common carotid artery while blood drained from an incision in the right jugular vein. There couldn't have been much blood left, considering the amount of spatter at the scene.

If only this were The Old Man on the slab instead. Whitmore would have gladly surrendered his weekend then. But it wasn't, and Whitmore wondered if it ever would be. He'd been waiting five years for The Old Man to die, and still the decrepit bastard kept going strong. Would the family business ever become his?

Five long years since doctors had given The Old Man six months to live. If anything, his health had improved since the diagnosis; his body was stronger, and his mind sharper. Wasn't dementia supposed to cause brain cell degeneration and not a reformation? Whitmore didn't understand it. The Old Man was a phoenix who had somehow risen from the ashes of terminal illness.

Whitmore tried to envision The Old Man's worn face and body on the table, but all he saw were the handsome, lifeless features of twenty-nine-year-old Davy Clough, a Caucasian male from Arlington, Virginia. God, what was it going to take for The Old Man to waste away? Why couldn't he possess Davy Clough's courage, slash his wrists, and be done with it? Was Whitmore going to have to kill The Old Man himself to claim what was rightfully his?

Whitmore had poured his heart and soul into the business. For what reward? He'd earned his mortuary science degree and joined the firm as chief embalmer at age twenty-four. The Old Man was sixty-three at the time and had promised Whitmore a piece of the business within two years and full control within five. Ten years later, Whitmore was still waiting.

Not only was The Old Man still the sole proprietor, but he hadn't even offered Whitmore the title of Funeral Director. A perfunctory carrot to be sure, but one that would have given Whitmore the prestige among his peers he so craved. The Old Man remained the face of the business, while Whitmore was the dutiful worker. A pathetic arrangement, to be sure.

It was also the last arrangement he'd allow The Old Man to dictate. Whitmore's weekend off had been promised, and he'd be damned if he was going to capitulate this time. He'd already packed his clothes and filled the Porsche's tank. Bridgette was waiting for him at the Atlantic Beach cottage, her naked body sparkling on the bedsheets like a sapphire.

She did things for free that most men had to pay for in darkened back alleys and seedy hotels. She especially liked to role-play, pretending to be dead while Whitmore "examined" her magnificent body. He decided that no amount of money or complaints from The Old Man would cause him to miss the exhilaration Bridgette so eagerly offered.

The sooner he finished the embalming, the sooner the fun could begin. With renewed motivation, he worked quickly, straightening the L-shaped cannula and pulling it away from the electric aspirator. He positioned himself behind Davy Clough's face, which Whitmore had earlier restored to a peaceful expression.

With gloved hands, he lifted the sharp metal trocar and punctured the abdomen two inches above the navel. He listened for the telltale sound, maneuvered the instrument into the stomach and intestines, and nodded with satisfaction as the machine began removing bodily fluids.

Embalming wasn't required by North Carolina law. However, any corpse transported across state lines had to be embalmed first to prevent decomposition. Clough lived in Virginia, which meant his remains would certainly be shipped home for burial. By the time Dr. Burton located the next of kin and received embalming authorization, Whitmore planned to be neck-deep in Bridgette's carnal juices.

Under no circumstances did he intend to cut short his well-deserved break, returning Saturday or early Sunday merely to embalm a body he knew required embalming anyway.

Although embalming a body in North Carolina without family consent was illegal, Whitmore wasn't worried about consequences. The funeral director would receive the blame. For once, The Old Man could take the heat. Whitmore had his own heat to generate with Bridgette, as soon as the aspirator finished sucking out Davy Clough's guts.

***

Samantha Burton pulled up the contact information on her laptop. At 7:22 a.m. on a Saturday, it was still too early for her liking, but she had a job to do, and she took her work seriously. According to the report she'd received, the sheriff's department had spent the previous evening searching for Davy Clough's family. He had left the emergency contact field blank on his registration form, and their initial database searches had come up empty.

The report detailed the search results: no social media presence on Facebook, Instagram, TikTok, or LinkedIn. No address listings on standard people-search engines. Even the county's LexisNexis subscription had returned nothing initially for any David or Davy Clough from Arlington, Virginia.

She had been informed that Deputy Rhodes had finally suggested checking the hotel's Wi-Fi logs, which revealed that Clough had accessed several news websites and journalism databases. For once, the deputy's excessive enthusiasm seemed to have paid off. A deeper investigation uncovered that David Edward Clough worked as an investigative reporter for *The Capital Review*, a magazine specializing in stories about political corruption and national defense.

Samantha believed this explained Clough's scrubbed online presence. Reporters covering sensitive topics often minimized their digital footprints to protect their sources and avoid retaliation from the subjects they investigated. Some even went undercover for months.

Notifying the next of kin was never easy. Samantha was still finding the right words when a soft, sophisticated female voice answered the phone.

She cleared her throat and said, "I'm trying to reach a Cynthia Clough or someone related to David Edward Clough of Arlington, Virginia."

After a long pause, the soft voice asked, "Who's calling?"

"Are you Mrs. Clough?"

"What's happened to my son?" The voice remained cool and controlled, devoid of emotion.

The detached tone bewildered Samantha. "Mrs. Clough, I regret to inform you that your son died yesterday in his hotel room. The preliminary cause of death appears to be suicide."

"Did you find his notebook? His personal papers?"

"Excuse me?"

"I asked whether you found his notes."

Samantha frowned, struggling to understand the woman's priorities. Was this shock? Cynthia Clough's way of processing her son's death? She decided to proceed cautiously. "Mrs. Clough, perhaps you didn't understand."

"I understood perfectly. My son is dead, and you think he killed himself, which is utterly ridiculous. Do you know what he did for a living?"

"Yes, I believe he was a journalist."

"Did you know my son had been receiving death threats for the past two weeks? The last one said he would be 'cut into little pieces and fed to the sharks'?"

Samantha didn't know how to respond. Was this woman telling the truth, or were these the desperate ravings of a grieving mother in denial?

"Was he, Dr. Burton?" Cynthia Clough asked. "Cut into little pieces and fed to the sharks?"

Samantha couldn't believe what she was hearing. "No, ma'am. He died from blood loss due to cuts to his wrists."

She thought she heard the woman chuckle. A chuckle. At the news of her son's death.

"You know, Dr. Burton, I've tried for years to get Davy to see a doctor for regular checkups, but he never would. Do you know why?"

"No, ma'am." Samantha found it increasingly difficult to maintain her professionalism. She was beginning to suspect that Cynthia Clough's mind had snapped, and she didn't know whether to feel compassion or pity.

"My son wouldn't see doctors because he had a phobia of needles and became violently ill at the sight of blood. Please tell me, Dr. Burton, how could someone like that find the courage to slash his own wrists?"

Samantha's exasperation reached its limit. The woman was clearly in denial, grasping at any theory that avoided accepting her son's suicide. "Perhaps it would be better if I connected you with local law enforcement. You can discuss your concerns with them."

"Oh, I'll be contacting law enforcement, all right. The state police, the FBI, and anyone else who can help prove that my son was murdered and that Kendall County officials are incompetent."

The line went dead. Samantha stared at the phone, shaking her head. Grief manifested in strange ways, but Cynthia Clough's reaction was one of the most disturbing she had encountered. The woman hadn't shed a tear, hadn't asked about her son's final moments, and hadn't even inquired about claiming his body. Just accusations and conspiracy theories.

Samantha closed her laptop and rubbed her temples. She needed to document this conversation carefully. When Cynthia Clough began making wild accusations to state and federal authorities, the county would need a record of her unstable mental state.

Still, one detail nagged at her: the blood phobia. If true, it would make self-inflicted wrist wounds unusual, though not impossible. People in extreme emotional distress could overcome their deepest fears. She had seen it before.

But she hadn't seen any evidence of death threats in Clough's belongings. Sheriff Helm would have mentioned them. Unless he had pocketed them along with the suicide note.

Samantha pushed the thought aside. She had a death certificate to complete and a mortuary to notify. Mac Whitmore would be irritated about working on a Saturday, but that was his problem. Her job was done. Davy Clough's death was officially a suicide, and no amount of maternal denial would change that.

***

"The woman's a crackpot," Samantha said. "She implied we were incompetent and said she was going to involve the SBI, the FBI, heck, maybe even the CIA for all I know. I'd watch my back if I were you."

She loathed the inside of Sheriff Helm's office. The photograph of the sheriff surrounded by the local Hooters girls, the mounted six-point buck's head prominently displayed above his desk. Even worse were the smells: musty cigar smoke, half-eaten Mexican food, stale farts. The morgue was a more pleasant environment.

"Well, if she thinks she's going to come down here and start some crap, she's got another thing coming," Helm said, chomping into an enchilada.

"Take it easy. She may be in denial, but she's still a bereaved mother." Samantha couldn't imagine Cynthia Clough's pain. She and Ken had two sons: a sophomore at East Carolina University and a junior at Kendall County High School. Losing one so tragically would have sent her spiraling into unimaginable despair.

"I don't care who or what she is." Helm leaned back in his chair and took another bite. Green mole sauce spilled out, staining the front of his uniform. "She ain't gonna tell me how to run my investigation."

"What investigation? I ruled the death a suicide."

He lit a cigar, and Samantha knew he had done it simply to provoke her. Her brother had died three years ago from lung cancer, and everyone in town knew how much she detested smoking.

"Then I got nothing to worry about." He puffed on the cigar, and Samantha tried not to inhale the thick smoke. "Sounds like you're the one who better watch her back."

She turned her face away from the acrid fumes. "I can tell you right now that Cynthia Clough will question every aspect of the investigation. She has money and connections. No one will be immune to scrutiny or criticism, including you."

"I got nothing to hide." The sheriff was smiling, but Samantha thought she detected concern underneath. Helm may have had nothing to hide in this case, but he had plenty of other skeletons in the closet should someone with Cynthia Clough's resources start digging.

"You like being sheriff, don't you?" Samantha pointed a finger at Helm's chest. "You have just as much to hide as the rest of us, so I suggest you drop the macho man routine and get with the program."

"Hey, there ain't no damned woman gonna come in here and threaten me! I ain't your husband. You don't get to tell me when to get on my knees and beg!" His face reddened, but then he seemed to deflate, apparently remembering he wouldn't be sheriff without Ken and Samantha Burton's help. He took a deep breath and mumbled, "So what are we gonna do?"

"We're going to cooperate fully with Mrs. Clough and wait for the storm to blow over. We have the truth on our side."

Helm nodded and gobbled down the last of the enchilada.

"And we're going to make sure Mrs. Clough gets her son's note-book back," Samantha said.

"His what?"

"His notebook, notes, personal papers. Mrs. Clough seemed very concerned about them."

"We didn't find a notebook or personal papers. Just his clothes and a wallet."

Samantha felt sweat forming on her brow. "Nothing? No notes? Mrs. Clough said they were important."

"Just the suicide note."

"Jesus." Samantha closed her eyes, trying to visualize what a mountain of trouble looked like when it hit an industrial fan.

Chapter 3

Michael Saville was sampling his morning coffee while keeping an eye on ESPN's SportsCenter, paying such scant attention to the Sunday edition of the *Kendall County Courier* that he almost missed the twenty-four-point headline in the bottom-right corner of page six: "Virginia Man Commits Suicide in Local Motel."

With his interest piqued, he lowered the television volume and carefully read the modest one-paragraph account:

David Edward Clough, 29, of Arlington, Va., was found dead in his room Friday evening at the Kendall County Country Inn. A housekeeper discovered the body when she attempted to clean the room and received no response after knocking repeatedly. Medical Examiner Dr. Samantha Burton ruled the death a suicide. No further details were available at press time.

Saville couldn't believe his eyes. He turned off the television, folded the newspaper, and reached for the telephone. The unmistakable drone of Jack Mayfield, senior agent at the FBI's Greenville, North Carolina resident agency, answered after the third ring.

"Seven o'clock on a Sunday morning, Mike?" Mayfield said, undoubtedly checking his caller ID. "This better be good."

"Sorry, Jack, but do you remember the kid who came to the office Thursday afternoon? The investigative reporter from Virginia?"

Mayfield likely hadn't seen the paper. He lived within the Greenville city limits, where *The Daily Reflector* served as the primary news source. Saville, on the other hand, resided about twenty miles away near the Pitt County-Kendall County border and received both local newspapers.

Mayfield coughed. "The conspiracy theorist who claimed he was working on a story that reached the highest levels of the federal government? Yeah, I remember. What was his name?"

"Davy Clough."

"What now? Did he figure out that aliens from Area 51 assassinated Kennedy?"

"I don't know, Jack. The kid raised some intriguing points. Maybe we should have listened more closely."

Mayfield scoffed. "What for?"

"A maid found the kid dead in his motel room over in Kendall County. The medical examiner is calling it a suicide, but I'm not convinced. I'd like to drive over there."

"Come on, Mike. The kid obviously had mental health issues. I could tell that in the fifteen minutes we talked to him. Why would you question the ME's findings?"

"My gut," Saville replied. "And twelve years of experience as an FBI field agent."

"Samantha Burton is the ME over in Kendall County, right? She knows what she's doing."

"The kid said his life was in danger."

"That's what all the loons say." Mayfield sighed audibly. "He also claimed he had documents that could prove his theories, but he couldn't show them to us just yet. Phantom documents, Mike. We're already stretched thin, and now you want to chase after a wild goose."

"He was doing his due diligence, remember? That's why he came to Kendall County. He was meeting someone for dinner who could authenticate those documents."

"That's just great, Mike. A mystery ghost to verify phantom documents. Who was he meeting? Beetlejuice? Deep Throat?"

"Indulge me, Jack." Saville tried to contain his frustration. "I know you think it's a waste of time, but I'd like to perform some due diligence of my own. The kid's dead. It's the least we can do."

Saville sipped his coffee, which had turned cold during their conversation, and waited for Mayfield's response. It took longer than he expected.

"Forty-eight hours," Mayfield finally said. "That's all the time I'm giving you."

"Thanks, Jack."

"Did you say this kid was from Virginia?" Mayfield didn't wait for a reply. "I'll have to work up some interstate commerce BS so we can legitimize our involvement. Don't make me look like a fool, Mike."

"I won't, Jack. I promise."

It was a promise he hoped he could keep.

***

"I'd like my son's body autopsied," Cynthia Clough said. "My husband is a physician, and he has a colleague who teaches pathology at the East Carolina University School of Medicine. I've already been in contact."

No doubt, Samantha Burton thought. *The only person you haven't contacted is the President.* Since arriving in Kendall County an hour ago, Cynthia Clough had reached out to the mayor, the medical examiner's office, the county commissioners, motel management, and the sheriff's department. That was why Samantha found herself in Sheriff Helm's orbit again. They were all gathered in the sheriff's main conference room, which smelled just as unpleasant as his office.

Cynthia Clough looked nothing like Samantha had expected. After their initial phone conversation, Samantha had envisioned a sophisticated, well-dressed, snippy, high-maintenance woman. Instead, Cynthia was tall and heavyset, with dark, spiky hair that fell to her shoulders. She wore a pale smock and little makeup or jewelry. Frumpy was the first word that came to Samantha's mind as she stared across the conference room at the bereaved mother.

"You understand, Mrs. Clough, that under North Carolina law, only the medical examiner or the district attorney can order an autopsy at government expense," Samantha said, keeping her tone professional. "If you want an autopsy performed on your son, you will be responsible for the full costs of the procedure, which typically runs—"

"Money is no object," Cynthia interrupted. "I'll simply recoup the costs in my malpractice lawsuit against you, the county, the sheriff's department—"

"Hey, hold on just a minute!" Helm interjected. "Why do you want to sue us? We haven't done anything wrong."

Cynthia touched her hand to her cheek. "All of you should pay for your incompetence. A murderer has gone free because of it." She glared at Helm and then at Samantha. "When the autopsy results come back, I'll have my proof."

"I'm sorry you feel that way," Samantha said. "I can assure you—"

"You'll be sorry, all right."

Samantha had heard enough. Her patience and empathy evaporated. "Where is Dr. Clough now?" she asked pointedly.

"Excuse me?"

"Your husband. You said he was a physician. I would have expected him to be here considering the circumstances."

Cynthia rose from her chair. "How dare you! My husband is very busy. He doesn't have time—"

"To bury his own son?"

Cynthia sank back into her seat, eyes ablaze. With anyone else, Samantha would have expected tears after such a harsh verbal attack, but not from this hard-hearted woman. Samantha refused to back down now that she had gained the upper hand.

"You do whatever you have to do," Samantha said. "But I don't think I'm alone in this room when I say that growing up with detached, self-serving parents who only care about lawsuits and their own careers provides a pretty powerful motive for suicide."

***

As a professional courtesy, Michael Saville's first stop was the Kendall County Sheriff's Department. The FBI aimed to coordinate with local law enforcement or, at the very least, keep them informed when conducting investigations in their jurisdiction. Kendall County was part of the Greenville resident agency's Area of Responsibility. Saville had worked cases there before, although it was rare due to the county's small size and low violent crime rate.

He'd also worked alongside Sheriff Dwight Helm before; he wasn't looking forward to it again. Saville considered the sheriff a blunt instrument, though he acknowledged Helm was largely responsible for the county's impressive crime statistics.

Shortly after 4:00 p.m., Saville pulled into the sheriff's department parking lot, only to find that Helm had already left for dinner.

"Likes to eat early, doesn't he?" Saville remarked to the young deputy behind the front desk, whose nameplate read W. M. Downing.

"He was in a meeting all afternoon and didn't have time to eat lunch," Downing replied.

Saville flashed his badge and ID, knowing they would impress, perhaps even intimidate, the small-town officer. "How long have you been with the department, Deputy Downing?"

"Wow, I've never seen a real-life FBI agent before." He gestured toward Saville's black leather credential case. "Mind if I see it?"

"Sure, as long as you give it back."

Downing caressed the gold badge, focusing on the eagle that surmounted it. "All we have are these stars," he said, pointing to the six-point shield on his chest.

"There's a lot of history in those stars," Saville said, returning his credentials to his jacket pocket. "They used to be made of copper, or so the story goes. That's where the name came from. Cops."

Downing looked down at his uniform. "No kidding?"

"No kidding. Were you on the scene when the reporter's body was recovered Friday?"

"The one at the Country Inn? Yeah, I was there."

"Anyone else?"

Downing indicated an older deputy who was busy typing at a desk in the corner. "Deputy Rhodes was there. He and I searched the room while Sheriff Helm questioned the witnesses."

"Which witnesses?"

"There was the maid who found the body, Miss Rodriguez. She's the only one, I guess."

"Who else worked the scene?"

"Well, there was Dr. Burton, the medical examiner, and Mac Whitmore from the funeral home who picked up the body. That's about everyone, I guess."

Saville felt like he was pulling teeth. "Where's the body now?"

"On the way to the medical school, I imagine. Mrs. Clough was pretty upset earlier."

"Mrs. Clough?" Saville asked.

"Davy Clough's mother. That's why the sheriff was in the meeting. She wants her son taken to Greenville for an autopsy. She thinks he was murdered."

"Great minds think alike," Saville whispered under his breath. "Deputy, do you know where I can find Mrs. Clough?"

"Sure do. She's in the conference room talking on the phone with some lawyer about suing our asses off."

Chapter 4

The hearse carrying Davy Clough's body departed Whitmore's Mortuary at 4:37 p.m. and arrived forty-six minutes later at Pitt County Memorial Hospital in Greenville.

Dr. Franklin Lyman, Professor of Forensic Medicine at East Carolina University's Brody School of Medicine, was already in the autopsy suite, scrubbed and waiting, when they brought the body in.

Although Lyman had known the Clough family for over thirty years, he had never met Davy and recalled that Dr. Clough rarely mentioned his son. Lyman and Bernard Clough had attended different medical schools, but both had specialized in anatomic and clinical pathology. They met while serving their residencies together at Lenoir Memorial Hospital in Kinston, thirty miles south of Greenville, and had bonded like most young doctors who weren't working twenty-four-hour shifts, chasing gold-digging coeds, or freebasing cocaine.

Lyman fell in love with a coed and eventually married her, but their marriage lasted only four years due to his uncontrolled drug habit. He remained in the area, working for nine years in Kinston before moving to the larger, more affluent Greenville. Although he had given up cocaine years ago, he still felt an affinity for the coeds at ECU, where there were plenty to admire.

Meanwhile, Clough returned home after completing his residency, married his college sweetheart, Cynthia, and secured a position at George Washington University Medical Center in Washington, DC. Over the next thirty-two years, he rose through the ranks to become Chair of the Department of Pathology, Director of Laboratories, and Chief of Chemistry and Flow Cytometry.

Clough also embraced his inner nerd, diving into cybernetics, algorithms, and computer programming. What began as a hobby soon turned lucrative, leading him to coauthor several successful patient tracking software programs that provided him with considerable extra income.

The two surgeons maintained sporadic contact, sharing phone calls and occasional emails, and socializing at conventions when time allowed. Lyman felt for the Cloughs over the loss of their son. Though he had no children of his own, his experience and interactions with emotionally devastated parents helped him understand that Bernie and Cindy had not been ideal mentors and were now struggling with overwhelming guilt over their parental shortcomings.

Then there was the tragic case of Davy's older sister, Tiffany, who had died under mysterious circumstances when Davy was just twelve. Lyman had conducted that autopsy as well. Her parents suspected suicide, but without a definitive cause of death, Lyman classified it as "undetermined."

The thought of burying two children in a single lifetime was not only heartbreaking; it gnawed at Lyman's soul.

Two muscular assistants, known as dieners, rolled Davy Clough's body next to the slanted aluminum autopsy table, lifted it from the gurney, and placed it down with a thud. Lyman was continually amazed by how matter-of-factly the dieners treated corpses, for whom comfort was no longer a concern.

Bernard Clough's words echoed in Lyman's mind as one of the dieners slid a plastic body block underneath Davy's back, causing his chest to protrude outward while the arms and neck fell back, allowing maximum exposure for trunk incisions.

They had spoken on the phone just that morning.

"I know I haven't been a good father, and I won't pretend otherwise," Bernard said, his voice hushed and melancholic. "But dammit, Frank, I know my son didn't kill himself. He wasn't depressed like Tiffany. He was excited about his work and said he was in the middle of a bombshell that could win him a Pulitzer. Somebody murdered my son, and the least I can do is help him get the justice he deserves. I need you, Frank. Davy needs you. Don't let us down."

Lyman took a deep breath and stared into Davy's vacant eyes and colorless face. The body had obviously been embalmed, complicating his work and the search for clues. Why hadn't anyone mentioned this to him earlier?

No matter. He had a job to do and a vow to keep. One made to a grieving parent, the most solemn vow of all.

"Don't worry, Bernie, I'll make sure Davy didn't die in vain," he had told his friend, speaking with utter conviction. Now, all he had to do was follow through on that promise.

With a heavy heart and measured expectations, he lifted the scalpel and made a Y-shaped incision from the front of each shoulder to the xiphoid process, through the abdominal wall, and down to the pubic bone. This marked the beginning of the process he hoped would reveal, with medical certainty, the cause of death for this young man who had died far too soon.

***

Cynthia Clough kept Saville waiting for twenty minutes while discussing potential lawsuits with her attorney. At first, Saville listened intently, hoping to gain insight into Davy Clough's life and character, but he eventually tuned out once it became clear that the topics were limited to medical malpractice, wrongful death, and other legal matters.

When he grew tired of waiting, he produced his FBI credentials and displayed them.

"I'm sorry, Rex, but we'll have to continue this conversation when I return home," she said. "The FBI is here. Finally."

Saville folded his arms and introduced himself. He had never met Cynthia Clough but already knew enough about her type from past encounters.

"Thank God, intelligence at last." She dropped her cell phone into her designer purse. "Mr. Saville, I need you to find my son's murderer—"

Saville raised his hand. "I'm sorry, Mrs. Clough, but first, we need to determine if a crime has actually been committed. I understand the medical examiner ruled his death a suicide?"

"And I'm supposed to accept her word at face value? Look around you, Mr. Saville. Do these people honestly seem to have any idea what's going on?"

"I know Samantha Burton, and she's a competent physician," Saville replied. "And by the way, I'm one of 'these people.'"

"I wasn't referring to you," she said innocently. "Just the locals."

"I've lived here for several years, so I guess I'm one of the locals." He wasn't offended and gave her the benefit of the doubt considering her situation. "Why don't you take a seat and tell me why you think someone murdered your son?"

He gestured toward the conference table in the center of the room. She hesitated, her lips moving as if she wanted to speak, but ultimately chose silence and sat down.

"Your son came to see me Thursday afternoon," he said, taking a seat across from her. Her expression brightened. "He mentioned he was working on a story about government corruption and that the FBI would be interested."

"That's what I've been trying to tell everyone."

"But he didn't have any proof, or at least he didn't offer any. I had nothing to work with. He said he was in town to meet with someone who could provide definitive corroboration of his suspicions."

She nearly jumped from her chair. "Who?"

"He didn't say. I was hoping you might know."

She shook her head. "My son didn't confide in me often." Her voice began to crack. "We weren't very close, and that's my fault."

"Please, Mrs. Clough. Any information would be helpful. We need to find the person your son came here to meet. He could be—"

"The murderer?"

"Perhaps."

Tears welled in her eyes. "I'm sorry. I wish I knew."

Saville decided to let it rest, sensing the regret in her expression.

Just then, the conference room door burst open with a loud bang against the wall.

"What the hell is going on?" a voice boomed. It was Sheriff Helm, his cheeks flushed with rage. He clutched a half-eaten cheeseburger in his right hand. "Dammit, Saville! This is my investigation. What gives you the right to question a witness in my jurisdiction without my permission?"

"I don't need your permission, Sheriff."

"I requested his presence," Cynthia said, standing to face the sheriff. "It's clear you're not going to do anything about my son's death." She marched up to him and slapped the cheeseburger from his hand, sending it to the floor, where a pickle stuck to the top of his shoe. "You're too busy stuffing your face."

Saville struggled to suppress a laugh as he watched the haughty socialite confront the self-proclaimed "Bear of Kendall County." The humor faded when Helm clenched his fist, as if preparing to retaliate.

No punch came, but Saville grabbed the sheriff's arm and pinned it down. Helm, using his superior size and strength, shook himself free, sending Saville tumbling backward.

"I can assure you that the proper authorities will be notified of your unprofessional conduct," Cynthia said as Saville regained his balance. "Not only will I have your badge, but I'm sure Mr. Saville here will be pressing charges for assault."

"Will this complaint be made before or after the lawsuit?" Helm sneered, unfazed.

Saville adjusted his tie and brushed himself off. "I'm putting you on notice, Sheriff. The FBI is assuming jurisdiction and will be the lead agency in the Davy Clough death investigation."

Helm gritted his teeth, but he knew there was nothing he could do.

"You should receive formal notification from our Charlotte Field Office within the next twenty-four hours," Saville continued. "We expect complete cooperation from you, your department, and anyone else associated with this investigation." He jabbed a finger into Helm's massive chest, indifferent to the consequences. "As for me personally, Sheriff, I suggest you stay the hell out of my way. I won't be caught off guard next time."

Saville took Cynthia by the hand, and as they marched out of the conference room, he swore he could see steam pouring from Helm's ears, reminiscent of a scene he and his five-year-old daughter, Emma, had once watched together on Cartoon Network.

Chapter 5

They left the sheriff's office and headed straight to Pitt County Memorial Hospital to await the autopsy results. Throughout the drive, Saville seethed but kept his composure, recognizing the importance of maintaining his professionalism. He attempted to gather information but found little success. Cynthia Clough, equally outraged by Sheriff Helm's conduct, repeatedly responded to questions with, "By the time my lawyers are finished, I'll own Kendall County."

Saville discovered little of value; most of what he learned was already known to him. During the ride, it became apparent that Cynthia's evasiveness stemmed not from deception but from genuine ignorance about many details concerning her son, which struck Saville as tragic.

He empathized with her situation. He only got to see his daughter Emma every other weekend and for two weeks during the summer. Even that schedule could be erratic due to his job and ongoing investigations, with Uncle Sam's tolerance for family obligations leaving much to be desired.

Yet, he felt he knew everything about Emma: her favorite foods, her favorite color, and the name of her best friend. Did Cynthia know these things about her son? He doubted it, and she'd had twenty-nine years to learn. Emma was only five. God, he hoped he never reached that point in his relationship with her. She was all he had left besides his work.

When they arrived at the reception area next to the autopsy suite, Dr. Lyman was already waiting. Dressed in a white coat and pressed shirt, he exchanged quiet words and a long embrace with Cynthia, which Saville found inappropriate but withheld judgment on given the tragic nature of their reunion.

After shaking hands with Lyman, they moved to a row of metal chairs in a nearby room marked "Patient Confidentiality Area."

Once seated, Saville got straight to the point. "Doctor, do we have a homicide on our hands?"

Lyman hesitated before responding. "Honestly, I just don't know."

"What do you mean you don't know?" Cynthia erupted. "How can you not know?"

Looking exhausted, Lyman replied, "Cynthia, please. I can't be certain until the toxicology results come back. My full written report should be available in approximately three days."

"Three days!" Cynthia burst into tears. "We can't wait that long, Frank! A murderer is getting away!"

Lyman reached out to console her, but she pushed him away, drying her eyes with the sleeve of her smock. "Tell me, Frank," she said with sudden intensity. "What happened to my son?"

Lyman sighed. "At this time, the evidence doesn't support a definitive conclusion."

"Dammit, Frank." She grabbed his arm. "That's my little boy you just examined. I'm begging you to tell me the truth."

Lyman glanced at Saville, seeking support. The FBI agent offered what little he could. "This is a potential criminal investigation, Dr. Lyman. Please be honest and give us your professional opinion."

Lyman nodded. "Unfortunately, the gross exam was inconclusive. Aside from the absence of hesitation marks, there's no evidence contradicting the medical examiner's finding that Davy killed himself."

"Hesitation marks?" Cynthia asked, her tone calming.

"There weren't any," Lyman explained. "Typically, suicide victims hesitate with the blade, making shallow cuts as they gauge their pain tolerance. Davy didn't do that. The cuts were very deep, almost in a hacking motion, down to the tendons. It's unique but not unheard of."

"Any other distinguishing marks?" Saville inquired.

"No bruises or defensive wounds. Nothing indicating Davy was beaten or restrained."

"Davy was scared of blood," Cynthia said. "Cutting himself would have made him sick."

"His blood alcohol content was elevated," Lyman noted. "How often did Davy drink?"

"Sometimes. I'm not sure."

"We know he drank shortly before he died; we just don't know the precise time. Even if he was afraid of blood, alcohol can trigger a suppressed phobia response." Lyman reached for Cynthia's hand again, and this time she didn't resist. "We won't know much until the lab completes the vitreous humor testing and analyzes Davy's stomach contents and tissue distribution."

"Could he have been forced to drink? Is it possible the suicide was staged?" Saville asked.

"Anything's possible. We'll know more in a few days."

"Davy wouldn't have," Cynthia said, her tears returning. "He wouldn't have put us through this agony again."

"Again?" Saville asked.

Cynthia looked at Lyman, as if expecting him to fill in the blanks. He understood her pain.

"Davy's sister was nineteen when she ingested a fatal dose of ethylene glycol."

"Antifreeze," Saville replied absently.

"Yes, antifreeze," Lyman confirmed. "We could never determine if her death was an accident or..." He trailed off, searching Cynthia's eyes for the right words.

"Suicide?"

"Tiffany knew what she was doing," Cynthia said. "Her death devastated our family. Davy was heartbroken. He and his sister were very close."

"She was an honor student and a champion swimmer at George Washington," Lyman said, his voice subdued. "I can't imagine."

"No, you can't," Cynthia replied. "You don't have children. I've lost two."

"I'm so sorry, Cynthia," Lyman said.

Saville stood up, trying to steer the conversation away from sorrow. "So, as of now, Dr. Lyman, you're unable to state conclusively whether foul play was involved in Davy Clough's death. Is that correct?"

"Unfortunately, yes. Until the lab results are complete."

"My son's murderer is a free man," Cynthia hissed.

Lyman simply stared at the floor.

***

It was almost midnight when Saville dropped Cynthia off at her hotel and returned home. She was still upset and implored him to stay with her until she felt better. Unsure how to respond, he handed her a business card and left without even shaking her hand. She tried to hide her disappointment, informed him she would be returning home in the morning, and asked him to keep her updated on the investigation.

Saville didn't have the heart to tell her the investigation was likely over. Instead, he promised to do everything in his power to bring her son's killer to justice. He wasn't proud of himself. Not only had he declined to comfort a distraught mother, but he had compounded her misery by making a promise he might not fulfill. He could always justify it to himself as an act of compassion.

His apartment was empty except for photographs of Emma that brought him joy: her preschool graduation, her fifth birthday party, her first dance recital. All the special moments he had refused to miss in the seven months since the separation.

There was also a portrait of Emma and her mother. Saville stared at it for some time. Jennifer Saville remained a beautiful woman, with dark hair and haunting hazel eyes, just as she had been seven years ago on their wedding day. She had come into his life quite by accident.

He remembered it as if it were yesterday. How she sat behind her desk at the FBI Training Academy in Quantico, her sleek legs beneath a knee-length denim skirt, black heels, and a matching blouse, her hair tied up with a ribbon. He had definitely taken notice but was informed right away that she was off-limits.

"Jennifer Greer doesn't date agents," his Investigative Training Unit instructor had warned. "Believe me, we've all tried."

That wasn't good enough for Saville. Challenge accepted. He refused to take no for an answer. He used every spare moment during the weeklong refresher training to speak to her and compliment her. When he returned to the Miami field office, he called, emailed, and wrote often. Nine months of persistence—his colleagues jokingly called it stalking—finally paid off. She agreed to go out with him upon his return to Quantico, a trip he arranged shortly after by volunteering for a three-week temporary duty assignment to teach a class on cold case methodology, one of his specialties.

They became inseparable; she followed him back to Miami, eventually married him, and stood by his side when the FBI assigned him to the Greenville Resident Agency, a move that signaled the end of their marriage.

He tried to block thoughts of Jennifer as he lifted the phone and dialed Jack Mayfield's home number. Jack went to bed early and wouldn't appreciate being roused at this hour. Saville couldn't help it. He needed to talk to someone, or he'd be awake all night.

"Bloody hell," Mayfield said. "It's not enough that you drag me out of bed on Sunday morning? Now you have to keep me up at night too? Do you have something against sleep, Mike?"

"Sorry, Jack," Saville said for the second time in less than twenty-four hours. "I need to get a few things off my chest."

"And it can't wait until morning?"

"Probably, but you know patience isn't one of my virtues."

"Yeah, well, you can update your behavioral analysis training after I get you transferred to Juneau." Mayfield sounded teasing, but Saville could never be quite sure. "What's the problem?"

"Davy Clough," Saville said. "They autopsied his body tonight."

"And?"

"Inconclusive."

"This burning information couldn't wait?" Mayfield's annoyance came through the phone.

"I don't buy it, Jack. There's just something—"

"Are you a doctor now?" Mayfield cleared his throat. "When did you finish medical school?"

"Come on, Jack."

"A licensed physician declared the death a suicide, and another performed the autopsy," Mayfield said. "Isn't that enough for you? It's time to let it go, Mike."

Saville had no response. While pragmatism might dictate that the investigation be closed, countless unanswered questions suggested otherwise. He couldn't identify the problem but knew he had to rely on his experience and training to uncover the truth, wherever it might lead.

"I still have another day," Saville finally said. "You gave me forty-eight hours."

"Put it to rest. That's what I'm going to do. Get some sleep. We'll talk in the morning."

Mayfield hung up, leaving Saville with a knot in his stomach. Sleep wasn't an option tonight. He could manage one night without it, but he had to shake the sinking feeling that a murderer was slipping away, never to be caught.

Chapter 6

It rained on Monday morning in Washington, D.C. Heavy droplets pounded the streets, government buildings, and the waters of the Potomac River.

Sections of Independence Avenue were flooded near the Tidal Basin, prompting the National Park Service to close surrounding streets and warn commuters to find alternate routes. Both the West Basin Drive and Ohio Drive entrances to West Potomac Park were shut, creating massive traffic jams stretching back to the Kutz Bridge and Seventeenth Street.

Sergeant Lowri Pritchard had seen this all before. Every time it rained, it seemed. The six-year veteran of the United States Park Police had requested that the Federal Highway Administration investigate the flooding situation twice before, but her pleas had gone ignored.

When the President's motorcade gets washed into the Tidal Basin, maybe then they'll do something, she thought irritably.

Not that she expected anything different. The Park Police were the bottom feeders of the law enforcement hierarchy, despite having jurisdiction over all national parks and select federal properties. They were not only the nation's oldest uniformed law enforcement agency, beginning as the Park Watchmen under George Washington in 1791, but their duties were just as important, and the dangers just as real.

Yet somehow, they always seemed to lag behind the Metropolitan Police and the Capitol Police in prestige and influence. Even the airport and transit cops, along with the Bureau of Engraving and Printing Police, enjoyed better perks during budget season.

Would a Capitol cop be standing here now, drenched and barefoot with her uniform trousers rolled up to her knees, pumping water off the street? No way. Only the dedicated officers of the Park Police, Central District, D-1, had the "honor" of wading through filthy floodwaters. It was one advantage of being the district closest to the White House, Lowri guessed. Tedious work for sure, but so was protecting visiting dignitaries and assisting the Secret Service with presidential security, a duty the Park Police sometimes performed.

The rain had finally stopped about ten minutes ago, but the water had yet to recede. The goal was to have the roads and park reopened by 1:00 p.m., a deadline she found unrealistic. It was a few minutes past ten now, and she'd been working diligently without tangible results since her 7:00 a.m. shift began. Considering the frustrated chatter crackling through her radio, other officers throughout the park were facing similar issues.

Someone was voicing their opinion over the radio now, mentioning her name. She strained to hear above the swish of the retreating waters and the complaints of stranded tourists, whose cars snaked back along Independence Avenue as far as she could see.

"Hey, Sarge! Do you read? Over." The voice belonged to Joel Graves, one of her best officers, another asset wasted on flood control.

"This is Sergeant Pritchard," she said, keying the lapel mic of her portable radio. As the ranking officer on the scene, all problems and crises eventually found their way back to her. "What's up?"

"Got something here you need to check out. Southern quadrant. Next to Old Jeff."

"Old Jeff." Graves's nickname for the Jefferson Memorial.

"What is it?" Lowri asked, fearing the worst. Had graffiti artists once again defaced the memorial? Great. Now she could add janitor to her list of accomplishments.

"Looks like a body."

"Say again?" Clearly, she had misunderstood.

"Caucasian male, mid-forties maybe. Looks like he ate a bullet—"

"Don't mess with me, Joel. I'm not in the mood."

"This is serious, Sarge. We've got a real DOA over here."

Damn, damn, damn, Lowri thought. A dead man at the Jefferson Memorial. Just this once, she would have welcomed a little graffiti on the portico or a big "Bite Me" spray-painted across the face of the preamble. She swallowed the lump in her throat and shouted into the radio, "Call it in. I'll be there in ten."

***

First Lady Hellen Carney never regretted being named after a man. Hellen, son of Deucalion and Pyrrha, though some scholars believed he was also the son of Zeus. Her father had been a professor of classical studies at Duke University and was particularly fond of Hellenistic Greece, the period between the death of Alexander the Great and the onset of the Roman Empire.

He'd briefly considered naming his daughter after Helen of Troy, but that name was too common, and Dr. Ambrose Wiley had always told anyone who would listen that his daughter would grow up to be anything but ordinary. So why not "Hellen" instead, a name that commanded instant attention and respect for its originality and meaning? Hellen, the man who would become the forefather of the Greeks.

When she was younger, her name had proven beneficial to the future First Lady. Her professors at Harvard remarked on its uniqueness and accorded her special privileges. Or was it because they knew her father, who was renowned throughout academia? The same thing happened in law school, and later in the courtroom, where judges, especially those nearing retirement, noted the unusual spelling, usually just before inviting her away for the weekend.

She'd accepted a few of those invitations. Truth be told, she never truly distinguished herself professionally. Her legal career flourished only because of her charm and good looks. She understood the sacrifices necessary to survive in a man's world. By age thirty-one, she was a partner in one of North Carolina's largest law firms, and two years later, she met Woodrow Carney, chief judge for the United States Fourth Circuit Court of Appeals, recently divorced and thirteen years her senior.

They hit it off, she with her classic blonde hair and blue eyes, and he, one of the most powerful men in the judiciary and a rising star in the Democratic Party. Not even his insatiable sexual appetite, especially for younger women, stood in her way. She was no innocent herself. She satisfied his every need, in every way, and rode his coattails all the way to the North Carolina governor's mansion. Eight years later, the White House called.

That seemed like a lifetime ago. Two years into his second term, President Carney's approval ratings hovered in the mid-thirties, the lowest of his administration. The economy had worsened, and inflation was rising. To compensate for his dwindling popularity, the President had withdrawn into a protective shell, relying more on trusted advisors and less on family and close friends.

His staff formed his support network, and he avoided his wife except when it was politically necessary to be seen with her. They rarely slept in the same room and hadn't been intimate in more than a year. His perversions manifested in secretaries, interns, and all the vulnerable young women who strolled the halls of power with stars in their eyes. After fourteen years of marriage, she'd grown tired of his affairs and indiscretions, realizing that a behavior-modifying political reversal was not on the immediate horizon.

That's why she sought comfort from one of her husband's best friends.

Deputy White House Counsel Victor Farnsworth had grown up and attended high school with Woody Carney and then served alongside him in the North Carolina State Senate and the governor's mansion. When the White House beckoned, Farnsworth answered the call again. He was one of the President's first appointments. Carney originally offered him a more prestigious position than deputy White House counsel, but Farnsworth declined. "I'm just an old country lawyer from North Carolina," he told the President. "I've got no business inside the Beltway."

Farnsworth shunned the spotlight, the lavish Washington parties, and the controversies surrounding partisan politics, preferring to remain in the shadows where he could work in virtual anonymity. He was probably the President's best friend, but he didn't flaunt it. And he was handsome. What was there not to like? He even called when he said he would.

Except today.

He had promised to call before noon, but the First Lady's cell phone had yet to ring. *Where are you, my darling? Why do you keep me waiting like this?* They had spent part of the early morning together at his Georgetown apartment, a refuge from late nights at the office that prevented him from driving back to his home in the suburbs. They listened to the relentless rain pounding on the roof, under the watchful eye of the Secret Service agents sworn to secrecy by oath and loyalty. There was no concern about her husband discovering their rendezvous; he was in Florida, preaching to the choir at a fundraiser in Broward County. He wouldn't care anyway.

She had been inside The Green Room for nearly two hours, waiting impatiently and savoring the memories of her latest encounter with Victor. This room was her favorite in the entire White House. It was where Abraham Lincoln's son Willie was laid to rest and where James Madison signed the nation's first declaration of war in 1812, which ultimately led to the White House being burned down two years later. She retreated here when she wanted solitude, sometimes sharing her feelings with the beautiful portrait of Louisa Catherine Adams, the wife of John Quincy Adams. Someday, her own portrait would hang in this very room, where a future First Lady could seek her guidance and inspiration.

Right now, hearing Victor's voice would be inspiration enough. Please, Vic, why won't you call me? Are you unhappy? You certainly had a smile on your face when I left this morning. She giggled. What was it about him that always brought out her schoolgirl giddiness? Was it his deep Southern drawl? His gentlemanly charm? She felt like a teenager falling in love for the first time.

And it was love. No doubt about that. She was the First Lady of the United States, after all. She didn't engage in tawdry affairs; that was her husband's style, sleeping with interns in the Oval Office, slapping political donors on the back with one hand while grabbing their wives with the other. Hellen wasn't that vulgar. Or desperate.

The sun was finally breaking through the clouds. She decided that some fresh air might clear her head and ease her worries about Victor's mysterious absence. It didn't help. As she stepped onto the South Portico, she still couldn't shake Victor's smile from her mind. She checked her phone again. Maybe she hadn't heard it ring, and he'd left a message. Nothing. Perhaps she had forgotten to turn up the ringer and left the phone on vibrate. No, the volume was at its highest.

Where are you, Vic? You've never forgotten me before. Her thoughts wandered to forbidden love, commitment, and trust, even as the thundering thwap-thwap-thwap of the Park Police helicopter in the distance drowned out her concentration.

Chapter 7

The Park Police Aviation Unit operated three helicopters, designated Eagle One, Eagle Two, and Eagle Three, all based at the "Eagle's Nest" complex in Anacostia Park.

Eagle One was the helicopter that rescued five survivors from the icy waters of the Potomac River after Air Florida Flight 90 crashed into the Fourteenth Street Bridge on January 13, 1982. The two crew members were awarded the Department of the Interior's Valor Award, the U.S. Coast Guard's Silver Lifesaving Medal, and the Carnegie Hero Fund Medal.

The crews weren't in line for commendations this time, but Lowri was grateful they were at least airborne. The roads were still impassable and would likely remain so for a few more hours. All three Eagle units had been dispatched to the crime scene, transporting paramedics, investigators, crime scene technicians, and the on-call medical examiner.

Eagle One arrived first, twenty-one minutes after Officer Graves reported the location of the deceased to Central District dispatch. It landed on a narrow strip of grass between the Jefferson Memorial and the Outlet Bridge. Its rotors nearly clipped the cherry trees lining the Tidal Basin, and the downwash scattered some blossoms.

Lowri shielded her eyes with her campaign hat as the Bell 412EP twin-engine helicopter's blades slowed to a stop. Once it was safe, she flung open the cabin door and shouted, "This way!"

An investigator from the Major Crimes Section and a crime scene technician stepped outside. Lowri recognized the investigator and immediately suppressed the urge to grimace.

"Hey, Dollface, heard you got a 10-100." His name was Peter Sprague, the department's most arrogant homicide detective. "What do you say? Let's get together after we process the stiff?"

Lowri ignored him and gestured for them to follow her to the crime scene. She had worked with him several times before, and his disrespect seemed to grow with each encounter. Someone once mentioned he was going through a nasty divorce, but unless that had been dragging on for the past six years, more than just property division contributed to his obnoxious and sexist attitude. Some people were just jerks, unable to change regardless of their circumstances.

"First day back from vacation, and I've got to deal with this mess," Sprague complained as they trudged through the mud. "Ruined a new pair of shoes."

"Vacation, huh?" Lowri couldn't resist. "Where'd you go? Afghanistan?"

"I went sailing. What's it to you?"

Sailing. Of course. Sprague's boat was his most prized possession. She had heard him brag about it so often that she could recite the details: Suwannee 47 Cabin Cruiser, commercial model, duo-prop stern drives, lower helm station with full engine instrumentation, balsa-cored fiberglass deck and cabin. When he retired, he aspired to become a charter boat captain. Lowri regretted bringing it up. How could he afford such a nice vessel on a detective's salary?

The body was located approximately fifteen feet southwest of the Tidal Basin and forty feet from the Outlet Bridge. Sprague slipped on latex gloves and hovered over the dead man for a moment. "Sorry, Dollface," he said. "Looks like this one died with his clothes on."

"Shut up, Sprague." God, he was insufferable.

"I didn't know you were such a prude, Dollface. Let's see what we've got." He knelt beside the body, lying on its back with its head tilted slightly to the right, arms and legs fully extended. The fingers of the right hand were wrapped around a Colt .38 Special revolver, and trickles of dried blood stained the nose and mouth. "Got an ID?"

"Not yet. We're still looking for his wallet."

Sprague sighed. "Figures."

The crime scene technician stood next to Sprague, photographing the body from every angle while Lowri observed from the background. Four other officers were scouring the area with evidence collection bags, searching for any physical evidence, especially the wallet.

There was little for the remaining officers to do without risking contamination of the crime scene. The perimeter had already been secured, and there was no pedestrian traffic to redirect. No witnesses to interview either; West Potomac Park had been closed since 11 p.m. on Sunday. The torrential rains had started shortly afterward and continued through the night and most of Monday morning.

Sprague and the technician flipped the body onto its stomach. The exit wound was immediately evident, a large hole beneath the scalp, at least one inch in diameter.

"Gunshot wound to the mouth," the technician said, pointing with a gloved finger. "Bullet exited the back of the skull right here."

"Why did they call homicide?" Sprague whined. "This guy killed himself." He turned and shouted to everyone within earshot. "Looks like we have a suicide. Should be a .38 slug around here somewhere. The sooner we find it, the sooner we get out of here."

Taking into account the position of the body and the likely trajectory of the bullet, Lowri led her officers in a concentrated search within a one-hundred-foot radius. The slug wouldn't have traveled far. A large chunk of brain and skull was missing; the impact would have slowed the bullet considerably as it passed through.

They searched in vain for an hour, then expanded their search by another hundred yards. Still nothing.

By then, all three Eagle helicopters had come and gone twice, delivering more emergency personnel and equipment. The water level had dropped enough for others to arrive by four-wheel-drive vehicles.

The slug's probably at the bottom of the Tidal Basin, Lowri thought, knowing that the crack divers of the Marine Unit would eventually retrieve it if the lead investigator, Sprague, deemed it important. Lowri doubted that would happen, though. The victim had obviously taken a bullet, and the .38 in his right hand suggested a self-inflicted wound.

A simple gunpowder residue test would reveal the complete story, assuming the rain hadn't washed away the residue. If the wound was indeed self-inflicted, then the victim must have driven himself to the park. Somewhere out there, either in the parking lot or buried among the stranded, flooded vehicles, was the victim's car, and perhaps the key to his identity.

She pressed her lapel mic and said, "We should have an abandoned car that belongs to the deceased somewhere in the park. Search every empty vehicle and run every tag. John Doe needs a name."

There was another issue that troubled her: the absence of blood at the scene. A gunshot to the mouth, with an exit wound the size of Texas, should have created a significant mess. John Doe would have taken seconds to die, and the heart would have continued to pump for as long as it had oxygenated blood, sometimes for up to two minutes. So where was the blood?

The rain could have washed away some of it, but not all. Mud and soot covered the victim's white shirt and tie, yet there were no visible bloodstains. No blood was found beneath the victim's head, either.

Had the rain disinfected the scene? Or had John Doe been killed elsewhere and his body moved to the park?

What was she thinking? She'd been watching too many crime show reruns. This was Sprague's problem anyway.

"Hey, Sarge, get over here quick." It was Joel Graves's voice crackling over the radio. "Got a silver 2016 Ford F-150 abandoned in the east parking lot. Keys still in the ignition. Suicide note and everything. You won't believe who it belongs to."

Uh-oh, here we go again, she thought as she retraced her steps back to the crime scene and updated Sprague with the latest news: no slug had been found, but John Doe's car apparently had.

***

By 2 p.m., the First Lady's gloom and worry had devolved into outrage. She still hadn't heard from Victor Farnsworth, and worse, he hadn't even shown up for work yet. She couldn't believe he had taken advantage of her like that. Who did he think he was? She already had one man controlling her life, but at least he was the President of the United States. She would not play that role for someone as low on the hierarchy as Victor Farnsworth.

How many people had Victor told about their affair? How many of his friends had he confided in while drunk? Guess who I'm sleeping with? The First Lady.

The thought made her blood boil. But Victor Farnsworth wasn't that type of man. Was he? His words from this morning still echoed in her mind. *What am I supposed to do, Hellen? I'm falling in love with you. I know it's wrong...*

Lies. He didn't love her. He loved the thrill of being with her, the First Lady, the wife of his best friend and confidant. Betraying the President of the United States? Now that was power. It had finally happened. Victor was no longer the humble, courtly cavalier who disdained the political games of Washington. He was now a fully integrated Beltway insider who understood how politics really worked.

He still couldn't erase his words from her mind. *I can't help it. You're my soulmate, Hellen.* Is it possible for this to turn out well for us, or are we heading for disaster?

Disaster. Obviously. Victor had convinced himself that their relationship was doomed. He had saved himself from the scandal, realizing they could never be together without turning the Washington political scene upside down. Why was life so unfair? For the first time in her life, she was truly happy. Truly in love. A forbidden love. Was that its appeal? She couldn't think about that right now. Was she destined to remain miserable forever?

She shook her head and walked to her office in the East Wing, next to the President's theater and overlooking the Jacqueline Kennedy Garden. The television was on, tuned to MSNBC.

As she sat at her desk, the words "Breaking Story" flashed across the bottom of the screen, superimposed over live images of the Jefferson Memorial and the Tidal Basin, taken from an NBC news helicopter.

The screen switched to a shot of White House correspondent Amanda Torres, standing in the stone-paved area on the North Lawn near the North Portico, known as Pebble Beach. The White House loomed in the background.

"We are waiting for official confirmation, but sources tell MSNBC that the victim has been identified as Victor Farnsworth, deputy White House counsel..."

Hellen froze, breath catching as the newscaster's words sharpened into focus. She fumbled for the remote and cranked the volume.

"Farnsworth died of a single gunshot to the head. The death has tentatively been ruled a suicide..."

Hellen was no longer listening. She buried her head in her hands and fought back tears.

Chapter 8

Frustration soured Saville's mood. He tried to maintain a calm demeanor, but truthfully, he was tired of banging his head against the brick wall known as Jack Mayfield. Saville had been up all night, just as he expected, and to make matters worse, Mayfield had waited until after lunch to come to the office, citing a migraine. But Saville knew the real reason for Mayfield's delay: he didn't want to argue about the Davy Clough case.

"I need more time," Saville said, pacing in tight circles around Mayfield's office. "Dr. Lyman said the complete autopsy report should be available in a couple of days—"

"I gave you forty-eight hours. Twenty-four have already passed." Mayfield stabbed at a cinnamon roll with a plastic fork, not looking up. "Time's running out. We've got a full caseload."

"Come on, Jack." Saville had been using those exact words quite a bit recently.

"Dammit, Mike." Mayfield leaned back in his chair, clasping his hands behind his head. "We have cases that are more pressing. The First Citizens Bank robbery?"

"That case has gone cold."

"The identity theft ring?"

"Has been traced back to Romania. DIICOT says arrests are imminent. Our Legal Attaché in Bucharest will initiate extradition proceedings through the Romanian Ministry of Justice."

"Good work," Mayfield said, "but that still doesn't justify spending resources on an undetermined-death investigation."

"You promised me, Jack," Saville said, his words sounding like a dog begging for scraps.

"Need I remind you that the Bureau has already disciplined you once for insubordination?" Mayfield glowered. "I'd stand down if I were you. I doubt you'll get another chance."

The statement struck a nerve. Saville's stint in Miami had ended badly, leaving a black mark on his record that he didn't like being reminded of. Still, the lessons learned were slow to penetrate. His ingrained stubbornness was impossible to tame.

"I thought Jack Mayfield was a man of his word," he said, bracing for the consequences.

"Three days. No more." Mayfield finally looked up from his roll.

"What?"

"If the autopsy report doesn't provide solid proof, we're done. This case goes away forever," Mayfield said. "In the meantime, you'd better find something to convince me otherwise."

"Thanks, Jack. You won't regret it."

Mayfield rolled his eyes. "You said the same thing to Sullivan in Miami, just before he put you on a plane to Greenville."

***

Saville's first stop was the Kendall County Sheriff's Department, where he picked up a copy of Davy Clough's incident report. Sheriff Helm wasn't in the office, but he ran into Deputy Downing on the way out.

"If you're looking for the sheriff, you won't find him," Downing said.

"I'm not looking." Honestly, Saville didn't care if he ever saw Helm's face again.

"He's on medical leave. Undergoing surgery in the morning. Some kind of plastic surgery."

"Convenient," Saville said, especially considering the incident in his office. "Wish him a speedy recovery."

Downing laughed. "A gangbanger tried to hack his face off a couple of years ago. Finally getting it fixed. It's going to cost a bundle. He's taking donations if you want to contribute."

"I'll pass. That's what workers' comp is for."

"I guess. Deputy Rhodes is in charge until the sheriff gets back."

"I'll keep that in mind if I need anything."

He returned to his car and read over the report while sitting in the Kendall County Courthouse parking lot. It provided nothing he didn't already know: the position and condition of Davy Clough's body, an inventory of items found at the scene, and a terse, almost indecipherable narrative written by Sheriff Helm. Nothing warranted attention, except the shoddy police procedure. He pushed it from his mind as he drove his dark-gray Chevrolet Tahoe to the Kendall County Country Inn.

He found Belinda Chatwyn in her first-floor office and introduced himself.

She stood and said, "Praise Jesus! A real cop."

"I appreciate the compliment." Saville smiled. "But I'm sure—"

"It's not a compliment. It's the truth. You have no idea what the people of this county have to put up with."

Believe me, I do, he thought. Belinda wasn't a bad-looking woman, plain in a pretty sort of way. With no makeup, her dark brown hair was tied in a ponytail. She wore no wedding band, and Saville wasn't sure why he'd even noticed, except that he'd been lonely since the separation and was starting to think about such things.

"I'm glad you're here," she said. "I hope you find out who killed Mr. Clough."

"Who says anyone killed him? The medical examiner ruled it a suicide."

"You're here, aren't you? Since when does the FBI investigate a suicide?"

Saville nodded. The lady was perceptive.

"At least you're going to do something. The only thing that interested Sheriff Helm was my maid, Magdalena."

Saville wasn't surprised. Repulsive should have been Helm's middle name. "Is Miss Rodriguez on duty today?"

"Yes. Should I call her in?"

"Not yet." There was only one chair in the office. He leaned against the wall, clutching the leather portfolio that contained his case notes. "What can you tell me about Mr. Clough?"

"Not much, really. He checked in around two o'clock on Thursday afternoon and was supposed to check out Saturday morning."

"Did you check him in personally?"

"Yes."

"Was he carrying a bag or luggage?"

She paused for a moment. "One suitcase, a toiletries bag, and that briefcase he wouldn't let anyone touch."

"Briefcase?" Saville flipped through his leather portfolio, noting there was no mention of a briefcase in the evidence log.

"Yes. He held it like a baby. Magdalena was cleaning the waiting area, so I asked her to help Mr. Clough with his luggage. The way he wrapped his arms around it, you'd think that briefcase contained something sacred."

"Any idea what was inside?"

She shook her head. "I got the impression he would have killed me for asking."

"Were you present when Magdalena found Mr. Clough's body?"

"She told me right afterward, and then I called the sheriff's office."

"Did you see Mr. Clough's briefcase in the room before the police arrived?"

"I'm not sure..." She rubbed her chin. "Now that you mention it, I don't believe I did."

Saville pushed himself away from the wall. Had he just discovered the key piece of evidence he'd been searching for? Had someone removed the briefcase after Davy Clough's death, or had Davy hidden it himself to protect its contents?

"Does the motel have security cameras, Miss Chatwyn?" he asked.

"We're not that sophisticated."

Saville masked his disappointment. Security footage could have clarified much. "What was Mr. Clough's mood when he checked in?"

"His mood?"

"Did he seem happy? Depressed? Was he talkative?"

"Definitely not depressed. He was smiling and very chatty. He said he was in town for a few days on important business. He even asked if I wanted to show him around." A gleam appeared in her eyes. "He was joking, of course. I'm old enough to be his mother."

Davy's mother. He tried not to think about Cynthia Clough. "Did you see him after he checked in?"

"Yes, he came downstairs once to get change for the soda machine. He was still smiling and flirting."

Saville remained silent. While Clough's cheerful demeanor before his death supported the murder theory, definitive proof was still required. Mental health professionals recognized a phenomenon called paradoxical improvement, where individuals might appear to be in good spirits prior to suicide. Once someone decides to end their life, they may feel a sense of relief and peace, believing they have resolved their internal struggle. A behavioral instructor at Quantico once referred to it as "terminal happiness," though he quickly clarified that this was more of a law enforcement term than established clinical terminology.

Saville had seen it before: a sport-fishing boat owner in Miami found with his throat cut. Investigators initially suspected drug cartel involvement, but the man owed hundreds of thousands in back taxes and was about to lose his boat and home. Blood spatter analysis revealed arterial spray from a stationary position, eventually ruling out murder. Witnesses later stated that the man had "seemed fine" in the days leading up to his death.

Could something similar have happened to Davy Clough? Perhaps, but Saville's instincts suggested a different story. He continued the interview.

"Did Mr. Clough meet anyone here that you know of?"

"I didn't see him with anyone."

"Did he mention any names?"

She shook her head.

"You have a restaurant here, right?"

"The Country Corner."

"Did he eat there?"

She tapped the computer keyboard in front of her. "He had breakfast there on Friday morning and charged it to the room."

"Any other meals?"

She continued to scan her screen. "Not that I see."

Saville mentally constructed a timeline. Davy Clough checked into the motel around two p.m. on Thursday. He was in Saville's office spouting conspiracy theories just ninety minutes later. He was supposed to meet a corroborating witness for dinner that night. The next day, he was dead. Assuming the dinner had taken place, it didn't happen at the motel. The options in Kendall County were limited; eliminate the burger, chicken, and barbecue joints, and that left Applebee's, Ruby Tuesday, the sole Chinese restaurant, and Saville's favorite, Normandy Landing, a local WWII-themed spot. He would check there first after the interviews.

"Please ask Magdalena Rodriguez to come in," he said.

"Just so you know," she said, "her English isn't very good. She hasn't been in the country long. I mean—"

"She's undocumented."

"Yes, but..." Belinda hesitated. "She's a wonderful person and a very hard worker."

"Her immigration status is ICE's problem," Saville replied. "I just want to talk about Davy Clough."

"You won't turn her in?"

"No."

She sighed in relief. "I knew you were a good man."

He didn't feel like a good man. Jennifer didn't think he was a good man. Honestly, he didn't care about Magdalena Rodriguez's fate, whether she was deported or not. He had bigger concerns.

There was a walkie-talkie on her desk next to the computer. She pressed a key. "Magda, I need you in my office right away."

A few seconds of static followed, then a voice with a heavy Latino accent responded, "Yes, ma'am."

Magdalena arrived a few minutes later, looking frightened. Belinda must have sensed it too.

"It's okay, Magda," Belinda reassured her. "This gentleman is with the FBI. He wants to ask you a few questions about the man in room 157."

Magdalena still seemed unsure, her eyes darting around the room.

"He's not concerned about anything else," Belinda continued. "And he has nothing to do with Sheriff Helm."

This seemed to provide some reassurance. Belinda offered her chair, and the two women switched places. Magdalena's eyes remained fixed on Saville's every move.

"Tell me about the man in room 157," he said.

"I don't know nothing." Her tone was tense. "Like I told the sheriff, I went to clean his room and found him dead in the bathtub."

"Describe what you saw as best you can." Saville aimed to be patient and gentle.

Magdalena glanced at Belinda and then back at Saville. "Lots of blood. On the floor. In the water. The towels—"

"Wait. Towels?" He referred back to his portfolio and the evidence inventory. Again, no mention of towels.

"Two bloody towels on the floor next to the toilet," Belinda confirmed. "It looked like the floor had been wiped with them."

Saville stared at both of them. "You both saw these towels?"

Belinda nodded, while Magdalena replied, *"Sí."*

"Do either of you have any idea what happened to those towels?"

"Sheriff Helm took them," Belinda said.

"Put them in a bag," Magdalena added.

Saville nodded. Evidence collection bag. Sheriff Helm, of course, had obstructed the investigation at every turn, and now he was conveniently on medical leave. Who else would conceal evidence and contaminate the scene? Saville cursed himself for not realizing it sooner.

Chapter 9

A five-hundred-dollar-an-hour call girl of Cuban descent had just finished with President Woodrow Carney when he poured himself a Negroni and opened his box of Zino Platinum Crown Series cigars. A reward for a job well done. Since arriving in Fort Lauderdale four hours ago, he'd been busy. He'd delivered a flawless press conference at Fort Lauderdale-Hollywood Airport with Air Force One as a backdrop, posed for photos with the mayor, and enjoyed the best oral sex ever from this lovely Princesa. Broward County party leaders specialized in first-class treatment, and he traveled here on official business whenever possible.

He'd earned some time to relax. His fundraising speech at the Bahia Mar Yachting Center was set for seven p.m., giving him four hours to enjoy drinks, smoke a premium panetela, and take a brief nap. Soon enough, he'd be in the makeup artist's chair, getting pampered for the television cameras. Even his political opponents couldn't criticize his devilish good looks. Pundits often claimed he was the most handsome president since JFK, and Carney took full advantage of his sex appeal.

Local party officials were even sending a masseuse to his hotel to help him unwind and get to sleep after the two-thousand-dollar-a-ticket event ended around ten p.m. His overall popularity may have waned, but Carney remained a rock star in the Democratic Party, a two-term president adored by the progressive base, especially the wealthy liberals who took their cues from the Center for American Progress and the ACLU. With mid-term elections approaching, Carney's presence at fundraisers was increasingly valuable.

Dressed only in his bathrobe, he stirred the ice in his drink and stepped onto the balcony overlooking the Atlantic Ocean. His twelfth-floor luxury suite at The Atlantic Resort and Spa offered one of the best views in the city. The hotel was one of his favorites, his go-to accommodation whenever he was in town.

Two Secret Service agents stood on the balcony, exchanging worried glances as Carney breathed in the salty air.

"Mr. President, please go back inside," one agent urged. "It's not safe out here."

The balcony was an exposed area, leaving the president vulnerable to sniper fire and aerial threats.

"You guys are no fun," Carney said. "I just wanted to check out the *mujerzuelas* on the beach."

The other agent took him by the arm and led him through the sliding glass doors back into the room.

"I think I'll take a nap," Carney said, just as his chief of staff, Calvin Gates, burst in with four other Secret Service agents.

"For God's sake, Calvin—"

"Sir, we have a situation," Gates said, struggling to catch his breath.

Carney laughed. "We sure do. I'm running low on Campari." He scanned the room. "Who's going to make me another drink?"

"All the major news organizations are reporting that Victor Farnsworth died by suicide this morning," Gates said. "They found his body in West Potomac Park near the Jefferson Memorial."

Carney lifted his glass. "Life, liberty, and the pursuit of adultery." He laughed, gulping down the last of his drink. "Sleeping with my wife would make any man want to kill himself."

"Please, Mr. President. The press is expecting a statement."

"And receive one they shall." Carney set his glass on the coffee table. "When I'm finished extolling the virtues of Deputy White House Counsel Victor Farnsworth, no one will remember what a two-faced bastard he was."

***

At precisely 5:30 p.m., President Carney stepped behind the podium bearing the presidential seal in the fourth-floor Intracoastal Room to deliver a statement about the tragic passing of Deputy White House Counsel Victor Farnsworth. Reporters from all major national news outlets and many local organizations filled every available chair.

Carney cleared his throat, drawing on his chameleonlike ability to change his expression and temperament. It was a skill that served him well in moments like this. The manufactured sorrow seeped through as he began to speak:

"Thank you all for being here on such short notice. I know many of you traveled here to cover tonight's fundraising event, but I felt it was important to address you directly about the tragic news we received this morning. As you've reported, we lost a valued member of our administration today. Deputy White House Counsel Victor Farnsworth was found deceased this morning in Washington, and I wanted to take this opportunity to discuss his service to our country and express our condolences to his family."

He paused, looking out at the assembled reporters.

"Before I make my statement, I want to acknowledge that this is an active investigation, and I will not be taking questions about the circumstances surrounding Victor's death. Those inquiries should be directed to the appropriate law enforcement agencies. What I can share is about the man we've lost and the legacy he leaves behind. Victor dedicated his life to public service and to the principles that make our democracy strong. For the past six years, he served this administration with distinction, bringing his legal expertise and unwavering commitment to justice to some of our most challenging issues."

He paused again, allowing his calculated display of grief to register with the audience. He knew the press corps would respond exactly as he intended.

"Before joining the White House, Victor spent over two decades as a respected attorney in North Carolina, where he earned the trust of his community through his integrity and dedication to the law. He brought that same sense of duty and honor to Washington. Victor was more than a colleague; he was a trusted friend whose counsel I valued deeply. His legal mind was sharp, his judgment sound, and his loyalty to the Constitution absolute."

Carney's voice caught slightly.

"But perhaps most importantly, Victor was a devoted husband and father. Our hearts go out to his wife, Molly, and their two children, Bryan and Julie, during this incredibly difficult time. No words can ease their pain, but I want them to know that Victor's service to our country will not be forgotten. Thank you."

He stepped back from the podium. The room fell silent for a moment, then the barrage of questions began. Carney ignored them. Gates put his arm around the President and led him from the room.

***

Hellen Carney suppressed a scream when she saw her husband's face flash across the television screen. She'd long since stopped crying; her despair over Victor's death was overshadowed by confusion about why it had happened. Last night and early this morning, Victor had been full of bliss. A few hours later, he was dead by his own hand. What had caused such an abrupt change?

Yes, he often complained about the polarizing Washington pressure cooker and how a "good ol' boy" shouldn't be subjected to such nonstop demonization from the right. As if his humble background made him immune to criticism. She knew how badly he yearned for home, the small-town life to which he'd grown accustomed. He'd even found Raleigh overwhelming during her husband's governorship, and that was a city almost half the size of Washington.

Was Victor truly unhappy and homesick enough to put a gun in his mouth and pull the trigger? She refused to believe it. Then why? She had no logical answer and mourned the reality that Victor would never touch her again in his special way. In any way. Nausea stirred inside her as she watched Woody leave the podium, awestruck by his performance.

She envied his gift of being all things to all people while displaying the proper emotion, regardless of the context. His voice even cracked at one point during the speech. She could only imagine the heartfelt condolences the Broward County Kool-Aid drinkers would offer once they opened their checkbooks later that night.

Woody wouldn't even be there. He was flying back to Washington to prepare for Victor's funeral. As a captain in the United States Army Reserve, Victor would be buried at Arlington National Cemetery with full military honors. Services were scheduled for Wednesday at 4:00 p.m.

She would be there, along with most of Washington and a few foreign dignitaries. So would her husband, the man who knew more than he was letting on. She was certain of it. Only one question remained: Would he confess to her willingly, or would she have to resort to political blackmail?

He'd be riding high when he got back to the White House. For a few days at least, the public would forget about the poor economy, high gas prices, and record inflation as they united with their heartsick President. Without a doubt, Woody's poll numbers would spike at least five to ten points because of Victor's death.

It made her sick. Literally. She ran to the bathroom as bile rose in her throat.

***

Saville watched the President's speech from the Ruby Tuesday bar. This restaurant was his third stop. He'd already been to Applebee's and Normandy Landing, but none of the servers or hosts at either place recognized Davy Clough from the driver's license photo Saville had enlarged to a slightly grainy 5 x 7 image. Seconds after he entered Ruby Tuesday, the bar television buzzed with a Fox News special bulletin: "Top White House Advisor Found Dead," although few patrons or employees took notice.

Saville definitely did. He viewed himself as a political junkie, although he never let politics influence his judgment and always considered both sides of any issue before deciding. His law enforcement training mandated that he remain open-minded.

He waited for the President to finish and then asked the bartender to locate the manager. He was just exiting the kitchen when the bartender waved him over.

"Hey, Sherm! Cops are here."

"I'm sorry, but we're a little short-staffed," the manager said. His nametag read Sherman. Saville didn't know if it was a first or last name.

Saville introduced himself without showing his badge, sometimes only doing so when asked.

"I'll be glad to talk to you, but you may have to follow me around," Sherman said.

He placed two sizzling plates in front of a young couple seated at a corner booth and asked if they needed anything else.

"More tea," the young man said, pushing his glass to the end of the table.

As Sherman picked up the glass and headed to the tea brewer, Saville grabbed his arm and asked, "Do you remember seeing this man here Thursday night?" He showed him Davy Clough's photo.

"Sorry, never seen him before," Sherman said, refilling the customer's glass. "Wait, did you say Thursday? No wonder. I was off that day."

"Who was working?"

"I'll have to check the schedule. Give me a minute."

Sherman hurried the tea glass back to the customer's table and then disappeared behind a set of swinging double doors. What he called a minute turned out to be ten. He finally returned with two college-aged servers, both redheads with identical facial features.

"The twins were working Thursday night," Sherman said. "Felicity and Fiona."

Saville showed the photo, and Felicity spoke up immediately. "Yeah, I remember him. Dude liked to play grab-ass."

"Did you report it?" Sherman interjected with a concerned look. He turned to Saville. "I assure you, we do not tolerate sexual harassment at this establishment."

Saville ignored him. "Felicity, was this gentleman here with anyone?"

"Two other guys," she said. "They were all kinda rude. But I guess it's okay. They left a fifty-dollar tip."

"You always get the high rollers," Fiona added.

"Can you describe the men he was with?" Saville asked.

Felicity thought for a moment. "Well, one was kinda tall, had dark hair, glasses. Oh, and a birthmark on his left cheek that was cute in a Cindy Crawford sort of way."

Saville nodded, taking it all in.

"And he had an accent," Felicity blurted.

Saville's ears perked up. "What kind of accent?"

"A foreign accent, like he was from Brazil or Russia or someplace."

Saville sighed. "What about the other guy?"

"He's dead," Felicity said without hesitation.

Saville rubbed his forehead. "And how do you know that?"

"They just showed his picture on television. Poor guy blew his brains out or something in Washington, D.C."

Chapter 10

Lowri watched the ambulance transport Victor Farnsworth's body to the nearby George Washington University Medical Center. Sweat trickled down her forehead; the rain clouds had cleared, the sun was out, and nightfall was still at least ninety minutes away. The oppressive humidity that often made summer in the nation's capital unbearable had returned.

Was it the heat causing her discomfort, or the unsettling feeling that she had stumbled into a genuine Washington conspiracy? So many aspects of the Farnsworth case troubled her. The attending medical examiner had already ruled the death a suicide, despite the absence of blood evidence and the missing bullet. Detective Sprague had agreed, effectively halting any investigation pending the autopsy results. That was just the beginning.

When the body was discovered, the gun was still clutched in Farnsworth's right hand. In typical suicide cases, a .38 caliber firearm would end up several feet away from the victim due to its powerful recoil. A cadaveric spasm at the time of death could cause the fingers to freeze around the trigger, but such occurrences were extremely rare.

It also appeared that no one had checked for postmortem lividity at the scene. When a body is found lying on its back, blood settles in the lower parts of the body, creating a purplish-red discoloration. If someone moves the body after death, gravity redistributes the blood, altering the lividity patterns. While only an autopsy could definitively prove if a body had been moved, it was standard procedure for the investigating officer to make a preliminary assessment at the scene.

As far as she could tell, Peter Sprague had done none of these things. He glossed over several critical elements of the investigation like a rookie. Was he truly disinterested, or were more sinister forces at play? Lowri knew he wasn't incompetent; she could attest to that. So why the shortcuts?

"Oh, stop it, Lowri," she muttered to herself. "Your overactive imagination will get you in trouble someday."

"Talking to yourself again, Sarge?" It was Joel Graves's voice, now in the flesh. He was all man, with toned abs and a tanned face that seemed to conceal a deeper complexity. "You know what they say: it's okay to talk to yourself as long as nobody answers."

Lowri couldn't muster a laugh. What she craved were answers to her questions. "Anything about this case bother you, Joel?"

"Well, hello to you, too."

"I'm serious." Joel had been darting back and forth from the crime scene conducting searches, and they hadn't had a chance to talk. He probably hadn't had time to reflect on the matter.

"I'm not sure," he replied. "I mean, why are we even here?"

Lowri understood what he meant. In cases involving the deaths of government officials, the FBI typically assumed jurisdiction. The Park Police should have left once they identified Farnsworth.

"Any other time, Hoover's boys would be here stepping on everybody's toes," he continued. "So where are they?"

Did that explain Sprague's negligence? Did he realize he was about to be removed from the case?

"What did you think of the note?" she asked.

"What about it? The guy was obviously a little nutty, or he wouldn't have shoved a gun in his mouth. A standard suicide note."

Not quite. The note, meticulously folded and printed in red ink, was found on the passenger seat of Farnsworth's unlocked vehicle: *This town will chew you up and spit you out. I've had enough.* That was it. There was no mention of his wife or children, no goodbyes to friends or colleagues, no signature, and no philosophical ramblings typical of a troubled mind. Nothing to suggest the note was authentic.

"I think the note's a fake," Lowri said.

"Christ, Sarge. You still trying to score points with the FBI? Have you heard anything back from them yet?"

"They say my application's still being processed." Three months earlier, Lowri had applied for a position with the FBI's Behavioral Science Unit. Her passion was criminal profiling.

"You'll make a great little Clarice Starling one day," Graves said.

"Just not today?"

"Come on, Sarge, you know what I mean. Sure, there are some things about this guy's death that don't add up, but what does it matter? We're out of the loop anyway. Can't we spare his family some grief?"

"Even if it was murder?"

"That's a big if, Sarge." He checked his watch. "Our shift's over in an hour. What do you say we grab some beer and wings at that place you like in Foggy Bottom—"

"I don't know."

"Come on, Sarge. We'll get a little drunk and go back to my place—"

"Maybe," she interrupted. She didn't want to be alone tonight. Besides, how long had it been? Two months since she and Joel had been together?

"We can drink our sorrows away," he said. "The investigation's out of our hands now. It's time to let it go."

"Maybe," she repeated, declining to mention that letting it go was the furthest thing from her mind.

***

Jack Mayfield never left the office before six p.m., often staying even later depending on his caseload. Until Saville's arrival from Miami, the Greenville Resident Agency had been a one-man operation. One agent, Mayfield, and his administrative assistant, Rosena Wyatt, who had been with him for years. Mayfield had joined the Greenville office twelve years ago from FBI New York, the Bureau's largest and most demanding field office. Burnout was common there, and Mayfield was no exception. After seventeen years of chasing organized crime figures and other federal criminals, he suffered a complete breakdown.

He spent four months at a Bureau-approved psychiatric facility and another three recuperating at his brother-in-law's cottage in the Blue Ridge Mountains. Once he completed his recovery, he was transferred to Greenville, where the Resident Agent was moving on to bigger assignments at FBI Phoenix. Mayfield had remained in Greenville ever since, and the low-key environment suited him just fine.

Saville had seen no signs of Mayfield's previous mental health struggles. Although the senior agent could be old-school and abrasive at times, he worked hard and treated his subordinates fairly. Even now, as Saville updated him on the latest developments concerning the Davy Clough investigation, Mayfield processed the information like the seasoned agent he was.

"Two men have dinner together and then both kill themselves within three days in different parts of the country?" Mayfield said, leaning on his desk.

"Seems a little far-fetched."

"Damn right it does."

"Davy Clough said he was in town to meet with someone very important," Saville added. "Victor Farnsworth would certainly qualify."

"I have to admit, Mike, you were right. Maybe he was onto something."

Saville smiled, knowing how much it must have pained Mayfield to say those words.

"What about the third man?" Mayfield asked. "The one with the foreign accent?"

"In the interest of expediency, I've called in a forensic artist from the SBI."

Mayfield winced. Saville knew how much his boss disliked calling in outside agencies for help, but an official Bureau request for additional personnel could take days. North Carolina's State Bureau of Investigation promised to have someone here in hours.

"I'll forgive you this time," Mayfield said. "But don't go over my head again."

"Yes, sir." Saville grinned. Mayfield had forgiven him "this time" on at least a dozen occasions over the past year. "But I need your permission for something else. I believe Sheriff Helm is corrupt."

Mayfield's tone turned serious. "So do I."

Saville explained the missing bloody towels from Davy Clough's hotel room. "Helm's involved in this somehow. He's supposedly out on medical leave, but that's complete garbage." Saville shook his head. "I'm going to track him down and lean on him hard. I'll need your support when he starts complaining to Charlotte and Washington."

"I've got your back."

"Thanks, Jack."

"What about the autopsy report?" Mayfield asked. "That's going to determine how far we go with this thing."

"I have an appointment with Dr. Lyman tomorrow. He left a message with Rosena that the report was ready."

Mayfield nodded.

"I'd also like permission to fly to Washington—"

"Whoa, partner!" Mayfield raised a hand. "The Farnsworth case is strictly off-limits. Self-inflicted gunshot—"

"Horseshit, Jack, and you know it. Just like Davy Clough."

"I agree there are inconsistencies and coincidences that warrant further investigation." Mayfield pointed a finger at Saville. "But nobody has any concrete information, including us."

"I know there's a connection between the deaths of Davy Clough and Victor Farnsworth, and I'm going to find out what it is."

Mayfield pursed his lips. "Tread lightly, Mike. Remember what happened in Miami?"

"I do," Saville replied. He remembered so well that he feared it could happen again.

Chapter 11

F ive o'clock on Tuesday morning.

First Lady Hellen Carney woke shuddering in the Lincoln Bedroom, her hair damp and tangled with sweat. The nightmare had been terrifying.

Victor Farnsworth had been above her, whispering her name, his body warm against hers. She was lost in his rhythm until his hand slipped beneath the pillow. A pistol emerged, and without hesitation, he thrust it into his mouth and pulled the trigger.

The blast was deafening. Bone and brains splattered across the walls. His blood soaked her face and stained her naked chest. His body collapsed on top of hers, crushing her beneath his weight. She struggled to push him off, but the blood kept flowing. She was drowning in him.

"Victor! Why did you leave me?"

She bolted upright, gasping, the echo of the gunshot still ringing in her ears. She had slept only in fragments all night. Her husband hadn't returned from Florida until after midnight, and she didn't want to see him—not that she often did anymore. Sometimes she escaped to the futon in her office; other times, to the Green Room.

On this night, she had chosen the Lincoln Bedroom, which was always ready when the President was away.

The room had taken on her signature style. At her insistence, it had undergone a sweeping Victorian restoration. Gone were the dull, dated tones; in their place was a lavish palette of greens, yellows, and purples, an ornate white marble mantel, and a carved crown-like canopy that transformed the bed into a throne. She had admired it as she lay awake through the night, staring upward with thoughts of Victor until exhaustion finally claimed her. Only then had the nightmare begun.

But this nightmare felt more than just grief. The image of Victor's suicide gnawed at her because she couldn't believe it was true. Not Victor. His marriage might have been hollow, and his affair with her reckless, but his love for his children was unshakeable.

He always spoke of them. Bryan, his eighteen-year-old son, was a basketball star already being scouted to play at Duke. Julie, fourteen, was a gifted scholar and performer, having already starred in several theater productions. They meant everything to him. He would not have left them behind.

Which left only one conclusion: Victor Farnsworth hadn't killed himself. Someone had murdered him.

The realization hardened inside her, sending an icy shiver through her stomach. And what frightened her most was that she already suspected who it was.

***

Saville was already waiting in his car when deputies Billy Downing and Alfred Rhodes arrived at 7:00 a.m. to begin their twelve-hour shift.

They parked next to each other in the courthouse lot, both driving late-model, American-made pickups that had seen better days.

They exchanged brief words and then headed for the employee entrance.

Saville followed at a distance, neither deputy acknowledging his presence, though Downing glanced back once before disappearing inside.

The sheriff's department occupied the building's east wing. Saville caught up with them in the main corridor.

"Deputies, I need a few minutes."

Rhodes turned first. "Agent Saville, right? Alfred Rhodes, acting sheriff while Helm's out." His handshake was firm and professional. "What can we do for you?"

"You already know me," Downing said.

Saville nodded as they walked into Helm's office. Rhodes sat behind the desk while Saville took the visitor's chair in front. Downing lingered in the hallway.

"How long before Sheriff Helm returns to work?" Saville asked, all business.

"Want some coffee or something?" Rhodes gestured to Downing. "Billy, get me and Mr. Saville a cup of coffee."

"No thanks," Saville replied. "I asked you about the sheriff."

For the second straight night, Saville had slept poorly, and his grumpiness was evident.

"Nobody knows," Rhodes said, his eyes darkening. "He's on medical leave. HIPAA—"

"I know. Downing told me. Plastic surgery. Where's the procedure being done?"

"He didn't say. He's been very secretive about it."

Downing entered the office with two steaming cups. He placed one on Rhodes' desk and handed the other to Saville, who accepted it despite his earlier refusal.

"Are you planning on visiting Sheriff Helm in the hospital? Sending a card or flowers?"

"Outpatient, I think," Downing said.

"Recovering at home. I'll need that address."

"No, he mentioned something about staying at a friend's house."

"What friend?"

"Didn't say."

"Billy, how come you know so much about what's going on?" Rhodes asked, carefully testing the hot liquid.

"Sheriff Helm tells me everything," Downing beamed. "Calls me 'his boy.'"

"Has he called in to talk to 'his boy' since the surgery?"

"Nope."

Saville realized he was spinning his wheels and would have to track down Helm another way. He changed the subject.

Belinda Chatwyn and Magdalena Rodriguez reported that a pair of bloody towels had been found at the crime scene. "Where would they be right now?"

"Evidence locker, I assume," Rhodes said, taking another sip. "Billy, go check, will you?"

Billy left. Saville said, "Do you remember those towels? Helm supposedly bagged them himself."

"I remember them. Somebody tried to wipe up the blood . . ." Rhodes waved his hands. "I tried to tell the sheriff that the kid had been murdered, but he didn't want to listen. I'm just a lowly deputy. What do I know?"

"You seem to know a lot." Saville sampled his coffee now that it had cooled. "What can you tell me about working for Sheriff Helm?"

"He's a good cop, if that's what you're asking. A little un-orthodox, maybe."

"Unorthodox?"

Rhodes didn't hesitate. "He believes in getting the job done, no matter what it takes."

"Is he dirty?"

Rhodes looked away, surprised. "I don't... I really wouldn't know."

Saville took note; Rhodes didn't deny it.

The door swung open, and Downing reentered, arms empty. "No dice," he said. "All the Clough evidence is missing. Sheriff Helm logged it out Sunday night."

"Just before he left town," Saville noted.

Rhodes slammed his fist on the desktop.

Saville stood and handed Rhodes a business card. Helm's evidence tampering confirmed his suspicions, but it also meant time was running out. Whatever the sheriff was hiding, he was actively working to cover it up. "Call me when you hear from the sheriff," he said, knowing that was one call he would never receive.

***

The President concluded his daily thirty-minute briefing with National Security Advisor Wallace Lancaster at 8:45 a.m. His schedule typically allowed fifteen minutes to prepare for his next appointment, usually with either the Senate Majority Leader or the chair of the Congressional Black Caucus. Today, however, his agenda changed without warning.

The First Lady had been waiting in the West Wing corridor since 8:30 a.m. Chief of Staff Calvin Gates had managed to temper her frustration over being denied immediate access to her husband, persuading her to wait until the Lancaster meeting concluded. She acquiesced and waited in relative silence alongside two Secret Service agents stationed outside the Oval Office. The agents knew better than to attempt conversation; the White House staff had long ago dubbed her the "Ice Queen" for good reason.

The President escorted Lancaster to the northwest door and bid him farewell. Hellen wasted no time; she pushed past both men, strode across the presidential seal woven into the carpet, and dropped into the chair behind the Resolute Desk.

Gates stood stunned in the doorway. "I'm sorry, Mr. President," he said. "I told her you were occupied, but you know—"

Carney clapped a hand on Gates's shoulder. "No worries, Cal. A little marital bliss always gets my juices flowing."

"Would you like me to stay, sir?"

"Absolutely not, Cal. I can't have you intruding on my quality time with my wife."

Gates nodded and exited through the door to his adjacent office.

Once Gates was out of earshot, Carney dropped all pretense. "How dare you embarrass me like that?" he thundered, stepping toward the desk. "It's not enough that you were sleeping with my best friend? You have to make a scene in front of my staff?"

The First Lady sneered. "At least I chose a real man to sleep with, unlike the college girls and interns you prefer."

The President jerked back his fist but thought better of it.

"What's the matter, honey?" the First Lady smirked. "Not man enough? Wouldn't my next public appearance be a hit, pardon the pun, with my face bruised and battered?"

"People would just think you fell down the Grand Staircase during one of your drunken stupors."

"You're such a bastard."

"The bastard you married who's the Commander-in-Chief. Never forget it. Now what the hell do you want?" He glanced at his watch. "I have another meeting in ten minutes."

"Cancel it. I want to know why you had Victor Farnsworth murdered."

"Oh, for Christ's sake," Carney scoffed. "You've lost your mind."

Hellen stood. "Have I? You've already admitted you knew about Victor and me. You couldn't handle—"

"Don't flatter yourself." He almost spat the words. "I couldn't care less who you sleep with."

"You care about anything you can't control. And you can't control me."

"I haven't cared for a long time." He walked toward the door. "Now, if you'll excuse me."

"I'll tell *The Post*."

He laughed. "Sure you will."

"I'll leak it anonymously. They'll never identify the source."

"What, and tell the world what an ungrateful whore you are?" He stopped a few steps from the door. "You're nothing without me."

"Not just *The Post*. Every major news outlet in the world. Hannity, and Clay and Buck, too. They'll crucify you."

"They already do. Why not exhume Limbaugh and ask him?" He continued his march toward the exit.

She hurried around the front of the desk to block the door. "Where do you think you're going?"

"I told you. I have a meeting." Realizing she had no intention of moving, he sighed. "Forget it. I'll just move it to the Eisenhower Building." He stepped around her and opened the northeast door. Gates and the two Secret Service agents rushed to his side. "Stay as long as you like, darling," he said in his most civil tone. "We'll have lunch together. How about one o'clock?" He gestured for Gates to follow and started down the hallway. Three steps later, he turned and blew the First Lady a kiss before continuing on.

"Son of a bitch." The words echoed in the empty Oval Office. Hellen stood alone, calculating her next move. She wasn't certain how far she would go, but she knew one thing: she would make him pay.

Chapter 12

Olivia Hardy, a freelance forensic artist contracted by the State Bureau of Investigation, delivered her composite sketches in person to the FBI's Greenville resident agency just before noon. The ten-minute drive from her home office was routine; she primarily worked in Greenville, the headquarters for the Northeastern District's twenty-three-county coverage area.

She found Saville in his office. "I was hoping to catch you before lunch," she said.

With long auburn hair and striking blue eyes, Olivia appeared fresh out of college, but her demeanor suggested deeper experience. Saville had collaborated with forensic artists from the state crime lab's Graphics Unit and several freelancers over the years, but he distinctly remembered Olivia.

"Where did the FBI find you?" Saville asked, trying to sound casual despite his curiosity.

"Through the North Carolina Justice Academy's contractor database. Before going freelance, I spent seven years with the Greenville PD's Special Victims Unit. Seven years of dealing with sexual assault cases, child abuse, and domestic violence was enough for me."

Seven years, Saville thought. So much for the fresh-out-of-college theory. "What led you to forensic art?"

"I earned my BFA in Graphic Design from ECU and received specialized training at the Justice Academy. Honestly? Too many episodes of *CSI* in college." She smiled.

"That's quite a combination." He smiled back, a rarity for him lately. "Listen, since it's lunchtime, the least the Bureau can do is buy you lunch. You've done excellent work for us."

"No favors needed," she replied. "The FBI pays very well. But I have to decline. I have a meeting in Raleigh this afternoon. Rain check?"

"It doesn't have to be today. There are plenty of great places around here… wait, you're not a vegetarian, are you?"

"God, no," she laughed. "I work with law enforcement, remember? Give me ribs and beer any day."

"Ribs and beer it is. Just say when."

"What would Mrs. Saville say about that?" She glanced at his left hand, where his wedding band still circled his finger. He wasn't ready to take it off yet, even though the divorce papers were nearly finalized.

He looked down, the moment of levity evaporating. "I guess you're right. I'm the one who needs the rain check."

She studied him, her expression softening. "Ah, one of those situations." She handed him a USB drive and a portfolio case. "The work helped me through mine. Sometimes staying busy is the only thing that works."

Inside the portfolio were three progressive composite sketches on 11 × 14 drawing paper, showing the iterative development of the subject's features. A fourth image, a digitally enhanced composite, displayed remarkable detail. Most forensic artists produced sequential sketches that became more refined as witnesses recalled additional details. Her final computer-generated composite, created using specialized software like FACES, was high-resolution enough for distribution without quality degradation.

Saville examined each drawing, grateful for the distraction from personal topics. The final composite was exceptional: short black hair, clean-shaven, a heart-shaped face with a distinctive circular birthmark on the left cheek, wire-rimmed glasses with round frames, and close-set brown eyes.

"Someone you know?" Olivia asked.

"No, I'm just impressed by the level of detail. Honestly, I didn't think our witness would provide enough information."

"That girl's more observant than she seems."

"I think the artist deserves most of the credit."

She blushed, an unexpected reaction that made her seem more approachable. Saville returned to his desk, inserted the USB drive, and initiated a secure upload to the Forensic Audio, Video, and Image Analysis Unit (FAVIAU) at the FBI Laboratory in Quantico. Following chain-of-custody protocols, he placed the USB drive and hard copies in a tamper-evident evidence bag, completing the documentation for overnight shipment as back-up.

Once FAVIAU received the composite, their analysts would run it through multiple facial recognition systems—geometric feature analysis, eigenface comparison, and neural network algorithms—cross-referencing against the Next Generation Identification (NGI) database and other systems maintained by CJIS in Clarksburg, West Virginia.

Processing time varied based on case priority. With the Davy Clough case designated as Priority 4, Saville anticipated at least a two-week wait, possibly longer.

"I should head out," Olivia said. "Anything else you need from me, Agent Saville? Professionally speaking, of course."

The qualification made him smile despite himself. "You've been tremendously helpful."

She placed a business card on his desk. "About that rain check. My number's there for whenever you're ready. It doesn't have to be ribs; coffee works too." She paused at the door. "The work helps, but sometimes you need to talk to someone who understands what you're going through."

After she left, Saville picked up the card, running his thumb over the embossed lettering. For the first time in months, he felt something other than the emotional wreckage of his failing marriage. He tucked the card into his wallet before returning to the case file.

***

Saville felt unexpectedly optimistic as he drove across town to Pitt County Memorial Hospital for his two-thirty appointment with Dr. Lyman. He and Lyman had spoken by phone after Olivia Hardy's departure, and the medical examiner confirmed that both toxicology and pathology results were complete. He hadn't provided specifics over the phone, citing privacy protocols and preferring to discuss findings in person.

"I haven't told Cynthia Clough yet," Lyman had said ominously. "You need to be prepared before we deal with the onslaught."

The comment had been troubling, but Saville tried to remain optimistic. As he turned right onto Arlington Boulevard, he realized his mood was oddly buoyant. Olivia Hardy was the reason, however inappropriate that might be. She was attractive, intelligent, engaging, and probably fifteen years younger than him. She was also a Bureau contractor, which created ethical complications. Still, she'd made him feel less untethered for the first time in months, even if the feeling was temporary.

He understood that law enforcement relationships rarely worked. While cops theoretically made good partners because they understood the job's demands and dangers, reality proved otherwise. That mutual understanding often created additional stress rather than alleviating it. When your spouse worked outside law enforcement, they couldn't fully grasp the daily pressures, which paradoxically reduced marital tension. There remained a protective buffer of not quite knowing.

God knows he'd experienced enough marital tension, most of it self-inflicted. His marriage had consisted of seven good years followed by twelve months of deterioration as Jennifer grew tired of his chronic absence and emotional unavailability. She'd abandoned her career to raise Emma, and her resentment over his apparent indifference to that sacrifice had metastasized into something toxic. They'd tried maintaining the façade for Emma's sake, but both recognized the futility. Jennifer had publicly supported him after the Miami incident, but his misconduct and subsequent transfer to Greenville had been the final blow.

He fidgeted with his wedding ring, understanding why Olivia Hardy affected him. She reminded him of Jennifer when they'd first met, stirring complicated feelings. Best to forget about Olivia entirely. Davy Clough's case required his complete focus.

The hospital visitor lot was nearly full, and it took ten minutes to find a space. Drawing patients from across eastern North Carolina, PCMH remained busy year-round.

Saville found Lyman in his fourth-floor office behind his desk. "Can I get you anything, Agent Saville?" Lyman asked, rising to pour coffee from a carafe on his credenza.

"No, thank you." Saville took a seat. "I'm hoping you have helpful news."

"That depends on what you're hoping to hear."

"I need evidence about Davy Clough's death. What did you find?"

Lyman returned to his chair with his coffee. "I'm afraid you'll be disappointed. I found no evidence of a homicide. My official determination is suicide."

Saville sat in stunned silence. While he'd braced himself for this possibility given Lyman's earlier warnings, there was a difference between intellectual preparation and emotional readiness. The conclusion hit hard.

"What's your basis for that determination?" Saville asked.

"The evidence is circumstantial but consistent with suicide cases." Lyman paused. "The findings show that—"

"Please, Dr. Lyman, just get to the point." The medical examiner's tendency to hedge and qualify frustrated Saville, whose work demanded concrete facts.

"Pathology identified multiple demyelinating lesions in Davy's brain consistent with early-stage multiple sclerosis. Toxicology also detected therapeutic levels of two antidepressants, escitalopram and mirtazapine, in his blood. My assessment is that Davy was being treated for depression related to his MS diagnosis."

"More speculation than substantiation. I need something more definitive, Dr. Lyman."

"I contacted Davy's insurance provider. His father, Dr. Clough, prescribed both medications two months ago, which aligns with the probable onset of his MS symptoms."

"His father wrote the prescriptions?" Saville frowned. "That's a serious ethical breach. Doctors aren't supposed to treat immediate family, especially for psychiatric issues."

"It is highly irregular and violates AMA guidelines, but it isn't strictly illegal," Lyman replied. "It suggests a desperate desire for privacy. They likely wanted to keep the MS diagnosis and the resulting depression 'in the house,' so to speak. I understand this isn't conclusive proof of suicide, Agent Saville, but these are the facts we have."

Saville said nothing, sensing the investigation collapsing.

"I know this isn't what you expected," Lyman said. "However, the medical evidence leads to only one reasonable conclusion: Davy

Clough, suffering from a degenerative neurological disease, took his own life. Now, I need to find a way to inform his mother."

Cynthia Clough would not take the news well. Saville now understood what Lyman meant about the impending onslaught.

Chapter 13

Lowri spent nearly an hour in the hallway gathering her courage before knocking on her district commander's door at exactly eight a.m.

"Come in," Captain Rufus Morrow called out. Upon seeing her, he smiled. "Sergeant Pritchard. What brings you here?"

Morrow was a twenty-two-year veteran of the U.S. Park Police. Lowri had been in sixth grade when he joined, and over the years, he had become a mentor to her.

His office always impressed her with its orderliness. While most commanders worked behind stacks of case files and administrative paperwork, or at least created that illusion, Morrow's desk held only a laptop, a single manila folder, and a photograph of his late wife. He processed work so efficiently that he often appeared to be doing nothing at all.

"I need to discuss the Farnsworth case, sir," Lowri said, taking a seat across from him.

Morrow's expression flickered. "That's Detective Sprague's investigation, Sergeant."

Lowri had never seen Morrow raise his voice or lose his temper, even when reprimanding subordinates. She suspected this leadership style was why District One maintained what everyone claimed was a ninety percent retention rate, while other divisions lost officers to municipal departments and federal agencies.

"I was a first responder, sir. I helped secure the scene." Lowri kept her voice steady. "There are inconsistencies that concern me."

"You mean the minimal blood spatter and the missing bullet?"

"Yes, sir."

"The storm surge explains both," Morrow replied. "Hurricane flooding displaced or destroyed most of the physical evidence. You know what water does to a crime scene."

"But the body's position suggested—"

"Sergeant." She could tell she was pushing too hard; the slight tightening around his eyes gave it away, but he remained patient with her, as always. "You have good instincts. That's why you'll make an outstanding detective someday. But strong investigators don't manufacture mysteries where none exist. Sometimes a case is exactly what it appears to be. In twenty-two years, I've encountered maybe a dozen truly straightforward suicides. This is one of them."

"With respect, sir, how can we be certain without a complete investigation?"

Morrow opened the folder on his desk. "Detective Sprague interviewed fourteen witnesses. Farnsworth's colleagues confirmed he was struggling with political pressure. His wife stated he'd been depressed for months and had discussed leaving D.C. His therapist, with family permission, confirmed he was on antidepressants."

Lowri shifted in her chair but remained silent.

"The forensics are conclusive," Morrow continued. "GSR on his right hand, his prints on the .38, trajectory consistent with self-infliction. The medical examiner's preliminary findings indicate no defensive wounds and no signs of struggle."

"When will the full autopsy report be available?"

"Within forty-eight hours." Morrow rubbed a hand through his hair, a gesture she'd learned meant he was growing weary of the conversation. "The case is closed pending that report, Sergeant. Unless the M.E. finds something extraordinary, we're done. Victor Farnsworth committed suicide. I need you to accept that and return to your assigned duties."

"Sir, I believe—"

"What you believe isn't relevant without evidence." He softened his voice. "Lowri, I understand this is difficult. But sometimes, people in pain make permanent decisions. Our job is to document facts, not pursue theories."

Lowri stood. "Yes, sir."

"Good. I don't want to hear that you're still asking questions about this case. Let the man rest in peace. Are we clear?"

"Clear, sir."

She left his office with her doubts intact. Morrow could cite all the evidence he wanted, but she had seen the scene. The angles were wrong, the blood pattern inconsistent with the body position, and nobody had adequately explained why a right-handed man would shoot himself and end up sprawled on his back, arms and legs stretched out.

She didn't consider herself particularly spiritual, but she knew that Victor Farnsworth would never rest in peace until his killers were brought to justice.

***

"It's over," Jack Mayfield said. "The M.E.'s report confirms suicide. Are you ready to accept that Davy Clough killed himself?"

"No." Saville studied the photographs on Mayfield's wall, his gaze settling on one from Ground Zero, September 2001. Mayfield stood beside the attorney general, his face etched with grief that twenty-plus years hadn't erased.

Mayfield had been a case agent on the initial response team. Saville had heard the Bureau legend: Mayfield lost fourteen colleagues when the towers fell, including John O'Neill, the former FBI counterterrorism chief who had just started as World Trade Center security director. People still whispered that the loss had triggered Mayfield's breakdown two years later.

Mayfield leaned back in his chair. "Mike, the case is closed. The autopsy findings are conclusive. I can't justify allocating resources to a resolved death investigation."

"I've got two weeks of annual leave banked," Saville said. "Maybe I'll take Emma to D.C. She's never seen the Smithsonian."

"Don't do this, Mike."

"At least let me locate Sheriff Helm. Find out why he contaminated the scene. Even if Clough committed suicide, Helm's behavior suggests something else."

"We don't have his location."

"We do. I flagged his credit cards through FinCEN. He used a Visa at a hotel in Wilmington on Monday night. That's flight behavior, Jack. I can be there in ninety minutes."

Mayfield tapped his desk, a nervous habit Saville recognized from their time working together. "The Wilmington RA should handle this."

"Give me twenty-four hours, Jack." Saville held up his hand and crossed his fingers. "Scout's honor. If this doesn't pan out—"

"You'll be keeping me company in the unemployment line."

"I'll do better than that." Saville tried to smile. "I'll throw you the fanciest retirement party the Bureau has ever seen."

Mayfield shook his head. "Miami all over again. You never learn."

"Miami taught me plenty. Sometimes the obvious answer isn't the right one."

"Twenty-four hours, Mike. Not one minute more. And you report everything through official channels."

"Understood."

"And Mike?" Mayfield's expression hardened. "If this goes sideways, I can't protect you. Not again."

***

Saville couldn't stop thinking about Miami. Eighteen months ago, he had been leading the investigation into German arms dealer Gregor Lambrecht for trafficking in dimethyl methylphosphonate, a regulated sarin precursor chemical. Then everything had gone to hell.

Hours before the arrest team moved in, Lambrecht fled to Nordhausen, Germany. But not before he tortured and killed Special Agent Caroline Cochran after luring her to a musty, largely abandoned medical supply warehouse in Wynwood.

Caroline had been thirty-one, just eight months out of Quantico. Saville had been her training agent and blamed himself for missing the danger signs. When Germany denied the extradition request, citing insufficient evidence and EU human rights protocols, something inside Saville snapped.

He boarded a flight to Germany without authorization. His plan was simple: find Lambrecht in Nordhausen and bring him back, legally or otherwise. The Miami SAC immediately notified the International Operations Division. FBI Legal Attaché Berlin intercepted Saville at Erfurt-Weimar Airport before he could clear customs.

He spent seventy-two hours in administrative detention while the Office of Professional Responsibility decided his fate. The verdict: six weeks suspension without pay, forfeiture of his supervisory status, and immediate transfer. Only his twelve-year stellar record and his forty-seven successful felony prosecutions saved him from termination.

They sent him to Greenville, North Carolina, where the resident agency handled tobacco fraud and occasional bank robberies. SAC Jack Mayfield, known in the Bureau as a last-chance supervisor, would monitor his every move.

Miami was one of the Bureau's crown jewels: international drug cartels, terrorism task forces, public corruption cases that made headlines. Agents called it "The Super Bowl of Crime." Now Saville worked on reactive investigations in a town most agents couldn't locate on a map.

His career was effectively over. Unless...

Unless he could break something significant. The kind of case that could make Washington forget past mistakes. Was Davy Clough that case? The kid claimed his investigation reached "the highest levels of government." Every paranoid fantasist said that. But Clough had been different. Tight-lipped about specifics, refusing to share details even with the FBI. That very secretiveness made Saville believe him. Real whistleblowers protected their information; the delusional ones couldn't stop talking.

Or maybe Clough was simply another troubled young man facing a degenerative disease who chose his own exit. The MS diagnosis. The antidepressants.

Saville recognized the gravity of the situation. If he misjudged Clough, Mayfield wouldn't come to his rescue; the Bureau was unforgiving. However, if he was correct, that Clough had been murdered to silence him, then someone powerful was deeply concerned.

Regardless of the outcome, in twenty-four hours, Michael Saville would discover whether he had a future with the FBI.

***

The drive to Wilmington took two hours instead of the usual ninety minutes because of a jackknifed tractor-trailer on Highway 11 between Deep Run and Pink Hill, causing a three-mile backup.

Saville passed through Kendall County and stopped at the Sheriff's Office to see if Helm had made contact. He hadn't. Saville wanted Deputies Downing and Rhodes to know the FBI was still interested. Rhodes exhibited his usual calculating indifference, while Downing seemed genuinely unconcerned. Neither man appeared eager for their boss to return, and given Saville's observations of Helm's temperament, he understood why.

At 6:02 p.m., Saville pulled under the porte-cochère of the Wilmington Inn on Market Street, a boutique hotel in the historic district. He had only a credit card transaction and this address. No indication of whether Helm was still registered, whether the supposed surgery was real, or if the sheriff had already fled. It was a long shot at best.

Saville showed his credentials to the desk clerk, a college-aged kid named Tyler.

"I need to speak with the manager," Tyler said nervously.

While waiting, Saville watched the lobby television, where WWAY was covering Victor Farnsworth's state funeral. The camera focused on the President's stoic expression, then panned to the First Lady wiping away tears. The ABC News correspondent described the procession leaving the National Cathedral.

A woman emerged from the back office. "I'm Ms. Davidson, the manager. How can I help you?"

Saville displayed his badge again. "I'm looking for Dwight Helm, sheriff from Kendall County."

She checked her computer. "Mr. Helm checked in on Monday evening, Room 103. He's booked through Friday."

"Is he currently on the property?"

"His key was last used at 11:47 this morning, entering the room."

"I need access."

She hesitated. "Don't you need a warrant?"

"Not for a welfare check on a law enforcement officer who's been missing for three days." Saville's tone left no room for argument. The exception for exigent circumstances was valid, though he doubted the manager knew that.

Room 103 faced Market Street. The curtains were drawn tight, and a "Do Not Disturb" sign hung from the handle. A weathered Crown Victoria, clearly a decommissioned police cruiser, occupied the designated parking space.

"That's his vehicle," the manager confirmed. She rapped on the door. "Mr. Helm? Hotel management. We need to check on you, sir."

No response.

"He might be sleeping or at a medical appointment." She looked uncomfortable. "I really shouldn't—"

"Ms. Davidson, I have reason to believe Sheriff Helm may be in danger."

She swiped her master keycard and pushed open the door.

Then she screamed.

The familiar smell hit Saville first, before his eyes processed the scene. Helm's body hung from the ceiling fan mount, three feet from the unmade bed. He'd been dead for hours; lividity had settled in his lower extremities. A leather belt was wrapped around his neck, the other end tied to the fixture. He was naked, with adult magazines scattered across the bed and nightstand.

"Call 911," Saville ordered, but Davidson had already fled.

Saville stood in the doorway, careful not to contaminate the scene. He noted the positioning: the body faced the door, not the bed. The magazines looked staged, too neat for someone engaged in autoerotic behavior. The belt was Helm's duty belt, sturdy enough to hold him but an unusual choice when the bathroom had a standard cloth robe hanging on the door.

Two suicides in one week, both connected to Davy Clough's investigation.

Saville pulled out his phone and called Mayfield. "Jack? We have a problem. A big one."

Chapter 14

A moving truck blocked half the driveway at Victor Farnsworth's three-story townhouse in Gunter Square, two miles from Fort Belvoir. Thursday was Lowri's regular day off. She had told no one about her plan to visit Victor's widow in Fairfax County; Captain Morrow would have suspended her on the spot. She knew she was risking her career, but she couldn't let this go.

Two burly men with crew cuts and tattoos were maneuvering a baby grand piano through the front door as Lowri approached. She waited until they'd cleared the threshold before speaking.

"I'm looking for Mrs. Farnsworth," Lowri said.

"Upstairs," the tall man replied without looking up.

Lowri entered through the open door and climbed the stairs. She could hear crying from the hallway and followed the sound to the master bedroom. She knocked on the doorframe. "Mrs. Farnsworth?"

Molly looked up from the bed, dabbing her eyes with a tissue. She sat surrounded by framed photographs and a half-packed moving box. As Lowri approached, she noticed sheets of expensive stationery layered in the box, each one monogrammed in elegant script. The name at the top caught her eye: Molly Tennyson Farnsworth.

Tennyson, like the poet. Molly's maiden name. Lowri had not been an exceptional student, but she had always been an avid reader. The town library had served as her weekend refuge, a quiet sanctuary where she could discover books her family could not afford to purchase. "The Lady of Shalott" had captivated her imagination during tenth-grade English. Something about that doomed woman in her tower, dying from a curse she could not escape. Her teacher had explained it as a commentary on art and isolation, but teenage Lowri had interpreted it as a tragic love story.

Lowri thought of Tennyson's doomed lady as she watched Molly. Even in mourning, the widow was strikingly polished—ash-blonde hair that spoke of expensive salons, the kind of refined beauty that fit naturally into Victor's political world. She was the type of woman who belonged at embassy parties and state dinners, while Lowri's romantic history consisted of mechanics and construction workers who considered Olive Garden upscale dining.

"I'm sorry for your loss." Lowri reached for Molly's shoulder, then hesitated. This felt intrusive, a violation of a private moment. She should leave and come back another day. But the movers downstairs were already loading boxes. By tomorrow, Molly Farnsworth would be in another state, and any answers she had would go with her.

Molly took Lowri's hand and looked up with reddened eyes. "Who are you, dear?"

Lowri introduced herself and handed Molly another tissue.

"I've already spoken to the police," Molly said, dabbing at her eyes. "A Detective Sprague, I believe."

Lowri sat beside her on the bed, glancing at the array of photographs. "This isn't an official visit, Mrs. Farnsworth."

"You're not in uniform."

"No, ma'am. I'm off duty."

Molly lifted one of the pictures, a wedding photo of a young couple obviously in love. "Victor was such a handsome young man, don't you think?"

"And you were a beautiful bride."

"The happiest day of my life." Fresh tears appeared. She accepted the tissue Lowri offered but didn't use it, just held it in her lap.

"Mrs. Farnsworth, I was one of the first officers on the scene when they found your husband."

She stared at the wedding photo. "Was he peaceful, Sergeant Pritchard?"

"Yes, ma'am." What else was she supposed to say? As peaceful as possible for a man whose brain matter was scattered across West Potomac Park.

"Do you think he took his own life?" Molly's tone grew serious. She was no longer crying.

Lowri considered her response. Any criticism of Sprague's investigation, any disruption of the established narrative, could terminate her career, assuming she hadn't already accomplished that merely by coming here. However, she had come for a specific purpose: the truth. "No, ma'am, I don't," she said. "I believe he was killed elsewhere and his body was moved to the park."

Molly sniffed. "He despised Washington, and he missed home. I simply can't believe he would inflict that kind of trauma on Bryan and Julie." She reached for another framed photograph, this one showing her husband standing beside a tall young man in a basketball jersey. "Especially Bryan."

Lowri noted that the kids were nowhere around. "How are your children coping?"

"As well as can be expected. They went back to North Carolina with Victor's parents after the funeral yesterday." More moisture appeared in her eyes. "Do you believe my husband was murdered, Sergeant Pritchard?"

Lowri hesitated, then remembered her purpose: the truth. "Several aspects of the crime scene were inconsistent." She discussed the body's position, the missing bullet, and the absence of blood evidence without being overly graphic.

"Are you implying that Detective Sprague is incompetent?"

Lowri grimaced. Exactly what she didn't want Molly to think, even if she believed it herself. "No, ma'am. I'm just bothered by a few things I saw, and I wanted you to know."

"Detective Sprague doesn't know you're here?"

"Nobody knows I'm here, and I'd appreciate it if you kept it between us."

Molly picked up the remaining pictures and arranged them in the moving box. "Do you think President Carney had something to do with my husband's death?"

Lowri's eyes widened. "Excuse me?"

"President Woodrow Carney. Victor was having an affair with his wife."

Lowri gasped, the air escaping her lungs. "The First Lady? Hellen Carney?" She loved a good sensational headline, so why had she never heard this allegation before?

"Yes, that's right," Molly replied. "I've known about it for a while. It was common knowledge in Washington circles."

Lowri stood, her mouth agape.

"It's impossible to keep secrets in this town," Molly continued. "I heard President Carney was furious."

"Did you tell Detective Sprague about this?" Lowri finally asked, struggling to believe that the President of the United States might have murdered her husband.

"Of course I did. I'm not sure he took me seriously, though. He dismissed it as hearsay and said grief makes people imagine things."

Lowri found herself questioning Molly's credibility. Did Molly genuinely believe Woodrow Carney orchestrated Victor's death? More importantly, did she have proof?

"That's a serious accusation," Lowri said. "Do you have any concrete evidence—"

"Only a wife's intuition."

That wasn't enough. "How long had this affair been going on?" She almost said "alleged affair," but knew that would provoke Molly's hostility. Lowri needed her to keep talking.

"I found out a few months ago," Molly said. "I confronted Victor, but he denied it, of course. I loved my husband deeply and made many sacrifices for him, both personally and professionally. I even had cosmetic surgery to make myself more attractive, more photogenic." She sighed. "To no avail. I was never glamorous enough for him. Not like Hellen Carney. He hurt me deeply, Sergeant Pritchard, but he didn't deserve to die."

"Did you consider divorce?"

"We agreed to postpone any decision until our daughter Julie graduated high school. She's fourteen."

Lowri calculated that Julie was probably a freshman. Staying together for the kids rarely worked out. "How did you find out about the affair?"

"Just the usual suspicions. Late nights at the office that kept getting later, unexplained perfume scents he attributed to his female staff." She shifted uncomfortably on the bed. "My fears were confirmed when one of Victor's aides saw him kissing the First Lady outside his office. It wasn't just a peck on the cheek."

"Who is this aide, and how can I reach him?"

"Henry Gilmore. I assume he's back home in Indiana. Hellen Carney had him fired shortly after."

"Do you have a phone number?"

Molly got up from the bed and walked to one of the few remaining pieces of furniture, an oak highboy. "It's in my address book." She pulled a purse from the bottom drawer and rummaged through it. "Here it is." Her demeanor had shifted entirely; no trace of tears remained.

Lowri took out her notebook and pen, always on hand even off duty, and wrote down the number.

"Please give Henry my regards when you speak to him," Molly said. "That man gave up his career to tell me the truth."

Lowri nodded. "Can you think of anyone else who might have wanted to harm your husband?"

"Certainly," Molly replied. "Me. Do you know what it's like to watch the man you love destroy everything you've built together? To smile at dinner parties while everyone whispers about his affair?" She stared at her hands. "I thought about killing him every single day for the past six months. But it turns out I couldn't even work up the nerve to leave him, let alone murder him."

***

Hellen Carney had not spoken to her husband since Victor's funeral, and only then because the cameras were rolling. The funeral had been somber, with many attending, friends, family, colleagues, and even minor diplomats from several foreign governments paying their respects.

There had been many tears, including hers, which flowed even when the cameras were not focused on her. In contrast, the President manufactured tears for the networks.

Even Molly Farnsworth had cried, despite Victor insisting that his wife despised him. But Molly's tears seemed genuine. Had Victor simply been telling Hellen what she wanted to hear?

Hellen felt confused and conflicted. Her emotions oscillated like a pendulum since Victor's death, and now a familiar ache settled behind her eyes. Sorrow, anger, and back to sorrow, trapped in a destructive cycle. Sorrow for losing Victor and for her own desperate circumstances. Anger at her husband for... what exactly?

For having Victor killed? She still refused to believe that Victor had taken his own life. Her husband didn't even seem to care that she had been sleeping with Victor. Yet one fact contradicted the other, didn't it? If her husband was indifferent to the affair, why would he have ordered Victor's death? What would his motive be? Wounded pride? Something deeper that she couldn't comprehend?

Her husband might be a power-obsessed autocrat who responded poorly to criticism, but he wasn't a fool. Only a fool posing as the President of the United States would order an assassination of Victor. If not her husband, then who else wanted Victor dead?

Molly. Obviously. That treacherous aide, Henry Gilmore, had informed her about the kiss. Hellen had made him pay for his betrayal, but the damage had already been done.

Victor had always described Molly as a jealous, manipulative predator who concealed her hostility behind vacant eyes. Had her suppressed rage finally erupted in the most calculated way imaginable? Perhaps, but how? How had the devoted wife accomplished it?

Hellen resolved to discover the truth. She could barely contain her envy of Molly's audacity and cunning.

Chapter 15

With Jack Mayfield's authorization, Saville slept late Thursday morning and reported to work at noon. The previous evening had been spent assisting the Wilmington Police Department with its investigation into Sheriff Helm's death. Saville had voluntarily provided a witness statement and background information as needed. The crime scene had been pristine, with no bloody towels or evidence linking to Davy Clough.

Officially, the FBI would remain uninvolved in the Helm case unless the Wilmington PD requested federal assistance. Unofficially, Jack Mayfield would monitor the investigation and keep Saville informed of developments.

Helm's preliminary cause of death was labeled "strangulation by autoerotic asphyxiation." Saville couldn't dispute the medical conclusion, but he could challenge the classification of death: accidental, pending autopsy results.

Accidental. Bullshit. Saville sat at his desk and unwrapped the turkey sandwich he had prepared before leaving home. Three men were dead: Davy Clough, Victor Farnsworth, and now Sheriff Helm. All under suspicious circumstances. All staged to appear as suicides or accidents. Even a rookie could detect the deception. Mayfield was starting to recognize the pattern, signaling that this might indeed be the high-priority case Saville had been seeking.

He could not wait any longer. The urgency consumed him. He took a bite of his sandwich and burst into Mayfield's office.

Mayfield was on the phone. He cupped a hand over the receiver and glared. "Dammit, Mike. Don't you ever knock?"

Saville dropped into a chair, remaining silent while Mayfield continued his conversation. He recognized it was Mayfield's wife, Ida, just from hearing one side of the exchange. Saville had never heard so many "yes, dears" in such a short span.

"One o'clock. Yes, dear. I'll be there." He hung up the phone. "I'm meeting my wife for lunch, and no, you're not invited. What do you want?"

"When do I deploy to Washington?"

"You don't," Mayfield replied. "I'm still waiting for authorization from Charlotte."

"What are they waiting for? Signed confessions?"

Mayfield raised a hand. "I'm on your side, Mike. But without Charlotte's approval, there's nothing I can do."

"There's something I can do." Saville shot to his feet. "I can request emergency leave."

"Dammit, Mike." The phone rang again. Mayfield lifted the receiver. "Just wait a minute."

Saville sank back into his chair out of respect for his supervisor. He knew Mayfield was right. Without proper authorization, expenses would go unreimbursed, and support would vanish. Careers could end. If he traveled to Washington without permission, the Bureau would likely fire him. Was he willing to take that risk? His heart said yes, but his head knew better. If he succeeded and earned a promotion to a larger field office, then what? He couldn't just leave Jennifer and Emma behind to satisfy his own ambitions. What kind of father and husband would he be then?

Mayfield listened for several moments without speaking, then said, "Yes, sir," and hung up the phone. "There's a secure message coming in that you need to see."

Mayfield waited a few minutes, monitoring his computer screen. He tapped several keys, and the office printer behind him hummed. He turned to retrieve the pages. "Washington has ordered us to back off. The Davy Clough investigation has been transferred to the Counterintelligence Division."

"Counterintelligence Division?" It was the Bureau's unit responsible for domestic espionage and terrorism cases. "What the hell, Jack?"

"They've identified the third man, the one who dined with Clough and Farnsworth." Mayfield flipped through the documents and handed Saville a photograph. "His name is Hillel Mond. He's attached to the Israeli embassy in Washington and is considered one of Mossad's most lethal operatives."

Saville struggled to catch his breath, grappling with the mixed emotions of vindication for being right about Davy Clough's murder and the frustration of losing the case. "Jesus, Jack," was all he could manage to say.

Mayfield placed a reassuring hand on Saville's shoulder. "You've been ahead of this case from the start, and you deserve full credit for that. You've earned some time off. Why don't you submit a leave request? I'll see if I can get it approved by the end of the day. I hear the nation's capital is beautiful this time of year, with the cherry blossoms in full bloom."

Saville smiled, wishing he could express his deep respect and appreciation for Mayfield without sounding foolish.

***

Lowri stopped at a convenience store on Telegraph Road to buy a prepaid flip phone. Once in her vehicle, she dialed the number for Henry Gilmore in Indiana, provided by Molly Farnsworth.

The phone rang repeatedly. Just as she was about to hang up in disappointment, a shaky female voice answered, breathless.

"May I speak to Henry Gilmore, please?" Lowri asked.

The woman's breathing quickened and became labored. "Who is this?"

"My name is Lowri Pritchard, and I'm with—"

"My son is dead, Ms. Pritchard. Do not call here again."

"Wait, please!" Lowri shouted in desperation, pressing the phone tighter against her ear, anticipating a disconnection. Instead, she heard the woman's shallow breathing continue. "Thank you for not hanging up, Mrs. Gilmore. Please accept my condolences."

"McLaughlin."

"Excuse me?"

"My name is Ruth McLaughlin. I remarried when Henry was a toddler."

"I'm so sorry, Mrs. McLaughlin." Lowri gripped the steering wheel with her free hand as she explained the reason for her call and mentioned that Molly Farnsworth had provided the number.

"Molly Farnsworth." The woman's voice turned bitter. "Such a manipulative woman."

Lowri blinked in surprise. "What makes you say that, Mrs. McLaughlin?"

"Both she and her husband. Truly despicable people. My son would still be alive if he hadn't gotten involved with them."

"What happened to your son?" Lowri asked.

"Car accident. Apparently, the brakes failed. He was driving to pick up Victor at the airport when he slammed head-on into a tree."

A chill ran through Lowri. "Wait, what?" She stared at the phone as if it had transformed into something alien. "Victor Farnsworth?"

"Yes." Ruth cleared her throat audibly. "Victor said he wanted to apologize personally for Henry losing his job. Such a fraud. I begged Henry not to meet him."

"When was this?" Lowri pressed.

"Last Thursday morning. Victor claimed he was traveling to a meeting in North Carolina. Henry was just a stopover as far as Victor was concerned."

Lowri's mind raced, making connections. "What happened to your son's car, Mrs. McLaughlin? You mentioned brake failure."

"The State Police concluded he took a curve too fast and lost control. There was evidence he tried pumping the brakes, but..." Her voice broke, and Lowri could hear muffled sobs through the phone. "They couldn't definitively establish mechanical failure. The car sustained too much damage for proper testing." She was crying openly now. "My husband believes we should file a wrongful death lawsuit."

Against whom, Lowri wondered, though she kept that question to herself. "Do you know why Victor Farnsworth fired your son?"

"He refused to discuss the details. Only that Victor hadn't wanted to fire him and was forced to by someone with higher authority."

"Did he identify this superior?"

"He wouldn't say. I met Victor and Molly Farnsworth twice when I visited Henry in Washington. I despised them both."

Lowri took a deep breath. "What do you believe happened to your son, Mrs. McLaughlin?"

"I believe my son had information that certain people wanted buried, and that Victor Farnsworth arranged his murder to protect those secrets. Then guilt consumed Victor, and he took his own life. The consequences finally caught up with him, and he couldn't face the reckoning." Her voice grew resigned. "I suppose this is the closest thing to justice Henry could have hoped for, God rest his soul."

***

A Secret Service detail of eight agents in three vehicles transported First Lady Hellen Carney to Fairfax County and Molly Farnsworth's townhouse. All eight agents had objected to the operation, citing inadequate reconnaissance and the sensitive nature of the situation as grounds to postpone or abort the mission. They were all aware of her affair with Victor and had participated in the cover-up. Ultimately, they had no choice but to comply with her directive.

Hellen recognized her impulsiveness, but this meeting was crucial. Molly was leaving town for good, and Hellen needed to confront her, perhaps even acknowledge what she suspected Molly had accomplished. They had grown up together in North Carolina and had known each other for over forty years, sharing more similarities than anyone realized.

The advance team swept the townhouse while the perimeter team secured the surrounding area. Agents ordered two movers loading boxes to vacate the premises and return in two hours. The taller one resisted and was briefly restrained in flex-cuffs before cooler heads intervened.

Once the movers had departed in their truck, the protection detail escorted the First Lady inside. Only scattered living room furniture and wall art remained. Hellen found Molly in the kitchen, packing silverware.

"Clear the room," Hellen instructed the agents, who reluctantly withdrew to positions outside.

"To what do I owe this honor?" Molly asked, brandishing a steak knife but not dropping it into the moving box.

"Planning to use that on me?" Hellen inquired.

Molly examined the blade. "You'd enjoy that, wouldn't you? I'm sure the Secret Service has standing orders to shoot to kill. I wouldn't survive three steps."

"They do, and you wouldn't." The First Lady's mouth curved into a stiff smile.

"Perhaps that's what I want. Without Victor—"

"Spare me the theatrics."

Molly dropped the knife into the box. "At least I genuinely loved my husband."

"And I didn't?"

"You exploited him for entertainment. For revenge against your husband."

"Initially, perhaps—"

"Victor just wanted to be left alone." A tear gathered in Molly's eye. "To complete his term and return to practicing small-town law. He despised Washington. He never felt comfortable around people like you and Woody."

Hellen's eyebrows arched at the casual use of the President's nickname.

"Victor was naïve. He didn't understand the game. The career politicians devoured him."

Hellen's expression turned contemptuous. "He lacked sufficient ambition. That's your real complaint."

Molly stared at the floor. "With Victor's charisma and appearance—"

"He attracted the First Lady of the United States," Hellen interjected.

"You seduced him for your own amusement."

"But I didn't murder him."

"No one claimed you did."

"You possessed the strongest motive," Hellen stated.

"Who says anyone killed him? The authorities ruled his death a suicide. Besides, numerous people had motives."

Hellen's expression hardened.

"Your husband should head that list," Molly continued. "He was the one being betrayed."

"He's the President of the United States. He's not that reckless." Hellen reflected that he was indifferent to the affair anyway.

"One person suspects your husband's involvement." Molly lifted a business card from the counter and flicked it across the room toward Hellen. "An off-duty Park Police sergeant came here asking a lot of questions."

Hellen bent to retrieve the card. It read: Sergeant Lowri Pritchard, United States Park Police. Lowri, what sort of name was that? More unusual than her own. "What did this Sergeant Pritchard want to know?"

"She believes Victor was murdered."

"So do I."

"Then perhaps you should speak with her." Molly turned back to her packing, signaling the conversation's end.

Hellen pocketed the card and moved toward the door. Two Secret Service agents immediately flanked her to provide escort. For once, Molly Farnsworth had offered sound advice. Hellen did need to contact this meddlesome Park Police officer. She would do so right after she leaked to conservative media outlets that Molly had conspired with the President to eliminate Victor Farnsworth.

Eliminate two problems simultaneously, as it were.

Chapter 16

Following a forty-minute layover in Charlotte, American Airlines Flight 618 from Greenville to Washington touched down at Reagan National Airport at 9:47 on Friday morning.

Saville had slept through most of the flight, which had departed Pitt-Greenville Airport at 5:43 a.m. He purchased the ticket with his personal credit card and was self-financing the entire operation. This remained an unauthorized mission, technically vacation leave, and no Bureau funds could be used. Jack Mayfield had promised eventual reimbursement, but Saville doubted even someone as experienced and politically astute as Mayfield could achieve that bureaucratic miracle. As he waited for his luggage at baggage claim, Saville recognized this as a calculated investment that might yield significant career dividends.

Mayfield wasn't the only person whose capabilities Saville questioned. He was operating without authorization and lacking Bureau support. More concerning was the nature of his target: a highly trained assassin, not just any government operative. Hillel Mond was Mossad-trained, and Israeli intelligence was arguably one of the most disciplined and lethal organizations on the planet.

Was Saville operating beyond his capabilities? He preferred not to entertain that possibility. His FBI training offered limited advantage in this scenario. The Bureau emphasized strict adherence to procedures and regulations, skills that stood in stark contrast to the tactics employed by foreign intelligence operatives, who often operated outside legal boundaries and conventional constraints. As a New Agent Trainee (NAT) at Quantico, Saville had been conditioned to prioritize analytical thinking, then defensive tactics, and to resort to lethal force only as a last measure. For operatives like Mond, killing was instinctive and frequently the first choice.

His military experience might provide some advantage. He had served as a platoon leader in Echo Company, 165th Military Intelligence Battalion, during Operation Iraqi Freedom. As a young officer responsible for surveillance and reconnaissance missions in hostile environments, he had successfully guided his team through the perils of post-invasion Iraq, balancing field operations with analytical precision, which earned him the respect of the soldiers who relied on his judgment and composure under fire.

Though he lacked the tactical field experience of someone like Mond, he understood the psychological profile that shaped such operatives. That expertise had to count for something. Or was he merely rationalizing an inevitable failure?

He picked up a white Chevrolet Malibu from the Enterprise counter and began reviewing Mond's biographical intelligence, which Mayfield had obtained from the FBI's Terrorist Screening Database. He had already committed the information to memory.

Born in Vancouver, British Columbia, to Jewish immigrants in 1979, Mond moved to Israel with his family five years later. At eighteen, he enlisted in the Israel Defense Forces, eventually becoming the youngest officer in IDF history, attaining the rank of Rav Seren, equivalent to lieutenant commander in the Israeli Navy.

His recruitment into Mossad occurred on an undisclosed date. Six years ago, he arrived in the United States as a *katsa*, the Hebrew term for case officer, specializing in the recruitment and management of foreign assets. Specific operational details remained classified, as Mossad maintained one of the most compartmentalized structures in global intelligence. Intelligence reports indicated his frequent returns to the Middle East, sometimes for extended periods, and analysts suspected his involvement in three of Mossad's most high-profile targeted eliminations: Imad Mughniyeh, Hezbollah's military chief, killed by a car bomb in Damascus; Mahmoud al-Mabhouh, a senior Hamas commander, assassinated in Dubai by a team using sophisticated forged documents and exotic toxins; and Mohsen Fakhrizadeh, Iran's chief nuclear scientist, eliminated near Tehran through a remotely operated weapons system.

Mond's tactical brilliance matched his ruthlessness. To call him a formidable adversary would be a gross understatement. Did Saville realistically have any chance of locating this ghost and bringing him to justice? Or should he retreat and hand the case over to Intelligence Division specialists?

Saville couldn't answer that question, but his pride wouldn't allow such easy capitulation. More importantly, he had promised Cynthia Clough that he would find her son's killer. Although professional necessity motivated the promise more than genuine compassion, he refused to break faith with a grieving mother.

His Bureau career depended on it. Perhaps even his sanity.

***

Cecelia Leehan cut into her veal, relishing her position as the senior correspondent for the press corps. She had long abandoned any pretense of journalistic impartiality and was a lifelong Democrat and hardcore progressive, unafraid of who knew it. This contrasted sharply with most of her colleagues in the White House Press Corps, who shared her political views but concealed them to maintain access, especially during Republican administrations.

Over the past six years, she and the First Lady had developed a close friendship, often lunching together in the private White House family dining room. Cecelia enjoyed unprecedented access to the First Lady and frequently called to discuss topics that politically connected women of their generation found compelling.

Hellen had even alluded to her affair with Victor Farnsworth during their conversations, trusting Cecelia's discretion when sensitive subjects arose.

Cecelia relished her role and the power it brought. She often boasted to Hellen that she had experienced everything Washington had to offer, including romantic liaisons with over one hundred journalists from around the globe, both male and female. She had never crossed the line with a sitting president, though members of the executive staff remained fair game and valuable sources.

"Have you noticed that new correspondent from *The Boston Globe*?" Cecelia asked, pausing between bites of her specially prepared meal.

"The one young enough to be your son?" Hellen replied.

"He spent last night at my Georgetown apartment. I showed him a few of my old tricks. He wept afterward, saying I reminded him of his mother."

"Jesus, Cecelia."

"My romantic life is my elixir of youth. You should consider it."

Hellen sighed and sipped the Chardonnay she preferred with lunch. Cecelia noticed her friend's hand trembling slightly as she lifted the glass.

"Oh, Hellen, imagine the damage we could have inflicted in our teenage years." She took another enthusiastic bite of veal. "I haven't spoken with you since Victor's death. How are you holding up?"

"It's been challenging, but I'll endure." Hellen winced and pressed a hand to her stomach before reaching for her wine again.

"Is there anything I can do to help?"

Hellen took another sip, savoring the bouquet. "Actually, yes, Cecelia. Assuming you're amenable."

"You know better than to question that." Cecelia leaned across the table and grasped Hellen's hand. "You're one of my closest friends. There's nothing I wouldn't do for you."

"I hope you mean that." The First Lady's eyes scanned the dining room. It was nearly empty, Cecelia noted. The staff had learned to avoid Hellen during her lunches, especially when her volatile temper surfaced. Satisfied that no one was eavesdropping, Hellen said, "I don't believe Victor committed suicide."

Cecelia patted Hellen's hand. "I understand your grief, but don't let conspiracy theories consume you. They're particularly vicious in this city."

"This isn't speculation. I know who murdered him."

Cecelia withdrew her hand and reached for the wine bottle instead of her glass. "My God, Hellen. You're serious."

"Woody was having an affair with Molly Farnsworth."

Cecelia poured wine into her glass and drained it in one motion. "What exactly are you suggesting, Hellen?"

"Woody and Molly conspired to eliminate Victor. I haven't determined who actually pulled the trigger—"

Cecelia raised her hand. "Hellen, you were sleeping with Victor. And now you're claiming that Woody and Molly..." She paused, shaking her head. "It sounds like an episode of *Jerry Springer*."

"I understand how it appears." Hellen's face crumpled, tears forming in her eyes. "They did it to wound me and exact revenge on Victor."

"That's an enormous leap from adultery to homicide." Cecelia shook her head. "What makes you so certain—"

"Woody essentially confessed yesterday." Tears streamed down Hellen's face. "He was gloating about it. 'This is what happens when you mess with the President of the United States,' he said." She buried her face in her hands. "How can I live with myself if I allow him to escape justice?"

Cecelia stood and embraced the First Lady, Hellen's mascara staining Cecelia's silk blouse. "What do you want me to do? We need concrete evidence. This would be the largest political scandal in American history."

"You don't need to act directly." Hellen dabbed her eyes with a linen napkin. "Once conservative media outlets grab hold of the story, they won't let go. Public opinion will handle the rest."

Cecelia returned to her seat, touching her cheek thoughtfully. "And how would they obtain this information?"

"Thirty-two years in Washington, Cecelia. You have connections throughout the media landscape. A strategic leak—"

"My God, Hellen. Do you comprehend what you're asking?"

Fresh tears welled in Hellen's eyes. The woman could cry on command, Cecelia noted. "I'm not asking; I'm pleading. Victor was a kind, decent man. I loved him, Cecelia."

"You're not only asking me to surrender the biggest story of my career, but you want me to deliver it to the people I despise most. I simply don't know—"

"Consider the service you'd provide to the country."

Cecelia scoffed. "Don't invoke patriotism with me, Hellen. My faith in American institutions died during the Reagan years."

"I'll compensate you handsomely after I'm elected to the Senate."

"Elected?"

"Can't you picture it, Cecelia? The betrayed wife of a murderous, unfaithful President running for office herself? It's a story North Carolina voters won't be able to resist." Hellen raised her glass. "Imagine the sympathy vote! After my election, I'll make sure you become the most influential journalist in Washington."

"I'm already the most influential journalist in Washington."

"You're not aging gracefully, Cecelia. Soon, those junior reporters, like your Boston correspondent, will look for inspiration elsewhere. Do we have an understanding?"

The calculated cruelty of the remark stung more than Cecelia had anticipated. She replied without hesitation. "Understood," she said, clinking her glass against the First Lady's.

Chapter 17

Saville owed Cynthia Clough something, didn't he? A visit, an update, or at least an acknowledgment that he was in town working on her son's case. As the victim's mother, she held undeniable moral authority. Yet Saville hesitated; he wasn't sure he could trust her discretion. If she caused any trouble or alerted FBI Headquarters, his career could be jeopardized.

He could fabricate a story, claiming he was assigned to Washington as the lead investigative case agent. But he believed in consequences; lies would eventually surface and ruin him.

Twice, he picked up the phone in his hotel room and dialed her number. Twice, he hung up before anyone answered. He regretted not staying in Greenville to handle the First Citizens Bank robbery like a dutiful field agent. Bank robbery was one of the most foolish crimes a perpetrator could commit, with an eighty percent clearance and conviction rate. Why wasn't he satisfied with closing that case and adding another easy win to his already solid performance record?

Promises. He had made them to both Cynthia and Jennifer, assuring Jennifer that after his transfer to Greenville, he would do whatever it took to restore his standing in the Bureau. Anything to regain her respect.

Yet here he was, embroiled in an unauthorized operation, just like in Miami. Was this his fate, to remain on the periphery, excluded from the inner circle? Perhaps it was time to accept his destiny and acknowledge that he would never become one of the Bureau's conventional agents.

But he was a skilled investigator. No one could dispute that, and those skills were exactly what he needed now to identify Davy Clough's killer and honor his commitment to Cynthia. He wanted to demonstrate to Jennifer that she was mistaken about his character flaws. Solving this case would force her to see him as someone who refused to surrender his principles, giving her no choice but to reconcile with him.

Once more, he lifted the handset and dialed Cynthia's number, this time feeling determined and confident when her voice answered.

***

They met at the Ragtime Restaurant and Bar, a modest establishment a few miles from the Tancred Motel, where Saville was staying to save money. He didn't expect to spend much time there anyway. Ragtime featured an eclectic mix of late 1890s jazz memorabilia alongside contemporary sports collectibles, primarily celebrating local DC area teams. The mid-afternoon clientele consisted mostly of middle-aged men, and Saville suspected they were either unemployed or seeking refuge from monotonous lives, or both. He envied that kind of predictable existence.

"This is my favorite place in Arlington," Cynthia said as they settled into a booth in the bar area. "It was Davy's favorite too. He met his wife, Marcia, here."

"Davy was married?" This was new information for Saville.

"Ex-wife, but I still treat her like a daughter." She glanced up at the young server who approached to take their drink order. "Davy could be difficult to live with," she said, then ordered a Bloody Mary, extra spicy.

"Water, please," Saville said. He looked at Cynthia. "I'm on duty."

Cynthia laughed. "Oh, I doubt that, Agent Saville. I suspect this visit is more personal in nature."

Saville hesitated, unsure of her implication. She had already offered to visit his hotel during their recent phone conversation, an invitation he had declined to maintain professional boundaries. He searched for the right words, finding it more challenging than he had expected. "I'm sorry, Mrs. Clough. I believe there's been a misunderstanding."

She giggled more loudly this time, clearly having exceeded her alcohol tolerance before arriving at the restaurant. "Oh no, Agent Saville. Not that kind of personal. Personal as in your visit is not entirely official, shall we say?"

Saville scrutinized her. How had she figured this out?

"I'm not as naïve as I appear," she said. "If the Bureau genuinely wanted to interview me, they would have sent a local agent. Elementary logic."

Saville remained silent. She had completely exposed him. The server returned with their beverages. Cynthia announced to the entire bar that she had developed an appetite and ordered a quesadilla with salsa.

"I'm happy to share," she said once the server departed, downing a substantial portion of her Bloody Mary in one gulp. "Two agents visited me last night. They suggested Davy was involved in espionage activities. I told them they were delusional."

"He dined with an Israeli intelligence operative named Hillel Mond the evening before his death."

"I've never heard that name, and I informed the other agents accordingly."

"He also had dinner with Victor Farnsworth, Deputy White House Chief of—"

"I know Victor Farnsworth's position. The other agents omitted that detail."

Saville leaned back, taking mental notes. The Bureau was proceeding cautiously, excluding Farnsworth's name from the investigation to avoid unnecessarily damaging his reputation. "How well did you know Victor Farnsworth?"

"What makes you assume—"

"I observed your expression when his name came up." Saville didn't elaborate, but it had been a mix of fear and contempt.

"I knew him socially. He was an acquaintance of my husband. I didn't care for him much."

"Socially? That was the extent of your relationship?" Saville's tone lost its diplomatic quality. She was hiding something, and he felt certain of it.

She started to respond but paused when the server returned with her appetizer. Cynthia's face flushed with indignation. "I'm absolutely certain that was the extent of it," she said after the server moved to another table. "I found him extremely discourteous."

"Where is your husband currently, Mrs. Clough? I need to interview him."

"I have no idea." She shrugged. "We've barely communicated since my son's death. He's in complete denial. Probably absorbed in his software development work. That's where he spends most of his time these days."

"Software development?"

"He helped create a new patient monitoring system." A sudden smile lit up her features. "I don't understand the technical details, but it's in high demand. The federal government recently offered to buy it for twenty million dollars."

Twenty million dollars. That sum, along with the settlements she anticipated from her pending lawsuits, certainly explained her optimistic demeanor. Saville tasted his water for the first time. The ice had nearly melted. "Do you or your husband understand why Davy dined with Hillel Mond and Victor Farnsworth?"

"That's the million-dollar question, isn't it, Agent Saville? Unfortunately, my son never discussed his professional activities. As I mentioned, we weren't particularly close."

Perhaps her husband had that knowledge, considering they had "barely communicated since my son's death." The entire family dynamic triggered Saville's investigative instincts.

"I'll arrange for my husband to contact you," she said, dipping a quesadilla piece into salsa. "I know the two agents who visited my home have no intention of solving my son's case. But you, Agent Saville. I could significantly advance your career if you identify Davy's killer."

"That sounds like attempted bribery." Saville was only partially joking.

"Consider it an investment opportunity," she said. "I know you came here independently to investigate my son's murder, and I'm grateful for that commitment." She finished her drink with another large gulp. "I also know you're financing this personally and that resources are limited. Otherwise, you wouldn't be staying at an establishment like the Tancred."

"It's adequate," he replied, wondering if his words sounded as unconvincing as they felt.

She stood and placed two hundred-dollar bills on the table. "My husband will be in touch soon." She slung her purse over her shoulder and patted her chest. "I still have your business card right here, close to my heart."

***

Lowri returned to work at midnight and was immediately confronted in the patrol room by a fatigued and hostile Peter Sprague. She had reported early for her shift, and only a few stragglers from the Traffic Safety Unit remained in the room. Most departed when Sprague entered. He had that kind of effect on people, treating fellow officers like incompetents.

"Working late hours, aren't you, Detective?" Lowri said, hoping that Sprague's presence was just a fatigue-induced hallucination. She was already exhausted from the shift change, having spent most of her day off obsessing over the Victor Farnsworth case. The statements from Molly Farnsworth and Ruth McLaughlin had consumed her thoughts during a time that would have been better spent sleeping.

"I hear you're not impressed with my investigative work," Sprague replied, ignoring her question.

Feigning ignorance, she said, "I don't understand what you're referring to." She braced herself for the inevitable verbal assault. At least it was preferable to Sprague's juvenile sexual innuendos.

"Sure you do, Dollface."

She removed her timecard from the machine and placed it in the designated slot. Sprague seized her arm and pinned it against the wall.

"What the hell? You're hurting me," Lowri protested.

"You think you're clever, complaining to Captain Morrow." He applied more pressure, causing her arm to throb. "Who do you think you are? Some kind of fucking Sherlock Holmes?"

He finally released her. She rubbed her arm to ease the pain. "I could file a complaint against you for that," she said.

"The word of a patrol officer against one of the district's most decorated detectives?" His tone matched the malice in his expression. "Go ahead. Let's see how that turns out for you."

He was right, and she knew it. Even if she could back up her claims, doing so would ruin her career. No one in law enforcement tolerated informants. Trust was everything. The line between survival and death. The Blue Wall of Silence was an unforgiving reality.

Clenching her jaw, she replied, "I only asked about the forensic evidence. Nothing specific about you."

"Morrow read between the lines. He tore me apart over it, saying you suggested my investigation was 'incomplete.'"

She remained silent, confirming his accusation with her lack of response.

"Just so you understand, Dollface, the autopsy report was completed today." He reached into his jacket pocket and pulled out several folded documents, a satisfied grin spreading across his face. "Seems I'm not so 'incomplete' after all."

She accepted the papers without resistance. As she unfolded the report, she began to examine the contents:

Cause of Death: Perforating Gunshot Wound, Mouth to Head

Findings: Examination reveals an entrance gunshot wound in the posterior oropharynx, located approximately 7.5 inches from the vertex of the skull. There is an associated defect in the soft palate, with tissue fragments containing probable powder debris identified in situ. The wound tract extends backward and upward, traversing the cranial cavity, with an entrance wound just left of the foramen magnum. Marked destruction of the brainstem and left cerebral hemisphere is observed. The track terminates with an irregular exit wound in the scalp and skull near the midline of the occipital region. No metallic fragments were recovered during the examination.

Toxicology: Postmortem toxicological analysis detected significant concentrations of trazodone in the decedent's system.

Opinion: Based on the described features, the gunshot wound was consistent with self-infliction.

The findings hit her like a punch to the throat. She noted the presence of trazodone, a prescription medication commonly used to treat major depressive disorder and anxiety, which was also popular among the addicts who frequented Lafayette Park.

Rubbing her eyes, she contemplated whether to offer an apology, then gasped when she saw the signature at the bottom of the report.

Signature of Pathologist: Dr. Bernard Clough.

"My God," she whispered. This revelation changed everything. Dr. Bernard Clough, known throughout law enforcement circles as "Dr. Suicide."

Chapter 18

President Carney suppressed a massive yawn as he ushered FBI Director Walter Shaffer into the Oval Office. It was six-thirty on Saturday morning, and neither man wanted to be there. The President preferred to sleep late on weekends unless pressing global events demanded his attention, which had become increasingly common in an unstable international climate. Even during busy weekends, he usually squeezed in a pre-dawn jog.

Today, thoughts of Victor Farnsworth's death prevented him from sleeping. He had awakened at four a.m. and could not return to bed. Too exhausted to run, he went directly to the Oval Office, intending to catch up on essential reading. Even that pursuit proved futile; he ended up watching television instead.

The seventy-two-inch flat-screen was typically tuned to MSNBC or CNN, but for reasons he couldn't explain, the President had selected Nickelodeon. Nothing like SpongeBob SquarePants to distract from global suffering.

"Sorry to drag you in so early on a weekend," Carney said, gesturing toward a chair. "You know I wouldn't have called unless it was critical."

"Of course, Mr. President."

Shaffer was another of the President's North Carolina allies, a former U.S. attorney and federal judge who had served as FBI Director since the beginning of Carney's first term. He was reliable and would follow directives, making him an invaluable asset to the administration.

"We have a situation, Walt," Carney said, pacing the white oak and pine flooring with his hands clasped behind his back. "The Victor Farnsworth investigation."

"We're fully engaged, sir. I understand you two were close friends."

"That's not the issue." Carney stopped atop the oval rug bearing the Presidential seal. "I need this investigation to disappear."

Shaffer sat in silence, then murmured, "I don't understand, sir."

The President surveyed the room, taking in Dallin's bronze sculpture of a Native American on horseback, titled *Appeal to the Great Spirit,* and Carlton's 1863 painting *Waiting for the Hour,* depicting enslaved people awaiting emancipation. He had selected both artworks for display in the Oval Office, drawing inspiration from them for his domestic agenda of cultural diversity and social progress. Six years in this office flashed before his eyes: the achievements, the rhetoric, the mistakes, and the crises. His legacy was all that remained. He refused to let everything he had worked for collapse because of his wife's and best friend's indiscretions.

"The First Lady believes I murdered Victor," Carney said.

"Sir, I'm certain—"

"I didn't, naturally. Hellen and Victor were having an affair."

"I wasn't aware, Mr. President."

Carney scoffed. "Of course you were aware, Walt. You wouldn't be competent at your job if you weren't."

Shaffer remained silent. The silence confirmed everything.

"Can you imagine the humiliation, Walt? To me, to the Presidency, if their affair becomes public knowledge?"

"Yes, sir."

"I would be destroyed. The media would feast on this."

"Yes, sir. Hannity, Levin—"

"To hell with Hannity and Levin," Carney snapped. "They'll attack me regardless. I'm concerned about our friends at MSNBC and CNN. They've supported me throughout my entire career, but they would have no choice but to pursue this aggressively."

"Consider it terminated, sir."

"What?" Carney said distractedly.

"The medical examiner ruled the death a suicide. There's no justification to continue. We'll simply issue a statement announcing our satisfaction with the ME's findings and declaring the criminal investigation closed."

"I need more than termination, Walt. This story must be obliterated, and its remnants scattered to the winds."

"Understood, Mr. President."

"There will be hard questions, Walt. You're going to face intense scrutiny, particularly from conservative media."

"I can manage it, sir. I learned the art of deflection from an expert."

Carney approached and placed his hands on Shaffer's shoulders. "Indeed, you did, Walt. Indeed, you did."

***

Lowri's shift ended at eight a.m. Five minutes before she was scheduled to clock out, she noticed a vehicle weaving erratically on Connecticut Avenue as it approached Dupont Circle. Conducting a traffic stop, she discovered that the driver was a visiting dignitary from the Embassy of Burkina Faso with full diplomatic immunity. Following established protocol, she issued no citation and escorted the intoxicated official back to the embassy. By the time she returned to the Central District substation on Ohio Drive, completed the incident report, and submitted it to her administrative commander for approval, it was after nine.

Since she was already at the station and well past her scheduled departure time, she decided to make productive use of the delay. She accessed the Park Police's Case Incident Reporting System and linked to the FBI-maintained National Incident-Based Reporting System to research Dr. Bernard Clough. His name appeared in thousands of cross-references throughout the databases, as he was one of twelve physicians working for the Office of the Chief Medical Examiner for the District of Columbia and had held that position for many years. She shuddered to think how many murderers might have escaped justice due to his questionable work.

She was searching for one particular case she had worked seven months earlier. During a routine patrol, Officer Joel Graves had discovered a body in the front seat of a company vehicle, a Nissan Rogue, on the fourth level of the parking garage across from Ford's Theatre.

The deceased was Todd Byers, a sales representative for Symmetric Technical Solutions, a software company in Research Triangle Park, North Carolina. Unknown to Byers, he was under internal investigation for embezzlement and theft of proprietary documents. Corporate executives indicated that he was scheduled to be terminated and arrested. Had he realized he was being targeted?

His injuries mirrored those of Victor Farnsworth: a single gunshot wound to the mouth, with an exit wound at the back of the skull. Investigators recovered the weapon at the scene but found no bullet, which was peculiar given that the windows were intact, no glass was shattered, and Byers had allegedly shot himself inside the vehicle.

Dr. Clough ruled the death a suicide, despite a responding paramedic's definitive statement that Byers had sustained a fractured jaw and a severely damaged right ear. These injuries were inconsistent with the wound trajectory but aligned with evidence of a pre-mortem beating. The autopsy report, however, omitted both injuries.

Only after Byers's family protested to the media did Clough revise his findings to "possible homicide." He apologized to the family, admitting he had rushed through the autopsy and might have overlooked evidence. Relatives petitioned for exhumation, but both a superior court judge and an appellate court denied their requests. The case was classified as closed and was never investigated as a homicide.

Notably, the paramedic who contradicted Clough's initial findings was later discredited after being arrested for possession of OxyContin and Vicodin with intent to distribute, despite having no prior history of substance abuse.

Due to this incident, along with similar questionable conclusions in at least two other cases, the major commanding the Criminal Investigations Unit sarcastically referred to Clough as "Dr. Suicide."

However, one aspect of the Byers case troubled Lowri the most: the lead detective was Peter Sprague.

***

At ten a.m., Saville had yet to receive the promised contact from Bernard Clough. Growing impatient with the delay, he reached out to an old military colleague who worked as a special attaché to the Department of Homeland Security for INSCOM, the U.S. Army Intelligence and Security Command at Fort Belvoir.

Saville dialed the main switchboard and waited through several transfers before hearing a familiar voice.

"Special Agent Mike Saville! I'll be damned," Lieutenant Colonel Van Romano exclaimed with genuine enthusiasm. "How did you know I'd be in the office on a Saturday?"

"You always were a workaholic," Saville replied. "Besides, the switchboard operator confirmed you were available."

"Well, how the hell are you? It's been what, eight, ten years since we last saw each other?"

"Three years. At the reunion in Chicago."

"Right. That entire weekend is a complete blur."

Saville still pictured a very intoxicated Romano diving off a third-floor hotel balcony into the pool below, striking the concrete bottom, and somehow emerging with only a scraped knee and wounded pride. Saville had thought Romano might have killed himself that night, but the man had always seemed to possess multiple lives.

"Hey, Saville, are you still married to that bombshell? What was her name... Jennifer?"

Saville felt a sharp pain in his chest. Jennifer had accompanied him to Chicago and clearly made an impression on his former platoon mates. The memory of happier times only intensified his current isolation.

"Living the dream," Saville said, unwilling to revisit the heartache of their separation.

"Hey, buddy, don't take this the wrong way, but did you bring her with you? Man, I'd love to catch up with both of you."

"Sorry," Saville said curtly. "This trip is strictly business."

"Damn shame. So what's going on? You sound tense."

"I need your help locating someone. Unofficially."

Romano's response followed a long silence, betraying his concern. "Uh-oh. That doesn't sound good."

"An intelligence operative attached to the Israeli Embassy. His name is Hillel Mond."

"Who did you say?" Romano's alarm was immediate, a complete shift from their casual conversation.

"Hillel Mond. He's supposedly a case officer with—"

"Where are you right now, Mike?" Romano's tone had become deadly serious.

"The Tancred Motel on Richmond Highway. I'm maybe fifteen minutes from Belvoir."

"I know exactly where that is, Mike. Listen to me very carefully. This is not a secure line. Stay exactly where you are and do not admit anyone to your room under any circumstances. I'm leaving the office immediately."

"Jesus, Van. What the hell is going on? You're scaring me."

Romano's voice dwindled to a whisper. "Mike, you've stumbled into something way above your clearance level. Make no more phone calls. Don't contact anyone else. Just sit tight until I get there."

"How long before—" Saville stopped speaking when he realized he was listening to a dial tone.

He stared at the receiver for several seconds before replacing it in the cradle. Romano's reaction had been far more intense than he'd expected. What kind of operation was Hillel Mond involved in that would provoke such an immediate and alarmed response from an Army intelligence officer?

Saville moved to the window and carefully surveyed the motel parking lot. Everything appeared normal, but Romano's warning echoed in his mind. He checked the door locks, ensuring both the deadbolt and chain were engaged, then settled into the uncomfortable chair beside the small table to wait.

Chapter 19

A person's appearance can change in three years. The man standing outside Saville's motel room door matched Van Romano's build and height. Saville searched for Romano's most distinctive features: the angular jaw and thick, dark eyebrows. The afternoon sun glaring off the window made positive identification difficult. The beard didn't help; Romano had been clean-shaven in Chicago. Minor discrepancies, perhaps, but Saville knew that in this business, minor discrepancies got operatives killed.

"Open up, Mike! It's me!" A fist hammered the door hard enough to rattle the window frame.

Romano's earlier warning replayed in Saville's mind: *This is not a secure line. Stay exactly where you are and do not admit anyone to your room under any circumstances.*

Saville weighed the possibilities. Foreign intelligence services could be monitoring government communications channels. He had contacted Romano through his office's direct line, supposedly secure, but nothing was guaranteed anymore. His pulse quickened.

"Come on, Mike! Let me in!" The man pounded again, then pressed a Department of Defense Common Access Card against the window. He held it steady while Saville examined the photograph, name, rank, service branch, and DoD identification number. It was Romano.

Saville unlocked the door, his palm slick against the deadbolt. As the man crossed the threshold, Saville drew his Bureau-issued Glock 19M and pressed the muzzle against the soft spot at the base of his skull.

"What the hell, Mike? You trying to blow my head off?"

Saville held his position for another heartbeat, studying the tension in Romano's shoulders and the way his hands remained visible and still. Trained responses. Saville lowered the weapon. "I had to be certain."

Romano rubbed the back of his head and winced. "Did you have to leave a mark?" Then he laughed and embraced Saville in a bear hug. Romano was lean and muscular. Saville felt the air compress out of his lungs. Same grip strength as Baghdad. Some things didn't change.

"Talk about leaving a mark," Saville wheezed.

Romano released him. "Now we're even." He moved to the window and swept the curtains aside. Saville heard a truck rumble past on the access road. Romano tracked it until it disappeared, then scanned the parking lot before turning back. "We need to extract you immediately. This location is compromised."

Saville dropped onto the bed. The cheap mattress springs groaned underneath. "Compromised how? What am I dealing with?"

"The same actors who eliminated Victor Farnsworth and Davy Clough."

Saville was stunned. In his peripheral vision, he caught Romano's hand drift toward his concealed carry position, then stop. Old habits. How did Romano come to possess this intelligence? "Hillel Mond?" He felt his stomach tighten.

"Unknown. That's what we're attempting to determine."

"What's INSCOM's connection to a homicide investigation?"

"I could pose the same question to you," Romano replied. "According to official channels, there is no FBI investigation. The medical examiner ruled Farnsworth's death a suicide, and the Bureau formally closed the case hours ago. What's your operational status, Mike?"

"I told you I was here unofficially."

"Define that precisely."

Saville provided a comprehensive brief, omitting nothing of substance, though he hesitated over certain operational details. He wasn't sure he could trust someone he hadn't seen in three years, but Romano had always been the sharpest and most dependable soldier in their unit. Saville remembered Fallujah, 2004: Romano had held position for fourteen hours providing overwatch, not moving even when insurgents passed ten meters from his hide site. He was the one operator Saville could count on to perform impeccably. He hoped that hadn't changed.

"How do you possess detailed intelligence about the Farnsworth and Clough investigations?" Saville asked.

Romano's expression hardened. "Because we monitor everything."

Saville nodded slowly. "Who told you the Farnsworth case was closed? Just yesterday, it was being transferred to the Counterintelligence Division." The information wasn't adding up.

"FBI Director Shaffer held a press conference an hour ago. He announced that the Bureau is satisfied that Farnsworth took his own life. Case closed."

"How could he reach that conclusion?"

"He faced immediate pushback," Romano replied. "Primarily from Fox News. They criticized him for a rush to judgment."

"They're right."

"Obviously."

"Who gave the order?" Saville pressed. "This must have come from the top."

"Without question." Romano glanced out the window, focusing on a sedan parked three spaces away. After a moment, an elderly woman stepped out with a shopping bag. Romano's shoulders relaxed slightly. "Shaffer wouldn't make that call on his own."

"Then who?"

"We're investigating that angle. Farnsworth had direct access to the President."

"I'll ask again, Van," Saville said, his patience wearing thin. "Why is military intelligence involved in the deaths of Victor Farnsworth and Davy Clough?"

"We have no interest in their deaths," Romano replied. "However, both men died shortly after dining with Hillel Mond, who is a high-priority intelligence target."

"Did Mond eliminate them?"

"Unknown."

"I thought you monitored everything."

Romano exhaled slowly. "We've monitored Mond for years. He's aware of our surveillance. It's a complex game of cat and mouse. At times, he slips past our watch; at others, we track him without his knowledge. While it's possible he committed both murders during a surveillance gap, it's unlikely."

"He has a history of targeted assassinations," Saville pointed out.

"Only against threats to Israeli national security."

"Who else could be responsible?"

"We're exploring multiple possibilities."

"Come on, Van. Give me something."

Romano wet his lips. "We know about the Kendall County meeting that Farnsworth arranged. Three weeks ago, Farnsworth approached Mond with a business proposal, allegedly for the U.S. government."

"Allegedly?"

"Farnsworth was freelancing. There was no official sanction."

"How do you know?"

"Two weeks ago, he and Mond traveled to Jerusalem together. We tracked them from Ben Gurion Airport to a safe house in the Rehavia neighborhood, a high-end area in the government district. There's no official record of the trip," Romano explained. "We contacted the White House, and they refused to confirm that Farnsworth even left Washington."

"The White House," Saville repeated, his mind racing through possibilities. "What was the nature of this business proposition?"

"I hate to sound repetitive," Romano said.

"You don't know." Saville's frustration mounted.

"We know Farnsworth was selling something, and Israeli intelligence was prepared to pay handsomely for it."

"Classified intel?"

"Possibly."

That would explain Romano's involvement. "What classified material could Farnsworth access?"

"Everything that crossed the President's desk: military intelligence, national security assessments, law enforcement briefings, policy papers, nuclear response protocols, CIA operational plans, NSA intercepts. They were friends. Who knows what else they discussed over dinner and cocktails?"

"Why would—"

"Why does anyone commit treason?" Romano interrupted. "Financial motivation, ideological conversion, or coercion. Especially coercion in Farnsworth's case."

Saville stared at him, confused.

"Farnsworth was having an affair with the First Lady," Romano stated bluntly.

Saville's expression went blank. The room felt stifling. He stood from the bed, paced a few steps, and stopped. His hands snapped open and closed. "How long?"

"Six months, that we can confirm. Possibly longer."

"Israeli intelligence may have discovered Farnsworth and Hellen Carney's relationship and leveraged it for operational advantage."

"Why would Israeli intelligence eliminate their asset?" Saville asked.

"Maybe they didn't. Others had motives."

Saville recalled his earlier thought. *This had to come from the top.* Someone with access to classified Pentagon communications. Someone with ultimate authority. The implications were staggering.

"You're investigating the President," Saville said.

Romano met his gaze, expression unreadable, saying nothing. A door slammed outside. Both men tensed until they heard children laughing.

"You think President Carney had Victor Farnsworth killed," Saville continued, "because of the affair or the intelligence compromise?"

"Potentially both."

"Where does Davy Clough fit into this scenario?"

Romano shrugged. "Perhaps his investigative reporting threatened sensitive operations. Maybe he was simply in the wrong place at the wrong time."

"He told me he was investigating something involving the highest levels of government. I believed him. His mother mentioned he had received threats."

"Mother knows best."

Saville ignored the subtle sarcasm. "What's our next move?"

"We go straight to the source."

"Which source?"

"Hillel Mond. We know he's involved, and we have his current location. It's time for a direct approach."

"Direct approach," Saville repeated, aware it wouldn't be a friendly chat.

Chapter 20

Two men in dark suits were waiting for Lowri when she clocked in at midnight for her second consecutive graveyard shift.

The men looked federal. Clean-shaven, athletic builds, earpieces. They displayed Secret Service Personal Identity Verification cards and asked her to accompany them. From their stance and tone, she understood it wasn't a request.

"What's this about?" Lowri asked, glancing at her fellow officers watching from across the patrol room. She suspected she already knew: Victor Farnsworth.

"You're wanted at the White House, ma'am," said the taller agent, who identified himself as Agent Sanchez.

"By whom?"

"We weren't given that information, ma'am."

Lowri considered her options. "I'm starting my shift. I need authorization to leave."

"The shift commander has already approved it," the other agent replied. "He called Captain Morrow at home."

"All right! Way to go, Sarge!" Joel Graves called from across the room. "You get the special candlelight tour."

"Shut up, Graves."

"Please, Sergeant Pritchard," Sanchez said. "We must be going. It's very late."

Yes, it was late, Lowri thought during the drive to the White House. A midnight summons indicated urgency. Whatever this was couldn't wait until her shift ended at eight. The implications intrigued her.

She sat in the back of the black Suburban, attempting to engage in conversation. No response. Sanchez might have nodded once, but it was so minimal it could have been nothing. She tried a different approach, commenting on his appearance and asking about his personal life. All she got was a tight smile.

As they turned onto 16th Street, she abandoned her attempts at gathering information. They were almost at the White House. She'd learn soon enough why she'd been pulled from duty.

They reached the Pennsylvania Avenue checkpoint. The Uniformed Division officers waved them through without inspection. This was notable. Pennsylvania Avenue in front of the White House had been closed to regular traffic since the Oklahoma City bombing in 1995. Only vehicles with specific authorization could pass.

The same expedited treatment occurred at the Southwest Gate. Sanchez showed his PIV card at the guard booth, and the Suburban continued up West Executive Avenue. Lowri had to surrender her service weapon at the checkpoint. Standard procedure, but the efficient entry confirmed that someone with significant authority had arranged this meeting.

She felt both privileged and uneasy. She drove past the White House daily on patrol and had worked perimeter security during state visits, coordinating with the Secret Service on motorcade routes. She'd met the vice president once and shaken his hand after escorting a donor to his ceremonial office in the Eisenhower Executive Office Building.

But she hadn't been inside the White House itself since a school field trip twenty years ago. She'd lived in D.C. her entire life, yet, like most residents, rarely thought about the government machinery operating around her.

She'd visited the Smithsonian exactly once and had never entered Arlington National Cemetery. Now, as Sanchez and his partner escorted her through the East Colonnade, past the Jacqueline Kennedy Garden and into the elevator to the State Floor, Lowri wished she'd paid more attention in her American Government courses.

***

Saville checked his watch. 12:38 a.m. The moon hung full and bright overhead; stars dotted the clear sky. Saville and Van Romano sat in Romano's white Ford Expedition, watching Hillel Mond enter a studio apartment on Virginia Avenue near the Foggy Bottom Metro station.

They'd been following him for an hour, ever since he left the Israeli embassy. He drove a black Dodge Charger with standard D.C. plates, indicating that Mond's midnight excursion was unofficial.

Tailing Mond had been effortless. Romano already knew the Israeli's destination, and Mond knew they knew. He waved at them when he left the embassy and called out *Boker tov* after stopping for Chinese takeout at a twenty-four-hour restaurant, kosher laws be damned.

"Three nights a week, he visits his mistress," Romano explained. "Three nights a week, someone from the intelligence community watches him do it."

Saville suppressed his distaste. The idea of a man Mond's age dating a college student made him uneasy, but the hypocrisy of his reaction troubled him even more. He had always seen himself as a devoted family man, the type the Bureau preferred in its agents. Loyalty had always been important to him. That's what he told himself. But Caroline Cochran was so young and beautiful. He had initially resisted her advances but ultimately succumbed to her considerable charms.

Who was he kidding? He had wanted her just as much as she had wanted him. From her first day in the Miami field office, they had shared an unspoken attraction that quickly escalated into an undeniable desire neither could resist.

Jennifer had sensed something was wrong in a way only a wife could. Saville had grown distant when they were together. She had tolerated it for a while, wrapped in denial, but then came Caroline's murder and Saville's reckless trip to Germany. His extreme reaction only confirmed her suspicions.

He had never admitted to the affair, and Jennifer had never confronted him. But the damage was done. In the months that followed, mistrust loomed between them like an invisible barrier that neither could breach. Eventually, they separated, and Saville felt lost on how to repair the damage.

He devised a plan: to tell the truth. He would confess everything to Jennifer, clear his conscience, and express his remorse about their marriage. He wanted her to understand the depth of his feelings for her and Emma. He couldn't predict her reaction; he could only hope for forgiveness.

"Rachel Hunt," Romano said.

"Sorry?"

"Mond's mistress. Rachel Hunt. A British national attending American University on a full scholarship. Political science major with an Arabic minor. She plans to work as a State Department translator after graduating next spring."

Saville was still grappling with his failing marriage when Romano's words sank in. "Arabic? Is that significant?"

"We don't believe so, but we're keeping all possibilities open. I understand the CIA is aggressively recruiting her."

Saville processed the profile: a senior in college, twenty-two or twenty-three years old, on a full scholarship. Clearly brilliant. An Arabic speaker. She had a promising future in the intelligence community, assuming Mond didn't compromise her first.

"Hope you brought reading material," Romano said, spinning his cell phone between his fingers. "Mond typically stays for about two hours before returning to the embassy. He rarely spends the night. It's the same pattern every time. He leaves, we follow. But tonight, we're changing the script."

"Changing how?"

"He'll expect the usual routine, so when he exits Rachel's apartment, his guard will drop, if only for a moment before his training kicks in. Our window is narrow. We have to move fast."

"Move?" Saville's unease grew with every word.

"He won't cooperate voluntarily, Mike. We'll need leverage."

"Jesus, Van, I'm a federal law enforcement officer. I swore an oath to defend and uphold the Constitution. What you're suggesting doesn't qualify."

"Against all enemies, foreign and domestic, Mike. Don't forget that part. Without any mental reservation or purpose of evasion. I believe that's the exact wording."

Saville shook his head. "I'm not a spy, Van. I can't operate outside the law." The irony hit him immediately: he was already doing just that.

"You were a spy once. What happened to that mindset?"

Saville wondered if involving Romano had been a mistake. "I was an analyst. You operators handled the wet work."

"Now you sound like a typical bureaucrat, washing your hands of the messy parts."

Romano hit the tailgate release and exited the vehicle. He lifted the rear window, reached into the cargo area, and retrieved a twelve-gauge tactical shotgun.

Dread washed over Saville. "What the hell are you planning to do with that?"

"Relax," Romano said, returning to the driver's seat with the weapon. "This isn't your average scattergun. It's equipped with less-lethal rounds."

Saville recognized it now: an Extended Range Electronic Projectile system, a long-range electroshock weapon that fired XREP rounds. Upon impact, the projectile's barbed electrodes would penetrate clothing or embed in skin, delivering pulsed electrical charges for twenty seconds, creating neuromuscular disruption. The current would override voluntary muscle control, causing uncoordinated muscle contractions and temporary incapacitation. Enough time to secure a target with restraints.

"So we're going to incapacitate and abduct an Israeli intelligence officer with diplomatic immunity?" Saville asked.

"This happens more often than you'd think, Mike. It just never makes the news. Welcome to my world."

Saville ran his fingers through his hair, wishing he were back in his own.

Chapter 21

Lowri could hardly believe her eyes. She had seen the First Lady before on television, magazines, and newspapers. Hellen Carney was even more striking in person. Shoulder-length blonde hair framed high cheekbones, and her tailored suit accentuated a figure that defied her fifty-something years. Lowri hoped she would look half as good at that age.

"I apologize for the inconvenience, Sergeant Pritchard," the First Lady said, gesturing to a wingback chair across from her desk. "I didn't think you'd mind being off the streets for a few hours."

"Yes, ma'am." Lowri sat down and surveyed the First Lady's office. The walls displayed a curated collection of photographs and paintings. The First Lady appeared in most of them alongside world leaders, celebrities, and power brokers. Some faces Lowri recognized, while others seemed familiar from news coverage, though she couldn't quite place them.

"Call me Hellen." The First Lady extended her hand across the desk. "We're all friends here."

Lowri shook the offered hand, trying to match the First Lady's firm grip without appearing overeager. She wasn't sure what protocol demanded in this situation. The Secret Service agents who had brought her here had offered no guidance.

The First Lady settled back in her chair and opened a manila folder on her desk. "You and I have a lot in common, Sergeant Pritchard."

Lowri's eyes widened. What could she possibly share with the most powerful woman in America?

"Lowri. Such a lovely name. Unusual spelling. We share that particular quirk."

"Yes, ma'am."

"Please. Call me Hellen," the First Lady insisted, her tone carrying a subtle edge.

"Yes, ma'am. I mean, Hellen."

"That's better." The First Lady turned a page in the folder. Her manicured fingernail traced down what appeared to be a personnel file. "Accept my condolences regarding your father. Did that tragedy contribute to your decision to become a police officer?"

Lowri dipped her head. The question struck closer than she had expected. "It had everything to do with it."

Her father had been a modest store clerk, a Welsh immigrant who raised his daughter alone after her mother died of cirrhosis when Lowri was still in diapers. When she was seventeen, two men entered his convenience store and shot him dead for the contents of the register. Less than two hundred dollars. She had been on her own ever since.

"I understand the killers were never caught?" the First Lady asked, still studying the file.

The familiar ache returned to Lowri's chest. She had vowed to find the men herself once she had the resources and authority. "They haven't been. It's a cold case now."

The First Lady nodded, her expression sympathetic. "Perhaps there's something we can do about that."

Lowri sat forward in her chair. "The cold case squad has reviewed it twice, but there's no physical evidence, no witnesses willing to talk."

"They don't have access to the resources that I do." The First Lady closed the folder and met Lowri's eyes directly. "I can have the investigation reopened immediately with federal assistance. DNA technology has advanced considerably. There might be evidence they missed."

Lowri didn't know what to say. "Thank you" seemed inadequate.

"Of course. That's what friends do for each other." The First Lady reopened the folder and turned another page. "Your parents were from Wales. That explains your name. It symbolizes victory and honor. I'm sure they would be very proud of the woman you've become."

"Thank you, ma'am." Lowri started to correct herself, but the First Lady said nothing, so she left it alone. "I never really knew my mother, but I miss my tad very much."

"You were born here in DC? At Howard University Hospital?"

Lowri sank back in her chair. Howard was the city's safety-net hospital, known for treating the uninsured and underinsured. "My family didn't have health insurance."

"Nothing to be ashamed of, Sergeant Pritchard. We all come from somewhere." The First Lady's tone remained neutral and businesslike. "My father named me after a mythological Greek warrior. He thought it would prepare me for the challenges of a male-dominated world."

"Did it?"

A slight smile crossed the First Lady's lips. "I'm sitting in the White House, aren't I?"

Lowri said nothing. The answer spoke for itself.

"Have you ever heard the phrase quid pro quo, Sergeant Pritchard? Do you know what it means?"

"Yes, ma'am." Hannibal Lecter had asked the same thing of Clarice Starling.

The First Lady continued examining the folder. "It says here you're a registered Republican."

Lowri looked away, unsure how to respond. Party affiliation shouldn't matter in law enforcement, but everything was political in DC.

"It's fine, Sergeant Pritchard. It also says you didn't vote in the last presidential election."

The tension in the room was palpable, and Lowri felt as if she were navigating a minefield.

"No matter," the First Lady said after a brief pause. "The selection of candidates leaves much to be desired."

Lowri touched her chin, unsure if the First Lady was joking or subtly criticizing her husband's campaign.

"A good conservative is just what I need. Someone who will pursue the truth no matter the political fallout." The First Lady's eyes fixed on Lowri with sudden intensity. "I hear you've been looking into the Victor Farnsworth investigation?"

"No, ma'am."

"My husband was having an affair with Molly Farnsworth." Her tone was flat and emotionless, as if she were reading from a grocery list.

Lowri struggled to hide her confusion. Did the First Lady know about her conversation with Victor's widow? Of course she did; that was why Lowri was here. She decided to stand her ground. "Molly Farnsworth claimed you were the one having an affair. With her husband."

The warmth faded from the First Lady's expression. "And you believe her?"

"I don't know what to believe," Lowri said, finally finding her voice. "All this politics and posturing. A man is dead, and everyone seems to be looking out for themselves."

She took a deep breath, surprised by her own boldness but relieved to express her thoughts.

"You're absolutely right, Sergeant Pritchard. Victor Farnsworth was murdered, and I know who is responsible."

"Who?" Lowri asked, recalling similar claims from Molly. Everyone seemed to have theories, but the certainty in their voices didn't lend credibility to their accusations.

The First Lady didn't hesitate. "My husband."

The matter-of-fact tone sent a chill down Lowri's spine. She had heard of the First Lady's ruthlessness but had assumed it was largely media exaggeration. Now, she wasn't so sure.

"Molly Farnsworth also accused your husband," Lowri said cautiously. "For a different reason."

"Molly used to be an exotic dancer." The First Lady's voice dripped with disdain. "When Victor met her, she was working at a gentlemen's club in Fayetteville, near Fort Bragg. She's always been opportunistic. Old habits die hard, Sergeant Pritchard."

"What does her past have to do with Victor's death?"

"Molly viewed her affair with my husband as a way to trade up. She's calculating and used her considerable charms to persuade my husband to eliminate Victor. She's always wanted Woody for herself."

The casual mention of "eliminate" made Lowri's stomach turn. "With all due respect, ma'am, I find it hard to believe the President of the United States would orchestrate a murder."

"Don't overestimate my husband, Sergeant Pritchard. He's intelligent, charismatic, and a brilliant politician, but he's also emotionally stunted." The First Lady's fingers drummed once on the desk. "Every powerful man has his weakness. Woody's weakness, which will be his political downfall, is his attraction to young women."

Lowri twisted a strand of hair around her finger, an old childhood habit resurfacing. "I'm not sure what you want me to do, ma'am."

"Quid pro quo," the First Lady replied, returning to the folder. "I'll ensure your father's case gets the attention it deserves, with the best forensic resources available. You continue your investigation into Victor's death and pursue the truth."

"I could lose my job if I investigate outside my jurisdiction."

"Work on your own time. Evenings, days off. Ask questions. Plant doubts about the official story. Suggest my husband played a role in Victor's death, and see what grows from those seeds."

"No one will listen to me, ma'am. I'm just a sergeant. I don't have that kind of influence."

The First Lady's smile returned, though it was colder now. "You don't need influence. Once the right questions reach bloggers and talk radio hosts, they'll run with it. The story will gain momentum, and the FBI will have no choice but to reopen the case. Public pressure will demand it."

"Ma'am, the scandal would destroy your husband's presidency."

"I can count on your complete discretion about this conversation, can't I, Sergeant Pritchard?"

The subtle threat was unmistakable. "I can't guarantee you'll come out of this unscathed."

The First Lady nodded slowly. "I've endured my husband's infidelities for twenty-three years, ignored and covered for him to protect his political career. Those days are over." Her voice hardened. "This time he's crossed a line. We're talking about murder, Sergeant Pritchard. How can I face myself if I do nothing? Victor was a good man. He didn't deserve to die."

Lowri noticed the change in the First Lady's tone whenever she mentioned Victor's name, a softness akin to the affection Lowri felt when she spoke about Joel Graves. "Is your conscience the only reason you want to bring your husband down?"

The First Lady ignored the question and reached beneath her desk. With visible effort, she lifted a banker's box and set it heavily on the desktop. "Victor's personal papers. I retrieved them from his office the day he died." She pushed the box toward Lowri. "I'll have Agent Sanchez carry it out for you."

"I can manage," Lowri said, eyeing the box. "What exactly should I be looking for?"

"With your skills as an investigator, I'm sure you'll recognize it when you see it."

"Why didn't Detective Sprague or the FBI find these documents?"

The First Lady laughed, a sharp sound devoid of humor. "Because I removed them before anyone searched Victor's office. I couldn't risk them falling into the wrong hands."

"The wrong hands? This is a murder investigation, ma'am."

"Except it's not anymore, is it? Why do you think the FBI closed the case so quickly? My husband made that call. Who else but the President could have shut down a federal investigation?"

Lowri maintained a neutral expression. "Perhaps it wouldn't have been closed if the FBI had seen these files."

"Don't be naïve, Sergeant Pritchard. What's in these files is exactly why the case was closed. That's why I need you. Someone outside the system to make sense of what's in this box."

Lowri weighed her options. Every instinct urged her to walk away, but the possibility of finally solving her father's murder was compelling. Could the First Lady's influence truly crack a cold case after all these years? Could she afford to pass up this opportunity?

"Don't worry about your job," the First Lady said, as if reading her thoughts. She glanced at the folder again. "When this is over, not only will we know who killed Victor and your father, but I'll also ensure your FBI application gets approved."

Lowri tried to conceal her surprise. How did the First Lady know about her application? Of course, she knew. She seemed to know everything.

The First Lady's tone grew serious. "You understand that once you leave this office, there can be no further contact between us?

If you try to involve me in any way, I'll deny this meeting ever happened."

Lowri nodded slowly. The implications were clear. She would be alone in this.

"You'll have questions," the First Lady continued, rising from her desk. "But you'll have to find the answers without my assistance. Starting now, I've never heard of Park Police Sergeant Lowri Pritchard. Are we clear?"

"Yes, ma'am." The words left a hollow feeling in Lowri's stomach.

"Very good." The First Lady moved toward the door, signaling the end of the meeting. Lowri stood and lifted the box; it was heavier than it appeared.

"Agent Sanchez will drive you back to your district." The First Lady paused at the door. "Oh, and Sergeant Pritchard? I told you to call me Hellen."

"Yes, ma'am," Lowri replied, relieved she wouldn't have to call her anything at all.

Chapter 22

Saville adjusted the binoculars Romano had given him. Through the lens, he watched Hillel Mond exit his lover's apartment at 2:47 a.m., closing the door behind him. As he reached the sidewalk, he turned right and began walking southwest on Virginia Avenue toward his car, parked two blocks away.

Following the plan he and Romano had devised, Saville slid into the driver's seat and guided the Expedition along the curb. The streets were empty, the night quiet. Most of Foggy Bottom's late-night activity revolved around George Washington University and the Kennedy Center, both well out of earshot.

Mond recognized the vehicle just as he had before. He raised his hand and waved as Saville pulled alongside. Saville kept his eyes on the Israeli while allowing the Expedition to coast. Mond maintained a steady pace, relaxed. In Saville's peripheral vision, Romano emerged from the shadows beside the apartment building, shotgun raised to his shoulder.

Something shifted in Saville's expression. Mond's training kicked in instantly. The Israeli drew a compact pistol from beneath his jacket and spun toward Romano's position in one fluid motion.

"Gun!" Saville shouted.

Two shots rang out, sharp cracks echoing off the apartment facades. The sounds reverberated down the empty street, unmistakably gunfire.

Saville instinctively ducked below the dashboard, gripping the steering wheel tightly. After a moment, he raised his head to see Mond collapse onto the pavement. The pistol skidded across the concrete, coming to rest against the front tire of the Expedition. Blood spread across Mond's yellow shirt from his right shoulder.

This wasn't the plan. Romano had promised a nonlethal takedown. The XREP rounds were supposed to incapacitate, not wound.

Saville slid into the passenger seat and pushed open the door. He dropped onto the sidewalk and grabbed Mond's pistol. Where was Romano?

Mond lay on his back, left hand pressed against his shoulder as blood seeped between his fingers. He stared at Saville with clear, pained eyes. No convulsions, no neuromuscular disruption. He was conscious and in control, bracing himself against the concrete, trying to rise.

"Romano!" Saville shouted, scanning the area. Then he saw him.

Romano lay crumpled several feet behind Mond, wedged between the building and the sidewalk. His chest was a gaping wound of exposed ribs and torn flesh where high-velocity rounds had pierced him. The shotgun lay beside him, unfired.

"Sniper! Get down!" Mond shouted through gritted teeth.

Another shot rang out, shattering the driver's side window of the Expedition. The bullet ripped through the headrest where Saville had just been sitting moments earlier.

Saville hit the concrete hard, Mond's pistol still in hand. He scrambled on hands and knees toward the Israeli, who had rolled behind the front wheel well of the Expedition for cover.

Lights flickered on in apartment windows as curtains parted, revealing faces pressed against the glass. Someone would call 911, and first responders would arrive within minutes.

Mond reached out with his uninjured arm. "Get me in the truck! We have to leave! Now!"

"We can't leave Romano," Saville replied, knowing his friend was beyond help.

"He's dead," Mond said flatly. He began crawling toward the rear passenger door, leaving a blood trail on the concrete. He reached for the handle and groaned, "Help me."

Saville stayed low and yanked open the door. He pulled Mond under his left arm and hoisted him into the back seat. Mond rolled onto the floor, crying out as he landed on his wounded shoulder.

A woman's scream pierced the air. Saville looked up to see someone leaning from a third-floor window directly above Romano's body. Another shot ricocheted off the building's brick facade, inches from the window, prompting more screams.

Survival instincts kicked in. Saville dove into the front passenger seat, scrambled into the driver's seat, and started the engine. He floored the accelerator, the speedometer hitting sixty as they raced down Virginia Avenue. He killed the headlights to reduce visibility and make the license plate harder to read, switching them back on only when they swung onto New Hampshire Avenue.

As they approached Dupont Circle, Saville checked the rearview mirror. Mond's face was pale, his expression focused despite the pain. A tactical error hit Saville hard: he had just helped a trained intelligence officer into the back seat while he drove. Did Mond have a backup weapon? Could he shoot Saville and take the vehicle? Basic operational security, and he had blown it completely.

But Mond was in no shape for aggression. The Israeli slumped against the rear seat, sweat beading on his forehead. His yellow shirt had turned dark red, and blood pooled on the leather upholstery. His left hand pressed against the wound, but his strength was fading.

"You need a hospital," Saville said, knowing George Washington University Medical Center was less than ten minutes away.

"No." Mond's voice was weak but firm.

"You're going to bleed out."

"No doctors. No hospitals," Mond insisted, more forcefully this time.

Saville glanced back. Mond had curled into a defensive position on the seat, protecting his injury. "I can get you to the embassy."

"No. Safe house." Mond caught his breath. "Columbia Heights. Thirteenth and Girard. There's a doctor."

Saville nodded, realizing he had no choice; he was in this mess too. He didn't know what awaited them at the safe house, but he pressed on, hurrying without drawing too much attention. The roads were mostly clear, and he made good time, though Mond likely didn't think so; the Israeli's moans and labored breathing came in waves.

Saville faced grim options. He was already implicated in whatever had just happened. Romano was dead, Mond was wounded, and someone had attempted to kill them all. He drove north, pushing the speed limit without being reckless. The streets remained mostly empty, but Mond's breathing grew more labored, punctuated by suppressed groans.

"Stay with me," Saville urged as he turned onto Florida Avenue. He made a quick left onto Thirteenth Street and spotted the intersection with Girard.

"There," Mond whispered, barely lifting his good arm toward a four-story brick and glass building on the corner. His eyes were starting to glaze over. "Back entrance."

Saville pulled around the building and parked near a steel door marked only by a security keypad. Mond was barely conscious.

"Code," Mond managed. "Two... four... one."

His voice faded. Saville jumped out and punched the numbers into the keypad.

"Yes?" A heavily accented voice came through a hidden speaker.

"Hillel Mond. He's been shot. He needs immediate medical attention."

The response was instantaneous. Three men burst through the door in less than thirty seconds. Two carried a tactical stretcher while the third held the door. All three had the build of soldiers and concealed weapons beneath their shirts.

They loaded Mond onto the stretcher and disappeared inside. Saville stood beside the building, adrenaline still coursing through him. His law enforcement instincts kicked in. Mond was at minimum, a material witness in multiple homicides, possibly a suspect. He couldn't just walk away.

Saville pulled out his FBI credentials and approached the door where the third man still stood guard.

The man drew a SIG Sauer P226 from his waistband in one smooth motion, the barrel trained on Saville's chest. "Stop."

"Easy," Saville said, holding up his badge. "FBI."

The man's expression didn't change. "Weapon. On ground. Slowly."

Saville didn't argue. He'd left Mond's pistol in the Expedition, but he still carried his service Glock. Moving deliberately, he reached into his jacket and withdrew the weapon from its shoulder holster using only his thumb and forefinger. He set it on the asphalt and slid it toward the guard with his foot.

The guard scooped up the Glock without taking his eyes off Saville. "Backup weapon."

"I don't carry one." Saville lifted both pant legs to show empty ankles. The Bureau required qualification for backup weapons, and Saville had never bothered with the paperwork or range time.

"Hands behind head. Interlace fingers."

Saville complied. The guard moved behind him, the SIG's barrel pressing against the base of his skull. "Walk."

They entered the building. The door sealed behind them with a mechanical click. Another guard was in the dim vestibule, cradling an Uzi Pro. He nodded slightly as they passed.

The guard pushed Saville forward with his free hand. They climbed two flights of stairs in near darkness. A single Star of David marked the wall between the second and third floors. The only sounds were their footsteps and Saville's controlled breathing.

On the third floor, they moved down a long corridor past multiple closed doors. The guard grabbed Saville's collar and stopped him at an unmarked door. "In."

He shoved Saville through the doorway. Bright surgical lights temporarily blinded him. As his vision adjusted, he saw six people in scrubs and surgical masks working around a hydraulic operating table, shouting instructions to each other in rapid Hebrew. Medical equipment lined the walls. IV bags hung from portable stands, and monitors displayed vital signs.

Mond lay on the table, intubated and connected to multiple machines. His shirt had been cut away, revealing the entry wound and surgical incisions.

One of the medical team, a woman with blood-spattered scrubs, broke away and approached them. She pulled down her mask, revealing a face lined with exhaustion.

"Lower the weapon, you idiot," she snapped at the guard in accented English. He immediately complied.

She studied Saville with dark, intelligent eyes. "You brought our friend here?"

Saville watched the medical team work. "Is he going to make it?"

"Yes. He lost significant blood, but the bullet missed the axillary artery. We're stabilizing him now." She pressed her palms together briefly. "*Elef todot*. A thousand thanks."

"Where am I?" Saville asked, though he had already guessed.

"I will explain everything once we finish here, Agent Saville."

The name stopped him cold. "How do you know who I am?"

But she had already returned to the operating table, mask up, hands reaching for instruments. She rejoined the urgent work of saving lives, the same work that had failed Van Romano, whose body lay cooling on a DC sidewalk while sirens wailed through the night.

Chapter 23

Lowri drove straight home at the end of her shift. She lived alone in a one-bedroom apartment near the U Street Corridor in Northwest DC. Her rent had just increased to $2,400 per month, utilities not included. On her $68,462 annual salary, she struggled in some months to cover expenses.

She lived simply, rarely indulging beyond occasional nights dancing at clubs with friends or grabbing beers with fellow officers after tough shifts. Her inability to cook meant she often ate out, which quickly drained her budget in DC.

The Park Police had no residency requirements, and Lowri knew she could find cheaper housing in the Maryland or Virginia suburbs. Yet, as a District native, she felt a strong need to stay in the city. If only the Park Police offered the same incentives as the MPD, whose officers enjoyed DC income tax credits, housing assistance, and property tax reductions courtesy of city council mandates.

Lowri had grown up in a row house in Mount Pleasant. The neighborhood had changed over the years, now home to Central American immigrants and young professionals. She hadn't returned since her father's death. His convenience store still stood boarded up on the corner of Sixteenth and Lamont, a painful reminder of memories she couldn't face.

One day, she hoped to find the strength to leave DC. She tried to convince herself she wouldn't miss it, but deep down, she recognized that was self-deception. The city's energy coursed through her veins: the power plays, the history layered in every corner, and the feeling of being at the center of what mattered. Her entire life, with its triumphs and tragedies, had unfolded within those sixty-eight square miles. Perhaps she would come to love Quantico once she started at the FBI's Behavioral Analysis Unit, assuming Hellen Carney lived up to her promise.

After leaving the White House, Lowri spent the remainder of her shift replaying the First Lady's words in her mind. She had made only one traffic stop, responding to a motorist with a flat tire who flagged her down on Constitution Avenue. But her thoughts were elsewhere.

Could she trust Hellen Carney? Like any political figure, the First Lady clearly had an agenda. It was evident she wanted to undermine her husband. But why? Was it simple jealousy? Lowri understood the anger that arose from infidelity; she had dated her share of cheaters and liars. Being a woman who carried a gun and spoke her mind had ended more than one relationship. She was strong-willed and independent, traits some men found threatening rather than attractive.

While Lowri had certainly fantasized about revenge on her ex-boyfriends, she wouldn't actually ruin their lives. She doubted the First Lady's motivations were that straightforward either. Hellen Carney wielded significant influence in her own right. At this point in her life and career, she no longer needed her husband's position to maintain her status. So why orchestrate his downfall?

The answer lay in how people like her operated. For the political elite, the drive to maintain power and social standing dictated every decision. Love and genuine intimacy were foreign concepts to them. They understood lust, but it was a lust for control, not connection.

Then there was the First Lady's claim about conscience: "How can I look at myself in the mirror if I do nothing?" The sentiment had seemed genuine in the moment, but was it? The public persona of the First Lady mirrored what Lowri had witnessed in private: a blend of calculating charm and ice-cold pragmatism.

Lowri struggled to read these people; she had no reference point for their motivations. Her work took her through DC's rougher neighborhoods, dealing with drug dealers, thieves, and occasional violent criminals. She understood desperation and survival, but the games played in Georgetown mansions and at embassy parties were beyond her comprehension. This gap in her experience was problematic. To uncover what happened to Victor Farnsworth, she needed to understand how his world operated.

The answer might lie in the box. Farnsworth's personal papers had been locked in her cruiser's trunk since she left the White House. Several times during her shift, she fought the urge to pull over and examine them, but caution prevailed. Possessing those documents could cost her badge and possibly land her in federal prison. Given what happened to their original owner, she might be risking more than her career.

Most likely, the papers contained nothing of value. The First Lady had certainly reviewed them and removed anything personally damaging or incriminating. Still, there might be something. Some detail Hellen Carney had overlooked or failed to recognize as significant.

Lowri returned to her cruiser parked in the narrow alley behind her building. The box felt heavier than she remembered. By the time she wrestled it up the stairs and through her door, sweat soaked through her uniform. She dropped the box onto her small kitchen table with a thud, likely annoying her downstairs neighbor.

She grabbed a Red Bull from the refrigerator, pulled out a chair, and opened the box. Hundreds of pages stared back at her: memos, reports, handwritten notes, and printed emails. Somewhere in this pile might lie the key to understanding why Victor Farnsworth had died. Or it might be nothing more than the sanitized remnants of a dead man's files, leaving her with more questions than answers.

Taking a long swig of her energy drink, she pulled out the first folder. It was time to uncover the secrets the President's friend had kept and determine whether those secrets were worth killing for.

***

Saville heard screams. Raw shrieks of pain that erupted in bursts, fell silent for moments, and then surged again with greater intensity.

It wasn't Hillel Mond. The cries came in Arabic, sometimes interrupted by harsh commands shouted in Hebrew. The sounds originated from the fourth-floor room adjacent to where Saville waited, confined by two guards after Mond's surgery.

Saville's room was comfortable enough, featuring a couch, a television, and a private bathroom, but no windows. The door locked from the outside, and a table in the center held a tray of kosher potato latkes, sour cream, and a pot of coffee that had gone cold hours ago.

Five hours had passed since they locked him in. He had eaten most of the latkes and drained the coffee pot. He had attempted to sleep on the couch, but the screams jolted him awake each time. His watch showed 8:40 a.m. Exhaustion and frustration vied for dominance.

The screaming stopped. Saville listened intently. This time, the silence held.

Suddenly, the door opened. The surgeon from earlier entered, accompanied by the same two guards who had brought him here. She had changed from blood-stained scrubs into a tan business suit and low heels. The transformation from emergency surgeon to intelligence officer was complete.

Saville stood as she approached, noting how naturally she moved despite what must have been an exhausting night.

"No need to stand, Agent Saville." She selected one of the remaining latkes from the tray. "I apologize for the extended wait."

"How's Mond? When can I speak with him?"

"Soon. The lieutenant commander is still recovering from surgery."

"I'm glad he survived," Saville said, keeping his tone professional. "But this is a federal investigation. I need to be notified the moment he's able to answer questions."

"Please, Agent Saville." She sat on the couch and gestured for him to join her. "We'll honor your request once our colleague is ready."

Saville sat, maintaining distance between them. "You knew my name before I identified myself. How?"

"You've been making inquiries about the lieutenant commander." Her voice remained pleasant but carried an edge. "We notice such things."

"Who's 'we'?"

"Those whose primary duty is protecting the State of Israel."

"Mossad," Saville said, more a statement than a question.

She extended her hand. "Major Ilana Zahavy."

Saville shook her hand, noting her introduction: Major, not Doctor. Military first, medical second.

"What is this place?" Saville asked.

"Where my country conducts intelligence operations within the United States."

Saville frowned. "That's illegal. You're operating on American soil without—"

"Without what?" Zahavy's expression remained neutral. "Without permission? Agent Saville, Israel is America's strongest ally in the war against terror. We share intelligence, coordinate operations, and prevent attacks that would kill thousands of your citizens." She paused, letting that sink in. "Sometimes governments look the other way when cooperation serves mutual interests. Your superiors understand this, even if you don't yet."

Saville wanted to argue, to cite statutes and jurisdictional boundaries, but he recognized the reality she described. He'd seen enough interagency cables to know that official policy and operational reality often diverged significantly.

"I heard screaming next door," Saville said.

She stood and moved toward the door. "Come with me, Agent Saville."

She led him to the adjacent room, with the guards following closely. She flipped the light switch, revealing a stark space. A metal table stood in the center, with an adjustable lamp suspended from the ceiling. Blood covered portions of the concrete floor. Some had dried to a rust brown, but fresh crimson pooled near the table legs.

"The man who was here," Saville began.

"Provided valuable intelligence."

"Where is he now?"

"No longer a threat."

A chill ran through Saville. "You killed him?"

"The prisoner was Bassam Al-Najjar, Community Liaison for the United Gaza Aid Network." Her tone turned clinical. "His organization funneled money that directly funded the October 7 Hamas attacks. He was executed for crimes against the State of Israel."

Saville stepped back. He understood the rage that followed October 7, 2023. He had seen the footage and watched his Jewish colleagues struggle with grief and fury. But summary execution violated everything he had sworn to uphold.

"You must understand, Agent Saville," she said, stepping closer to the bloodstained table. "Every day, we fight for our survival against enemies who seek our complete destruction. Passivity is a path to extinction. We confront them using whatever methods are necessary. It's how we've survived since 1948."

Saville carefully considered her words. "By executing an American citizen without trial?"

"We eliminated a terrorist. Perhaps we prevented your next 9/11 or spared another mother in Tel Aviv from identifying her children's remains after a suicide bombing."

Her voice trembled slightly at the end, and she quickly wiped her eyes with her sleeve.

"Forgive me," she said, regaining her composure. "Emotion is a luxury I can't afford. Israel cannot confront terrorists with velvet gloves. We lack the privilege of adhering to the Geneva Convention rules when our enemies recognize no rules and slaughter civilians without hesitation. Such restraint would be seen as betrayal in my country."

Saville chose not to argue. He understood her position intellectually, even if his training rejected it. The moral complexities of counterterrorism weren't his fight today.

A man in a white coat appeared in the doorway. "The lieutenant commander is awake. He's asking for the American."

Ilana nodded at Saville and turned to the doctor. "How did he take the news?"

"As expected. His recovery is in God's hands now."

The doctor left, disappearing down the corridor.

"What news?" Saville asked.

"Our colleague's injuries are severe," Ilana replied, her professional demeanor returning. "Based on the blood loss and tissue damage, we've determined he was struck by a 7.62×51mm NATO round, likely from an M24 Sniper Weapon System. The shooter was approximately six hundred meters away."

Saville processed the implications: American military ammunition and professional sniper tactics significantly narrowed the suspect pool.

"It's too early for a definitive prognosis," Ilana continued as she walked toward the corridor. "However, the lieutenant commander will probably never regain full use of his right arm."

The career implications were clear. Mond's fieldwork was over; he would likely spend his remaining years behind a desk, assuming he had any years left.

"When can I see him?" Saville maintained a neutral tone, suppressing both sympathy and satisfaction.

"He requested your presence. I'll check if he's ready." She paused at the doorway and turned back. "A word of advice, Agent Saville: keep your opinions about our methods to yourself when speaking with him. The lieutenant commander personally developed many of our enhanced interrogation protocols. He won't appreciate lectures on restraint from someone who has never faced existential threats to their nation."

Saville nodded, too weary to argue further. "Understood."

She returned within minutes. "Lieutenant Commander Mond is ready. Please follow me."

They walked down another dimly lit corridor. Saville noticed that the building's layout seemed intentionally confusing, with multiple turns and unmarked doors. Guards maintained their positions, one ahead and one behind.

Ilana stopped at a door marked only with Hebrew characters. She knocked twice, waited for a muffled response, then opened it.

"Five minutes," she said to Saville. "He needs rest."

Saville entered the recovery room, uncertain of Mond's condition or what truths the wounded spy might finally reveal.

Chapter 24

Lowri had been combing through Victor Farnsworth's personal papers for two hours, finding little of substance.

The contents of the box were spread across her kitchen table, filled with the expected memorabilia of a political life: greeting cards, letters, newspaper clippings, awards, and certificates spanning decades. A birthday card from Victor's children caught her eye. The childish handwriting read: "To the world's greatest dad. We'll love you forever. Bryan and Julie."

"Forever" had come sooner than anyone anticipated.

Notably absent was any correspondence between Victor and his wife, Molly. No love letters, anniversary cards, or photos of them together. Nothing to document their marriage. The omission felt deliberate rather than accidental. The First Lady had seemingly edited Molly Farnsworth out of her husband's history before handing over the box. This spoke volumes about Hellen Carney's feelings for Victor, more than any love letter could convey.

Lowri opened another Red Bull, her third in the past few hours, and resumed her search. Just as she was about to give up, her fingers brushed against a thick manila envelope wedged at the bottom of the box. The label read simply, "Photographs."

Inside were hundreds of prints, the kind typically developed at photo labs before everything went digital. She spread them across the table, organizing them chronologically.

The early photos captured Victor's childhood: baby pictures, school portraits, and high school football shots. Victor in his quarterback jersey, number 12. Victor at graduation, his parents beaming beside him. Then came professional shots from his government career: Victor shaking hands with senators, cabinet members, and even the President.

The military photos formed their own distinct collection. Victor as a fresh recruit at basic training, head shaved, wearing standard-issue PT gear, and holding an M16. Several shots of him in Marine dress blues, taken at formal events, followed by deployment photos from Iraq.

One image showed Victor in desert camouflage with his unit, all crowded around a Humvee. Someone had written on the back: "Kuwait, February 11, 1991–Desert Storm." Victor stood at the center, arms around his fellow Marines, all grinning despite the harsh conditions.

Just as Lowri was about to move to the next photo, she froze. She picked up a 5 x 7 print, holding it under her desk lamp. Same desert background, same Humvee, same Victor Farnsworth. But this time, he stood with just one other person.

Peter Sprague.

She blinked hard and looked again. The photo had aged poorly, its edges worn and colors faded, but the face was unmistakable. A younger Sprague. Thirty years younger, but definitely him. Same jaw structure, same way of standing with his weight shifted slightly to the left.

Her stomach turned. Sprague had never mentioned knowing Farnsworth. Not during the investigation briefings, not when he'd taken over as lead detective, and not when he'd pushed to close the case. A prior relationship, especially military service together, would have mandated immediate recusal. Every cop knew that. Sprague certainly knew it.

Which meant he'd deliberately hidden the connection.

Lowri examined the photo more closely. There was damage to the right edge where the photo had been torn. A third person had been in the original image, but only fragments remained: part of a shoulder in desert camouflage, the edge of a face revealing one eye and a portion of the nose, dark hair barely visible under what looked like a beret.

Not enough to identify anyone. She couldn't even determine if it was a man or a woman.

The tear looked old but deliberate. Photos didn't typically rip in such a precise vertical line. Someone had removed the third person from the image, and given the yellowing of the torn edge, they'd done it years ago.

Lowri set the photo aside and rifled through the rest, searching for another shot that might show the same group. Nothing. Every other Desert Storm photo displayed larger groups or different people entirely.

She leaned back in her chair, her mind racing through possibilities. Why had Sprague hidden his connection to Farnsworth? The obvious answer was that he wanted to control the investigation. But why? To protect Farnsworth's reputation? To bury something from their shared past? Or was he following someone else's orders?

The speed with which the case had been closed suddenly made more sense. Sprague hadn't been incompetent or lazy; he'd been deliberate. He had classified the case as a suicide before anyone could dig deeper, before anyone could discover connections that might lead to uncomfortable questions.

And the third person in the photo. Their identity felt crucial now. Someone had wanted them erased from this record. Was it Farnsworth who tore the photo? Sprague? The missing person themselves?

Lowri grabbed her phone but hesitated. She couldn't call Captain Morrow without revealing she'd disobeyed his direct order to drop the case. His words still rang in her ears: "Let the man rest in peace. Are we clear?"

The First Lady was also off-limits. She'd been explicit about cutting contact, threatening to deny their meeting if Lowri tried to involve her.

Confronting Sprague directly would be career suicide. A patrol sergeant accusing a decorated detective of corruption without solid proof? The department would close ranks around Sprague, and she'd be directing traffic in Anacostia by week's end.

That left Joel Graves. He'd understand her position. More importantly, he'd believe her. They'd been dancing around their feelings for months. Maybe it was time to trust him with both her discovery and her heart.

Lowri picked up the torn photo again, studying the visible fragment of the third person. Something about that partial profile nagged at her. The visible eye seemed familiar, but she couldn't place it. The nose appeared distinctive. Mediterranean or Middle Eastern perhaps, but the image was too damaged to be certain.

She photographed the picture with her phone, ensuring the torn edge was clear. Evidence of evidence. Then, she carefully returned all the materials to the box exactly as she'd found them. If anyone checked, she needed plausible deniability about how thoroughly she'd searched.

Her phone showed 10:47 a.m. Joel would be home by now, probably just getting up after working the overnight shift. She typed out a text, deleted it, and typed another. How did you tell someone you might have stumbled onto a conspiracy involving murder, the White House, and corrupt cops?

Finally, she settled on simple: "Need to see you. It's important. And complicated."

His response came within seconds: "Your place or mine?"

"Mine," she typed back. She needed to maintain control of the situation, and having the evidence here would help explain what she'd discovered.

She sent another text: "Give me an hour. Need to clean up first." She'd been in the same clothes since yesterday's shift, and exhaustion was making her punchy.

As she carefully returned the photos to the envelope, Lowri glanced once more at the image of Farnsworth and Sprague in Desert Storm. Two young Marines in the Kuwaiti desert, unaware that thirty years later, one would be dead and the other would be covering up his murder.

Lowri couldn't shake the feeling that the third person, torn away and lost to time, held the answer to everything.

If Farnsworth had been murdered for what he knew, the third person in that photo was running out of time.

***

Joel had cleaned up before coming over. He wore a fresh polo shirt, pressed khakis, and styled hair still damp from the shower. The cologne was new, something expensive that made Lowri acutely aware of her own exhausted state.

"Kind of early for a booty call, isn't it, Sarge?" He grinned as she let him in.

"This isn't a booty call, Joel. I need your help." She led him to the kitchen, where the box of documents still covered her table.

Joel tossed his keys on the counter and sat beside her. She slid the torn photograph across the table.

"Tell me what you see."

He picked it up, squinting at the faded image. "Desert Storm, 1991." He flipped it over to check the timestamp. "Photographer needs lessons. It's pretty grainy."

"Look at the faces, Joel. Do you recognize anyone?"

He studied it again. "Should I?"

"The man in the middle is Victor Farnsworth."

Joel brought the photo closer to his face. "Okay, yeah. I can see it now. Younger, but that's him."

"Now look at the man on his right."

"Which right? His right or my right?"

"Jesus, Joel. The one who isn't torn off." She pointed directly at Sprague's image. "Who does that look like?"

Joel examined the face more carefully, tilting the photo to catch better light. "I don't know, Sarge. This picture's over thirty years old."

"It's Peter Sprague."

His head jerked up. "Detective Sprague?"

"Take another look." She tapped the photo. "That's him. Younger, but definitely him."

Joel studied it again, his expression shifting from skepticism to uncertainty. "Maybe. Even if it is, so what? Lots of guys served in Desert Storm."

"Sprague never disclosed he knew Farnsworth. He was the lead detective on a case involving his old military buddy. That's a massive conflict of interest."

"Could be a coincidence."

"No." Lowri kept her voice steady, fighting the urge to shout. "There's more going on here, Joel. I need someone I can trust, and you're it."

His posture changed, leaning forward. "Okay, Sarge. I'm listening."

She took a breath. "Victor Farnsworth was murdered, and Peter Sprague is involved in the cover-up."

Joel's eyebrows shot up. "That's a serious accusation. Do you have proof beyond an old photo?"

"Can I trust you? Really trust you? What I'm about to say could get us both fired."

"You have to ask?" He looked genuinely hurt.

"The Secret Service agents took me to the White House last night."

Joel's mouth opened slightly, but he remained silent.

"I spent two hours with the First Lady. Hellen Carney believes her husband ordered Victor Farnsworth's murder."

"The President?" Joel laughed nervously. "You're saying President Carney had someone killed?"

"The First Lady thinks he was having an affair with Molly Farnsworth and that she convinced him to eliminate Victor."

Joel stood abruptly and walked to the refrigerator. He pulled out a Yuengling, twisted off the cap, and drank half the bottle in one long pull.

"It's noon, Joel."

"Yeah, well." He returned to the table, beer in hand. "You understand why this is hard to process? Why would the First Lady confide in you? No offense, but you're not exactly high up the chain."

The question stung; Lowri had been asking herself the same thing. "She said I'm far enough below the radar that no one will notice if I ask questions."

Even as she said it, the explanation sounded weak. Why would Hellen Carney trust a patrol sergeant with something this explosive? Why not the FBI? The CIA? Private investigators with proven discretion?

Joel sipped his beer, watching her carefully. His silence was worse than skepticism.

"You think I'm crazy." Lowri started collecting the photos, shoving them back into the envelope.

"I didn't say that."

"You don't have to." She dropped the envelope back in the box and stood. "I shouldn't have involved you."

"Sarge, come on."

"I need sleep before tonight's shift." She walked toward the front door.

Joel followed, picking up his keys from the counter. At the door, he paused. "Look, this is a lot to process. But I'm not dismissing it, okay? Just... be careful. If even half of what you're saying is true, you're in dangerous territory."

She nodded, not trusting herself to speak.

"We'll talk more tonight," he said. "After we've both had time to think."

She closed the door behind him and leaned against it for a moment before returning to the kitchen. The box sat on the table where she'd left it. She pulled out the envelope again, extracting the photo of Farnsworth and Sprague. Two Marines in Kuwait, young and unaware of how their paths would cross again thirty years later.

The torn edge where the third person had been removed seemed more jagged now, more deliberate. Someone had wanted that person erased from history.

Lowri wondered if she was next.

Chapter 25

The recovery room contained standard medical equipment: a hospital bed, IV drip, catheter, and vital signs monitor. A tray of surgical instruments sat beside the bed, forceps and hemostats sitting among other tools, all gleaming under fluorescent lights.

Major Ilana Zahavy stood next to Saville. A guard watched from the doorway. Hillel Mond lay motionless on the bed, his face pale and swollen, multiple lines running from his body to various machines. His eyes were closed, and his breathing was shallow. For a moment, Saville thought he might be unconscious. Then Mond's eyes snapped open, the sudden movement startling.

"Lieutenant Commander," Ilana said. "I hope you're feeling better."

"Yes," Mond answered with surprising clarity, though his appearance suggested otherwise. "This is the man who saved me?"

Ilana nodded.

"Leave us alone, please," Mond said.

Ilana moved to the bed and took his left hand gently, careful not to disturb the IV line. His right shoulder was heavily bandaged, the arm immobilized.

"Are you certain you're ready for this, Lieutenant Commander? You've suffered significant trauma."

"Please, Major. I already have a mother in Herzliya."

"Very well." She released his hand and walked to the door. "The call button is beside your bed. We'll be right outside."

Mond attempted to wave her away but could barely lift his arm. Ilana departed with the guard, closing the door behind them.

"Please sit," Mond said.

Saville took the chair facing the bed. The room smelled of antiseptic mixed with lingering smoke, an odd combination that triggered unwanted memories of Caroline Cochran's murder scene in Miami. He pushed the thought aside.

"I want to thank you, Agent Saville." Mond extended his left hand with obvious effort.

"That's not necessary." Saville leaned forward to shake it briefly, then sat back.

Despite saving the man's life, this remained a criminal investigation. Mond was still a suspect, possibly a killer.

"I know why you were following me," Mond said before Saville could begin. "The other man, Romano. Is he alive?"

Saville shook his head. "He didn't make it."

"I'm sorry. He and I had an understanding of sorts."

Saville felt a stab of guilt for how little he'd thought of Romano since the shooting. They'd served together in Iraq, sharing the bonds that only combat creates. Despite years of limited contact, Romano had immediately answered Saville's call for help. Of course, Romano had his own agenda regarding Mond, and it had gotten him killed. But he'd chosen to stand by Saville, placing himself in harm's way. Now he was dead, his chest blown apart on a DC sidewalk. That debt demanded justice.

But Saville was in dangerous territory. Unarmed, without backup, sitting in an Israeli safe house that might or might not have diplomatic immunity. Israel was an ally, but one that prioritized its own survival above all else.

"Who shot you?" Saville asked directly.

"The same people who killed Clough and Farnsworth."

The immediate admission surprised Saville. "Who are these people?"

Mond remained silent.

"This is a murder investigation, Mond."

"And this is sovereign Israeli territory. You have no authority here."

"It's a safe house in Columbia Heights."

"With extraterritorial status recognized by your State Department."

Saville wondered if that was true. Extraterritoriality typically applied only to embassies and consulates, but the U.S.-Israeli relationship often bent normal diplomatic rules.

"Three men are dead," Saville said. "I could have left you bleeding on that sidewalk."

Mond stared at the wall. Color slowly returned to his face. "Yes. I owe you my life."

"You had dinner with Farnsworth and Clough in Kendall County. Why?"

"Victor and I were business partners. We were negotiating with Mr. Clough, who threatened to expose our arrangement."

"What arrangement?"

"A classified project involving both our governments. Are you familiar with SAINTS?"

Saville searched his memory. "No."

"Systematic Analysis and Intelligence Tracking Software. Developed by Symmetric Technical Solutions in Research Triangle Park."

Recognition clicked. "I know Symmetric. Defense contractor, right?"

"Among other things. Farnsworth was brokering a deal between your Department of Homeland Security and Israeli intelligence. I was negotiating for my government."

"Why was DHS involved in a deal between a private company and Israel? Why not negotiate directly with Symmetric?"

"Two reasons," Mond said. "First, all sales of sensitive technology to foreign governments require State Department approval. Second, the version we wanted wasn't Symmetric's original product."

Saville waited.

Mond reached for the water pitcher. Saville poured him a glass, noticing how the Israeli's hand trembled as he drank.

The door opened. The guard entered, hand on his weapon. "Is there a problem, Lieutenant Commander?"

"No. Agent Saville is helping me drink."

The guard glared at Saville before withdrawing.

"Ignore Corporal Bashevis," Mond said. "I saved his life in Gaza. He's protective." He took another sip. "The SAINTS program was originally medical records software. Comprehensive patient tracking, treatment histories, billing, and standard hospital management systems."

"Sounds routine."

"Listen carefully. When patients enter the medical system, everything is recorded: blood type, DNA markers, biometric data, distinguishing features. Complete biological profiles."

"So?"

"Your Department of Homeland Security modified the software. They installed backdoor access for American intelligence agencies. Every patient treated at a facility using SAINTS becomes part of a searchable database available to the CIA, NSA, and FBI."

Saville processed the implications. "And Israel wants the same access."

"Exactly. The modified version Farnsworth demonstrated in Jerusalem would give us equivalent capabilities." Mond paused for another sip of water. "What makes this so valuable is the reach. The original SAINTS software, before modification, has already been sold to hospitals across Europe, the Middle East, and parts of Asia: Saudi Arabia, Egypt, Jordan, Kuwait. Any person born or treated in these facilities can potentially be tracked from birth to death once you have backdoor access."

"Creating profiles of potential terrorists before they become threats."

"Exactly. Once someone is flagged, we access everything. Physical descriptions, psychological evaluations, medications, vulnerabilities. Information that allows precise targeting."

"You mean assassination."

"Elimination of threats. The 9/11 hijackers were primarily Saudis. The London bombers were British citizens. Fort Hood, the Boston Marathon. Homegrown terrorists. Geographic boundaries are irrelevant."

"Did Davy Clough discover this?"

Mond's jaw tightened. "Americans and their privacy concerns. You debate civil liberties while terrorists plot mass casualties. In Israel, security is a matter of survival."

"I asked about Clough."

"He accused Farnsworth and me of stealing the software."

"From whom?"

"His father."

Saville recalled Cynthia Clough mentioning her husband's software work. A government contract worth twenty million. "Bernard Clough developed the original SAINTS?"

"He consulted for Symmetric on the medical components."

"Was the software stolen?"

"Yes. Farnsworth had DHS modify Clough's code without authorization. He demonstrated it to us in Jerusalem two weeks ago. We agreed to pay fifty million dollars."

Thirty million profit, Saville calculated. Buy for twenty, sell for fifty.

"That's just the beginning," Mond continued. "Britain, Spain, Italy, India, and even Russia have expressed interest. Potential sales could reach billions. Farnsworth would have made millions in commissions."

"So Clough tried blackmail instead of exposure?"

"Ten million to his father for the stolen code, another ten million to a Cayman Islands account for his silence."

"Giving you a motive for murder."

"Don't forget, Agent Saville. They tried to kill me as well."

"What about Bernard Clough?"

"I only know what his son said. A physician who worked with Symmetric."

"From my perspective, Israel had the most to gain from silencing Farnsworth and Davy Clough."

"The owner of Symmetric had more motive. His technology was being sold without his knowledge. He was supposed to attend our dinner in Kendall County to negotiate a legitimate arrangement but never showed."

"Who owns Symmetric?"

"Ken Burton," Mond replied. "One of your Kendall County neighbors."

The name sounded vaguely familiar. Saville had heard it around the office and seen it in local papers. Burton owned significant property in Kendall County and had connections throughout North Carolina's political and business landscape. But Saville had never investigated him. No criminal record, no federal complaints. Just another wealthy businessman in the region.

If Burton was involved in murder and espionage, the implications extended far beyond three dead bodies.

Saville stood. "I need to make some calls."

"Be careful, Agent Saville. Whoever killed Romano won't hesitate to kill you. They've shown their reach and capabilities."

"Any idea who 'they' are?"

Mond closed his eyes, exhaustion evident. "Someone with access to military-grade weapons and trained snipers. Someone who knew our exact location and movements. Someone with everything to lose if SAINTS becomes public."

"Burton?"

"Or your own government. Who else knew about your meeting with Romano?"

The question chilled Saville. He'd told no one at the Bureau, but Romano had military intelligence connections. How many people had Romano informed? How deep did this conspiracy run?

"Rest," Saville said. "We'll talk more later."

"There may not be a later," Mond replied, eyes still closed. "For either of us."

Chapter 26

President Woodrow Carney was enjoying the best part of his Monday routine: lunch and *The Young and the Restless*. He bit into his grilled cheese sandwich as Victor Newman declared his undying love for Nikki on the screen. After six years in office, this was one of the few pleasures that remained unspoiled by politics.

Victor Newman understood power. The character built an empire, destroyed his enemies, and always kept his woman. Lately, however, Carney found himself wincing at the character's first name. Too many unpleasant associations. But Nikki made it worthwhile. Melody Thomas Scott had been beautiful for four decades on screen.

Perhaps a White House reception for daytime television. Cultural appreciation. Or maybe just Ms. Scott. The Lincoln Bedroom had hosted many notable guests over the years.

The northwest door opened at 12:37. Calvin Gates entered without knocking, a privilege of his chief of staff position that Carney only occasionally resented.

"Pull up a chair, Cal," Carney said, not looking away from the screen. "These *Y&R* girls always get my blood pumping."

"There's no time, Mr. President." Gates's tone was all business, his default mode these days. "You need to hear this."

Nikki glided across the screen in blue silk, whispering something about kitchen furniture. Carney sighed and clicked off the television. His fifteen minutes of peace were gone.

"This better be important, Cal."

Gates was already at the entertainment console, fiddling with the radio tuner. Clay Travis's voice boomed through the Oval Office speakers, mid-rant about something. It took Carney a moment to focus on the words.

Victor Farnsworth. Suspicious death. White House involvement. Chicago-style politics.

"Clay and Buck?" Carney set down his sandwich, appetite gone. "You're interrupting my lunch for talk radio?"

"Just listen, sir."

Carney listened. The host was dancing around direct accusations, but the implication was clear: they suggested he'd had Farnsworth killed. After ten minutes of innuendo and speculation, Carney had heard enough.

"Where are they getting this garbage? Who's feeding them?"

"Unknown, sir." Gates lowered the volume. "But the narrative is gaining traction."

"Find the source, Cal. I can handle policy leaks, but this fiction dressed as fact is unacceptable."

Gates stood in his usual spot, halfway between the desk and the door, ready to act or flee as necessary. "He's essentially accusing you of ordering Farnsworth's murder. This could metastasize before the midterms."

"You think anyone who matters listens to conservative talk radio?"

"It's not Washington I'm worried about. This plays badly in swing states. Vice President Godwin could lose five points with independents."

Carney leaned back, propping his feet on the Resolute Desk, a habit that drove his wife crazy. "The election's two years away. Besides, you really think Godwin gets the nomination?"

"He's been your vice president for six years. He's the presumptive nominee."

The cheese in Carney's sandwich had congealed. He took a bite anyway, buying time to think. "Voters are exhausted with his climate evangelism. I only added him to the ticket for the Sierra Club votes. Eighteen months from now, he'll be making documentaries with Leo DiCaprio."

"Mr. President, we need to address these rumors before the mainstream media picks them up."

Carney laughed. His approval rating had nowhere to go but up. "What's the current number, Cal? Thirty-five percent?"

"Thirty-two, actually. But we should go on the offensive. If Republicans are orchestrating this, we make them pay in the midterms."

"I miss the old days, Cal. Before the twenty-four-hour news cycle. When journalists understood that some stones shouldn't be turned."

"The standards have certainly changed. Dan Rather makes one documentation error, career over. Meanwhile, talk radio can say anything."

"Handle it however you think best." Carney reached for the remote, ready to return to his soap opera. "But this is just noise."

"Sir, they're talking about murder."

"Last week they had me taking bribes from pharmaceutical companies. The week before, secret offshore accounts." The television came back to life. Nikki and Victor were heading toward the kitchen. "It's all theater, Cal."

Gates hadn't moved. The man could stand motionless for hours, a skill that unnerved foreign diplomats. "What if they have something concrete?"

"Then we deal with it. But right now, I have Secretary Austin arriving in fifteen minutes, and I'd like to finish my lunch."

"I'll have our media team prepare response options."

"You do that." Carney's attention had already returned to the screen. "And Cal? Find out who's talking to Travis. Someone inside is feeding him."

"Yes, Mr. President."

Gates left through the same door he'd entered, his footsteps barely audible on the thick carpet. Carney remained at his desk, the famous desk where Lincoln signed the Emancipation Proclamation, where Kennedy navigated the Cuban Missile Crisis, where Reagan won the Cold War.

Now, it supported his feet while he watched fictional rich people navigate their invented dramas.

The irony wasn't lost on him. Victor Newman would have already identified his enemies and destroyed them. Newman understood that power unused was power lost. But Newman was fiction, carefully scripted to always win in the end.

Real life was messier. Sometimes the best strategy was to do nothing, to let the scandal exhaust itself. The American attention span was approximately three news cycles. By Friday, they'd be outraged about something else.

On screen, Nikki was saying something about wanting Victor to prove his love. Carney turned up the volume. At least here, in this fictional universe, passion still meant something.

His phone buzzed. Gates, texting from just outside: "Travis now claiming he has documents."

Carney deleted the message and went back to his show. Documents could be dealt with. They always were. That's what he had people for.

But for the next thirteen minutes, until the secretary of defense arrived, he was just another American watching daytime television, wondering if true love could survive in a world built on lies.

***

Hellen Carney and Cecelia Leehan were listening to the *Clay &* *Buck Show* together in Cecelia's Chevy Chase townhouse, where five Secret Service agents were stationed outside.

The First Lady was surprised when Cecelia suggested they spend the afternoon monitoring the broadcast, observing the fruits of their manipulation taking root in conservative media.

When Clay Travis broke the scandal at noon, Cecelia retrieved a bottle of Château Margaux from her wine cellar. "Vintage 2005," she said, working the corkscrew with ease. "We should toast to our success."

"It's premature," Hellen replied, accepting the glass anyway.

"Nonsense. By evening, every network will be running this."

As they listened, Travis built the narrative, weaving together the threads Cecelia had strategically leaked through her network of sources. An hour into the broadcast, with the wine warming her blood, Hellen felt the professional boundaries between them shift.

Cecelia moved closer on the leather sofa. "You're tense," she observed, her hand finding Hellen's shoulder. "This should be a moment of triumph."

"I've never done anything like this before," Hellen admitted, and they both knew she wasn't referring to the media manipulation.

"Orchestrating your husband's downfall? Or this?" Cecelia's fingers traced along Hellen's collarbone.

"Both."

"I've been navigating Washington bedrooms for twenty years," Cecelia said, her reputation preceding her. "Power and pleasure are often intertwined in this city. But you... you're different."

The afternoon unfolded in ways Hellen hadn't anticipated. The wine, the adrenaline of their conspiracy, and Cecelia's confidence combined to dissolve her carefully maintained composure. She responded to Cecelia's touch with an intensity that surprised them both.

By three o'clock, Sean Hannity had picked up the story, claiming prior knowledge of inconsistencies in Farnsworth's death. Meanwhile, the Secret Service detail outside remained oblivious to what was transpiring in the master bedroom, focused on external threats while the First Lady crossed lines she never imagined crossing.

"God," Hellen breathed against Cecelia's neck. "Victor never... Woody certainly never..."

"Made you feel alive?" Cecelia finished. "Men like them don't understand women. They see us as accessories or obstacles, never equals."

The physical intimacy between them was intense and overwhelming. Hellen experienced sensations that left her breathless, her body responding in ways her marriage bed never had. Cecelia's expertise was evident, her touch knowing exactly where to linger, where to press, and where to tease.

At four-fifteen, CNN picked up the story, followed minutes later by MSNBC. The news tickers scrolled their carefully crafted scandal while Hellen lay tangled in the burgundy sheets, her skin flushed, her wedding ring abandoned on the nightstand.

"The Associated Press just posted," Cecelia said, checking her phone while her other hand remained on Hellen's hip. "Reuters too. It's everywhere now."

"I can't believe you accomplished this," Hellen said, still catching her breath. "Thirty-two years of connections?"

"Every journalist, every producer, every intern I've cultivated," Cecelia confirmed. "Even some conservatives who despise your husband more than they love their party. I called in every favor."

They watched the five o'clock news from bed, Cecelia's laptop propped on a pillow. Every network led with questions about Farnsworth's death and the White House's potential involvement.

"He'll be destroyed by this," Hellen said with satisfaction. "His legacy, his reputation, everything."

"And you'll emerge as the wronged wife," Cecelia added. "The sympathetic figure who knew nothing about her husband's crimes."

Hellen turned to study Cecelia's face. The journalist's pale skin glowed in the afternoon light filtering through the curtains. "What happens to us after this?"

"That depends," Cecelia said, pulling Hellen closer. "How much are you willing to risk?"

"I've already risked everything."

"No," Cecelia corrected. "You've invested everything. There's a difference. Investments can pay dividends."

Her hand moved with deliberate slowness down Hellen's body, making the First Lady gasp.

"Still sensitive?" Cecelia asked with a knowing smile.

"Everything is sensitive," Hellen admitted. "Everything is different now."

"Good," Cecelia said, leaning in for another kiss. "Different is exactly what Washington needs."

Outside, the Secret Service agents maintained their watch, unaware that the woman they were protecting had just orchestrated her husband's political annihilation while discovering desires she had suppressed for decades. The combination of betrayal and awakening left Hellen feeling more powerful than she had ever felt in the White House.

By six o'clock, #FarnsworthMurder was trending on social media. The President's press secretary was scrambling to respond. And in a Chevy Chase bedroom, the First Lady of the United States was learning exactly what kind of woman she really was.

Chapter 27

Saville tried to recall what he knew about Ken Burton. The software magnate had built his fortune packaging gaming software for consumers while selling advanced systems to the defense industry. Burton ranked among North Carolina's wealthiest residents.

Saville had seen Burton's estate featured on one of those architectural programs on TLC. A three-story Victorian with wraparound porches, it was the showpiece of Kendall County's only gated community. Burton divided his time between there and his Research Triangle Park headquarters, ninety minutes northwest.

Saville knew Burton's wife, Dr. Samantha Burton, through her work as the county medical examiner, though he'd never met either of the Burtons personally. Neither had a criminal record that would have crossed his desk. He'd run them through NCIC when he got back to the office.

If he got back to the office. The thought crept in unbidden.

Mond was right about motive. Burton stood to lose millions from the pirated software. But Saville's thoughts shifted to a more immediate problem: how long before someone connected him to Romano's death in Foggy Bottom? The shooting had occurred at night, but not in complete darkness. Could the woman screaming from her window identify him? Or Rachel Hunt, Mond's mistress?

His only consolation was that both American and Israeli intelligence were involved. If anyone could make the incident disappear and spin it as random street violence, they could. But that meant Romano would be buried without honors, his sacrifice unacknowledged. Another star on the wall at Langley, perhaps, though Romano wasn't CIA. More likely nothing at all: a John Doe in the DC morgue until someone made the body disappear entirely.

Saville pushed the thought aside. Everyone had known the risks. Romano died protecting an asset, even if no one would ever know it. The man had served three tours in Iraq, survived Fallujah and Ramadi, only to die on a sidewalk on Virginia Avenue. There was no justice in that. But Saville had learned long ago that justice and intelligence work rarely intersected.

He watched Mond drain his water glass and replace it on the tray. The Israeli had dozed for fifteen minutes. Saville was losing patience. His wrists still ached from the zip ties they had used to restrain him during the initial interrogation, before Mond had ordered his release. The Israelis were nothing if not thorough.

"Why didn't Burton show up for your meeting?" he asked.

"Unknown. Perhaps greed. Perhaps someone reached him first."

"What was his role supposed to be?"

"Selling legitimate SAINTS licenses to Israel."

"Because you needed the authentic version before installing the backdoor."

Mond nodded, then winced. The movement clearly pained him.

"Did Burton discover your plans for his software?"

"Perhaps he decided to handle matters personally."

Saville understood the implication but struggled to envision Burton as a killer. The man had generational wealth. Why risk life in prison over what amounted to pocket change for him? Unless Burton had motives beyond money. Pride, perhaps, or something darker. Saville had seen enough in his career to know that the rich often valued respect more than money. Being played for a fool might matter more to Burton than millions in lost revenue.

The door opened. Major Zahavy entered with Corporal Bashevis. The corporal's hand rested on his sidearm, a casual gesture that wasn't casual at all.

"Give us more time," Mond said.

Ilana ignored him, moving to his bedside. "I'm sorry, Lieutenant Commander. The Deputy Director has spoken with the Prime Minister."

Mond's expression darkened. In that moment, Saville saw the operative Mond had been before the shooting: cold, calculating, lethal.

"It has been decided at the highest level."

"This man saved my life," Mond protested.

"I'm sorry, Lieutenant Commander. He knows too much about our operations."

Saville felt Bashevis move behind him. Training kicked in. He cataloged exits: door blocked by Ilana, window reinforced, no other options. He glimpsed the shadow on the wall and recognized the stance. The garrote came fast.

Saville instinctively threw his hands up. The wire sliced into his wrists instead of his throat, sending a jolt of pain through his arms as blood rushed toward his elbows. He gasped, struggling to keep his footing on the slick linoleum.

He had to stay upright. If Bashevis got him down, he was finished.

He couldn't die here. Emma needed her father, despite the divorce proceedings. He wouldn't allow Jennifer's boyfriend, that investment banker Willie, to raise his daughter.

Saville roared as adrenaline surged through him. His legs steadied as he pushed back against Bashevis, using his larger frame as leverage. The room spun as they grappled, and the wire dug deeper.

He drove backward, slamming Bashevis into the wall. The Israeli's grip loosened for a moment. Saville twisted, his knee colliding with Mond's bed rail.

Bashevis cried out, and the pressure released.

Saville spun to see Bashevis on the floor, blood pulsing from a wound in his neck. Mond sat upright in bed, a surgical hemostat in his hand, its curved tips stained with blood.

Bashevis pressed his hand to his neck, his eyes reflecting the realization of a fatal wound: the carotid artery. He had minutes at most.

Ilana stood frozen. Saville knew she was armed, but she made no move for her weapon.

"God forgive me," she whispered.

"Don't just stand there!" Mond shouted with surprising strength. "Save him!"

Ilana stared at the floor. "But... the orders. Agent Saville—"

"Is leaving. Now."

"The Prime Minister—"

"This man saved my life! Help Bashevis, or I'll shoot you my-self!"

Ilana dropped to her knees beside Bashevis. "Yes, Lieutenant Commander."

Mond grabbed Saville's sleeve, pulling him close. "I owe you my life. But understand this: if you reveal this location or our operations, I will hunt you personally. As certain as there is a God of Israel."

Saville nodded, believing every word.

"Go! Now!"

Saville backed toward the door as Ilana frantically worked on Bashevis. Direct pressure wouldn't stop a carotid bleed. The corporal had minutes at best.

He hit the stairwell at a run. Three flights down, with no one in pursuit, he burst through the exit into the blazing afternoon sun.

His Glock was still inside. So was his cellphone. Romano's Expedition sat where they'd left it, but the keys were gone. He didn't stop to search.

He flagged a taxi at the intersection of 14th and Girard. "Take me to the nearest convenience store," he told the driver. He needed a burner phone. Something untraceable, paid for with cash.

"You okay, man?" the driver asked, eyeing him in the rearview mirror.

"Fine," Saville managed, pressing his sleeves against his wrists.

He was done. Finished. Let someone else chase ghosts and conspiracy theories. Let someone else be strangled in foreign safe houses. He'd write up a report, pass it to Mayfield, and walk away. Emma deserved a father who came home alive.

As the taxi moved through traffic, Saville stared out the window at normal people living normal lives. People who didn't know about SAINTS or assassins or diplomatic immunity for torture chambers.

The image of Romano's destroyed chest flashed in his mind, followed by Davy Clough's earnest face in his office just days ago. Victor Farnsworth's name in the headlines.

No. He pushed the thoughts away. He was done.

But somewhere in the back of his mind, a small voice whispered: Burton's still out there. Someone ordered that sniper hit.

He ignored it. For now.

Chapter 28

Joel Graves climbed into his black Toyota Tundra and drove to Lowri's DuPont Circle apartment. Her car wasn't in its usual spot. He parked anyway and knocked hard on her door. A dozen times. Nothing. Good. She wasn't home.

He walked back to his truck, relieved he wouldn't have to face her yet. The guilt from their conversation that morning still weighed heavily on his chest. She'd wanted him to believe her story. What was he supposed to do? Lie? Her theory was insane, even if parts of it might be true. He hadn't meant to hurt her; that was the last thing he wanted. He cared about Lowri. It wasn't love, exactly, though they'd slept together plenty of times.

Their relationship had never been about romance. They came together out of need, not tenderness. Physical release, not emotional connection. They didn't hold hands or linger in bed afterward. Neither had ever said the words "I love you." The closest they came to expressing feelings was through sex itself.

Still, Joel knew Lowri cared about him. He couldn't explain how he knew; he just did.

Now he'd failed her when she'd asked him to trust her. He wanted to believe her. He did. But the story was impossible. The First Lady secretly meeting with a Park Police sergeant to accuse the President of murder? It sounded like something out of a cheap thriller.

Lowri read constantly. Maybe her imagination had gotten away from her. Perhaps the stress of the job, combined with her fixation on Victor Farnsworth's death, had pushed her past some breaking point. Joel didn't want to consider that possibility. Lowri had always been solid, reliable. The officer everyone turned to when things went bad. The person Joel himself counted on.

He checked his watch: 7:57 p.m. The sun was setting outside Lowri's apartment. After leaving her place that morning, Joel had spent the day indoors with the air conditioning cranked up, working through a six-pack and his guilt.

His shift started at midnight. Plenty of time to sober up and handle something that needed doing.

He would find Peter Sprague on the second shift, ask him about Lowri's theory, and determine if that really was him in the photograph with Victor Farnsworth.

He would do this for Lowri. Get answers. Put this thing to rest.

He owed her that much.

***

Lowri had never confused sensuality with beauty. She knew she was not beautiful in the classical sense. The word was a delicate instrument, and her appeal was something blunter, more visceral. She attracted men and women who wanted immediate gratification rather than a lasting connection. A promise of friction and heat that appealed to those looking for a bonfire rather than a hearth.

It was a truth she had accepted in high school and had since learned to exploit. She disliked relying on her body, the transactional nature of her most effective tool. Yet she had used her sexuality to clear obstacles, from sleeping with her senior algebra teacher for a passing grade to navigating the stubborn hierarchies of law enforcement. She was not the prettiest or the smartest, but she possessed a potent combination of both. A formula that had always been just enough to get by. She did not consider herself a prostitute. Payment came in many forms besides money, and survival in a male-dominated world required a certain moral flexibility. She wished her intellect were her primary weapon, but biology had armed her differently, and she had long ago stopped apologizing for it.

Just as she was not apologizing for the phone call she was about to make.

His name was Ben Manning. They had dated briefly in high school. He was two years older, the varsity team's star left-handed pitcher. On prom night, in the back of a rented Cadillac, he had taken her virginity. She was a sophomore, he was a senior, and being his date had felt like validation. Even after he bragged about "busting her cherry" and the school labeled her "loose Lowri," she had still claimed him as her boyfriend.

When he left for Stanford, the calls stopped. The lesson was clear: her ability to influence men was more reliable than love.

Manning had returned to Washington after law school, joining the National Archives and Records Administration. He had transferred to the National Personnel Records Center in St. Louis, where he had successfully defended the government in two data breach cases involving stolen laptops containing military personnel files. The plaintiffs had demanded fifty million in damages. Manning got them to settle for eight. The settlements came in far below projections. She had watched his press coverage with complicated feelings. First love left marks, especially when it ended badly.

She dialed his private number, obtained through a law enforcement database she had access to. The number had cost her a favor with a contact at the phone company. Her throat tightened as it rang. If Manning refused to help, she had no backup plan. The official channels would take weeks. Weeks she didn't have.

He answered on the third ring.

"Bet you don't know who this is." She immediately regretted the weak opening.

"Sorry, I don't."

"Lowri Pritchard."

"Well, I'll be damned."

"It's been a while. I sent you some emails at work."

"Never saw them. Our spam filters are like Fort Knox."

She heard the lie but didn't challenge it. "How does it feel to be a big-shot attorney?"

"Just a civil servant who got his name in the papers." He paused. "I've thought about you over the years."

The admission surprised her. If true, he could have answered her emails.

"Pritchard?" he said. "Never married?"

"No."

"I never apologized."

"For what?"

"For prom night. For telling everyone."

"Make it up to me," she said, recognizing the opening. "I need a favor."

"What kind?"

"The kind that isn't exactly legal."

Silence. Then: "Okay."

"I need military records pulled."

"Lowri, just file a Freedom of Information Act request. With your credentials, two weeks tops."

So he knew she was in law enforcement. He had been keeping track.

"I can't wait two weeks." She let vulnerability creep into her voice, the same tone that had worked after prom.

"Are you in trouble?"

"Yes. That's all I can say."

"I'm an attorney with contacts everywhere."

"Please, Ben. Just do this one thing for me."

"I can't restore your reputation, but I can help you. Are you at your office?"

"It's after nine."

"I'm home. My work phone forwards here, and I can access the system remotely. Give me names, Social Security numbers, dates of birth, service information. Whatever you have."

"I don't have Social Security numbers."

"We'll manage."

She provided him with the details of Victor Farnsworth from the Washington Post obituary.

"That Victor Farnsworth? The Deputy White House Counsel?"

"Yes."

"Jesus, Lowri."

"I told you I couldn't discuss it."

She heard typing. "Victor Farnsworth. United States Marine Corps, Twenty-Fourth Marine Expeditionary Unit, 1989 to 1995. Honorable discharge. Purple Heart for wounds sustained during Operation Deliberate Force in Bosnia."

"Was he in Desert Storm?"

"Affirmative. The Twenty-Fourth MEU was deployed to the Persian Gulf."

"I have another name: Peter Sprague."

More typing. "Peter Arlen Sprague. Same unit, 1986 to 1997. Same deployments." A pause. "Interesting."

"What's interesting?"

"Your man graduated Scout Sniper School as the class honorman. He received the Navy and Marine Corps Achievement Medal for marksmanship. That's elite training."

The information sank in. Sprague had been a decorated sniper. Scout Sniper School accepted only the best marksmen in the Corps, with a washout rate exceeding sixty percent. It was a detail Sprague would brag about unless he had a compelling reason to hide it. Like murder.

"What connects these two?" Manning asked.

"Still working on that." She had spent the afternoon studying a torn photograph, trying to identify the third person. One name kept surfacing: Dr. Suicide. "Last name, I promise. Bernard David Clough." She spelled it out. "He possibly served as a medic with the unit."

Extended typing. "Negative. No Bernard David Clough in those records."

So Clough wasn't the third man. She had wasted time chasing a dead end. The name had appeared in three different contexts connected to Farnsworth. Now she would have to start over.

"I don't like this, Lowri. Military records are classified for a reason."

"I know the risks."

"Do you? Because I'm the one taking them."

"I need one more thing. Email me the complete roster for the Twenty-Fourth MEU as of February 1991. Send it to L dot Pritch—"

"Ben!" A woman's voice in the background. "Who are you talking to?"

"My wife. I have to go." The line went dead.

Lowri stared at the phone. Had she finished giving him her email address? She replayed the conversation in her head. Pritchard. She had gotten that far. But had she mentioned the domain? Her personal email was straightforward: L.pritchard 92@gmail.com. Manning was sharp; he would figure it out. He had to.

Lowri set down the phone. Two Marines from the same unit. One dead. One concealing his sniper training. A photograph with someone torn out.

The roster would reveal who else had been there. One of those names would explain why Victor Farnsworth had ended up with a bullet in West Potomac Park.

Chapter 29

The taxi dropped Saville at a 24-hour 7-Eleven on Georgia Avenue near Kennedy Street. He paid forty dollars cash for a sixteen-dollar fare and asked the driver to wait twenty minutes.

"Can't do it, man. Too rough around here to sit still." The driver pulled away before Saville could respond.

The area looked like a war zone. Broken glass littered the sidewalks. Gang tags marked every surface. Drug dealers manned the corners while addicts shuffled between abandoned storefronts. A group of teenagers in baggy clothes watched him from across the street, sizing him up. His suit marked him as either a cop or an easy target.

Inside, fluorescent lights buzzed overhead, with half the bulbs dead. The clerk sat behind bulletproof glass, watching him with vacant eyes. Security cameras covered every angle. The shelves were sparse, most good merchandise locked behind the counter. Saville bought the cheapest prepaid phone available and a twenty-dollar phone card. The Israelis had taken his Glock and his Bureau phone, but they'd left his wallet. He still had his credentials and credit cards.

He found a concrete picnic table behind the store, away from street traffic. The smell of urine and rotting garbage hung in the air. Graffiti covered the table and the surrounding brick wall. He kept his back to the wall and scanned the lot for trouble. His wrists throbbed from the garrote wire, and dried blood stained his shirt cuffs.

A homeless man pushed a shopping cart past the dumpster, muttering to himself. Two women in tight clothing walked by, eyeing Saville with professional interest before moving on. The sound of sirens echoed from several blocks away.

He thought about Emma. He hadn't spoken to his daughter in three days, and the need to hear her voice gnawed at him. Before the separation, he had barely noticed how much Jennifer handled the parenting. Work had always come first. Now he regretted every missed bedtime story, every school event he had skipped for a case. The divorce papers sat unsigned on his kitchen table back in Greenville.

Emma lived in Greenville with Jennifer, but Willie seemed to be there more often. Saville's unannounced visits drove them both crazy, especially when he showed up to find Willie's car in the driveway again. But Emma loved those surprise visits. She would run to the door yelling "Daddy!" and throw her arms around his legs. He always brought her something: stuffed animals from the mall, cheap jewelry from Claire's, anything featuring her favorite cartoon characters.

On his last visit, he'd brought her a Bluey doll. Willie had bought her a bigger, more expensive version the day before. The smug bastard had made sure Saville knew it too, holding up both dolls for comparison while Emma watched.

He dialed his home number. Jennifer answered on the fourth ring, her voice cautious.

"I want to talk to Emma."

"She's outside with her friends." Her tone turned cold when she recognized his voice.

"Can you get her? Just for a minute."

"She's having a tea party in the backyard. I'm not interrupting that."

"Please, Jennifer. I need to hear her voice."

"Who is it, honey?" Willie's voice carried through the phone in the background. The man was there again.

"Doesn't he work?" Saville said. "It's two in the afternoon."

"He has a very good job. And he knows how to prioritize his family."

His family. The words hit him like a punch to the gut. Willie was becoming Emma's father figure while Saville chased killers across the country. "Jennifer, please."

"I'm hanging up. Goodbye."

"Tell her I love her." But the line was already dead.

He stared at the phone, fighting the urge to hurl it into the street. What kind of job let Willie leave work whenever he wanted? Investment banking, Jennifer had mentioned once. Big money, flexible hours. Willie was practically living there now, and for the first time, it struck him that Jennifer was probably sleeping with another man. The thought made his stomach turn.

A police cruiser drove slowly past the 7-Eleven. The officers inside glanced at him but kept moving. Saville checked his watch. He needed to get moving before someone decided he was an easy target.

He dialed the Greenville Resident Agency. Rosena Wyatt transferred him to Jack Mayfield.

"I need help," Saville said.

"Where are you? You sound like hell."

"Still in DC. What do you know about Ken Burton?"

"Computer software guy from Kendall County. Rich, clean record. Owns half of Research Triangle Park. Why?"

"His name came up in the investigation."

"How? And where's your regular phone? This number came up unknown."

"Long story. I don't know much yet, Jack."

"Did you find Mond?"

"Yeah. He didn't kill Clough or Farnsworth. He actually helped me understand what happened."

Mayfield grunted. "You're not telling me everything. Are you in some kind of trouble?"

"Work with me here. I need a full background check on Burton. Financial records, business associates. Everything you can dig up. I'll call you back in a few hours."

He hung up before Mayfield could ask more questions. Then he dialed Cynthia Clough's cell phone.

"I need a ride," he said when she answered.

"Agent Saville. How nice to hear from you again."

He gave her his location.

"That's not a safe area. Are you all right? Was your car stolen?"

"No."

Her voice softened. "Do you have news about Davy?"

"Yes."

"I'll be there in twenty minutes."

***

It took Cynthia forty-five minutes to arrive, and Saville sweated through every one of them. The concrete radiated heat from the afternoon sun. His shirt clung to his back, and the smell from the dumpster grew stronger as the temperature climbed.

Twenty minutes in, two wiry youths covered in gang tattoos approached the picnic table. They wore red bandanas and oversized jerseys, moving with the predatory swagger of street dealers. Saville tensed, calculating distances to cover.

"You waiting for someone, suit?" the taller one asked, eyeing Saville's clothing with suspicion.

"Just catching my breath," Saville replied, keeping his hands visible.

The shorter one moved closer. "Nah, man. You look like five-oh. Or maybe DEA."

Saville slowly reached into his jacket, producing his FBI credentials and holding them up for both men to see. "Federal agent. Just waiting for a ride."

The taller man grinned, revealing gold teeth. "My bad. We just wanted somewhere to smoke." He pulled out a pack of Newports. "All good, agent man?"

Saville nodded and left the table. It was wiser to avoid confrontation in hostile territory. He moved to the street corner, pressing his back against a utility pole and keeping his eyes on the approaching traffic.

When Cynthia finally pulled up in a silver Mercedes-AMG SL Roadster, the car surprisingly fit the neighborhood. Drug money often bought expensive toys here. The convertible top was down, and her hair was pulled back in a ponytail threaded through a Washington Commanders cap. She appeared fifteen years younger than she had at the restaurant. Remarkably attractive without makeup and despite unremarkable features.

"Going my way?" she asked, reaching across the center console to open the passenger door.

Saville slid into the leather seat, relief washing over him as they pulled away from the corner. The car's interior smelled of expensive perfume and new leather.

"My goodness, Agent Saville. What brought you to this neighborhood?" She glanced at his hands gripping the door handle. "And what happened to your wrists?"

The cuts had reopened while he waited. Blood stained his shirt cuffs, and the wounds throbbed with each heartbeat.

"I was in a fight."

She accelerated through a yellow light, weaving between slower traffic. Her driving was aggressive but controlled. Saville wished she would slow down. He had survived an Israeli interrogation and years of street violence; dying in a car accident would be absurd.

"You need medical attention."

"No doctors," he replied firmly. "It looks worse than it is."

"I have supplies at home. I used to be a trauma nurse before I married Bernie. We met during his residency at Johns Hopkins." She took a hard right onto Connecticut Avenue. "Twenty-three years in emergency medicine. I know a deep laceration when I see one. You need stitches."

Saville shook his head. "That's not a good idea."

"I don't bite, Agent Saville. Besides, where else can we talk privately? You said you had news about Davy."

She had a point. He still needed to interview her husband about the SAINTS software, and he required somewhere safe to regroup and plan his next moves. The Israelis could be looking for him.

"Will Dr. Clough be there?"

"Hardly." The bitterness in her voice was sharp enough to cut glass. "He's at the hospital. He hasn't been home before midnight in six months."

Saville studied her profile as she drove. Something about Cynthia Clough had unsettled him since their first meeting. Something beyond her hostile attitude and threats of lawsuits. She was hiding something important; he was certain of it. Her eagerness to help seemed calculated, almost predatory.

But he needed shelter and medical attention. And if Dr. Clough eventually returned home, Saville could conduct the interview that might break the case wide open.

Maybe a few hours at the Clough residence was exactly what he needed.

He reclined the passenger seat and let the afternoon breeze cool his face. The Washington traffic moved around them in familiar patterns while Cynthia navigated toward whatever suburban sanctuary awaited. For the first time in eighteen hours, Saville allowed himself to relax.

The Mercedes purred through the streets, carrying him away from the violence and chaos of the morning toward answers that might finally make sense of three dead bodies and a software conspiracy reaching the highest levels of American and Israeli intelligence.

Chapter 30

Joel Graves called in sick at 11:30 p.m., thirty minutes before his shift was set to begin. He paced his small living room while listening to his shift commander, Lieutenant Javier Fuentes, berate him for the late notice.

Graves apologized and claimed food poisoning. "I've been in the bathroom for two hours. Something I ate didn't agree with me."

"You and your weak stomach," Fuentes said. "How many times have I told you gringo cops not to eat the street food?"

When Fuentes finally ended the lecture, Graves hung up and stared at his phone. The apartment felt too quiet, too empty. Rain drummed against the windows of his second-floor unit, and the neighbor's television bled through the thin walls.

He was about to betray Lowri's trust. She had no idea he was making this call and probably would never forgive him if she found out. But he couldn't shake the image of her wild eyes when she'd shown him that photograph. She was spiraling, obsessing over conspiracy theories that sounded like paranoid delusions. Someone had to help her before she destroyed her career.

Or maybe he was the one who needed help understanding what was really happening.

Graves dialed Peter Sprague's cell phone. The number was listed in the staff directory along with his extension in the Criminal Investigations Branch.

"Yeah?" Sprague answered after four rings. Background noise suggested he was still at the station.

Graves spent several minutes explaining who he was.

"I know who you are," Sprague interrupted. "You're the guy screwing Lowri Pritchard."

Graves felt his face flush. He wondered how Sprague knew about their relationship, then realized everyone on the force probably did. Privacy was an illusion in a tight-knit law enforcement family.

Maybe this call was a mistake. What could he possibly gain from talking to Sprague? The man was obviously crude and hostile.

"What's wrong, Graves? Nothing to say? I was giving you a compliment. Pritchard's a fine piece of ass. You're lucky."

"Don't talk about Sergeant Pritchard like that."

Sprague laughed. "Relax, man. Just guy talk. What do you want, Graves? I'm busy."

The dismissive tone stung, but Graves pressed on. "I'm worried about Lowri. She's obsessed with..."

"We have department shrinks for that."

"The Victor Farnsworth case."

The line went quiet. Graves could hear muffled voices in the background, the sound of footsteps on linoleum. "That case is closed."

"I know. But Lowri thinks you're involved somehow."

"I am involved. I was the lead detective."

"More involved than that. We need to talk. She has this photograph—"

"What photograph?"

Graves hesitated. He was too deep in to stop now. "You and Farnsworth when you served in Desert Storm. There's a third man with you."

Another long silence. "We need to talk about this in person, Graves. Not over the phone. Where are you now?"

"At home."

"I'll swing by after my shift ends. What's your address?"

Graves gave him the information and hung up. Immediately, he regretted revealing where he lived. Sprague wouldn't talk openly at the station, but inviting him to his apartment felt dangerous. He considered calling back to suggest a neutral location but decided against it. Sprague might refuse to meet at all. He walked to his kitchen window. The parking lot below was empty except for his Toyota pickup under the flickering streetlight.

He had wanted answers, but now he wondered if he had just made the biggest mistake of his life.

***

Saville sat motionless while Cynthia finished bandaging his wrists. The antiseptic she had applied earlier still stung, but the sharp pain was fading to a dull throb.

"Why did you quit nursing?" he asked as she secured the last strip of medical tape.

"The children," she replied simply.

Saville nodded. He was learning to appreciate the sacrifices mothers made for their families, the sacrifices Jennifer had made for Emma before their marriage fell apart.

"Better?" she asked, stepping back to examine her work.

"Yes. Thank you."

He flexed his fingers. His head felt clearer too. Thoughts of quitting the Bureau, abandoning the case, and walking away from everything were gone. He was ready to get back to work, though not being able to talk to Emma still gnawed at him.

"When will your husband be home?" He needed to interview Bernard Clough, and being alone with Cynthia in this house made him uncomfortable.

She shrugged. "When he finishes at the lab. I never know his schedule."

"Can you call him?"

"He won't answer. He doesn't like interruptions when he's working."

"Is he working on the computer program?"

"Probably. He doesn't discuss business with me."

"The SAINTS program?"

She hesitated. "I assume so."

"What do you know about SAINTS?"

"I told you, he doesn't discuss business matters with me."

"But you knew the government offered him twenty million for it," Saville said.

She glared at him. "I don't appreciate your tone, Agent Saville."

They sat at a massive oak dining table in a kitchen larger than most people's entire apartments. The house was in Country Club Manor, near the Washington Golf and Country Club. The imported tile flooring probably cost more than Saville's entire house in North Carolina.

"You still haven't answered the question," he pressed.

She stood and poured herself coffee without offering him any. He wondered if they employed household staff and where they might be.

"My husband and I discuss our finances," she said, not looking at him.

"Except when they involve his business dealings."

"What are you implying?"

"I'm trying to find out who murdered your son."

"Then perhaps you should focus your investigation elsewhere."

"How well do you know Ken Burton?"

She sat back down and took a sip of her coffee. "He's Bernie's business partner. I don't know him personally."

"You've never met him? Never had him over for dinner?"

"No. I've only heard Bernie mention him occasionally."

"Why didn't you tell me about Burton when you were in Kendall County? You knew he lived there and must have suspected a connection to Davy's presence in town."

"Why would I? What does my husband's software have to do with my son's death?"

"The Department of Homeland Security was stealing your husband's code from Burton's company."

Her head snapped back. "What are you talking about?"

Saville explained what he had learned from Mond: the secret meetings between Israeli intelligence and Victor Farnsworth, and the plan to sell modified SAINTS software to foreign governments for massive profits.

"The Israelis were prepared to pay fifty million for the back-door version," he said.

She stared into her coffee cup.

"Davy discovered what was happening and tried to warn Burton. That's what got him killed."

He left out Davy's attempt to extort ten million dollars from the conspirators. She was still grieving; she didn't need to know that her son's greed had sealed his fate.

"Did Bernie know?" Her voice mixed anger with sorrow.

"Only if Davy told him."

A tear rolled down her cheek. "He must know now. That's why he's never home anymore."

Saville understood. Guilt was eating Bernard Clough alive, keeping him away from his house and his wife. He knew about guilt. Caroline Cochran's death, his failed marriage, the wreckage of his relationship with Emma. Guilt was a familiar companion.

"I can't believe neither my husband nor my son trusted me enough to tell me what was happening," she said, her tears flowing more freely now as she got up to grab tissues from the counter.

"They were trying to protect you," Saville said, though he doubted his own words. This family seemed incapable of honest communication.

Her expression transformed. The tears vanished, replaced by cold fury, the same dramatic shift he had witnessed in Kendall County.

"My husband has some explaining to do," she said. "I think I will call him after all."

***

Lowri returned to work at midnight and was immediately dispatched to a traffic accident involving a suspected drunk driver on Rock Creek Parkway between Virginia Avenue and Calvert Street.

When she arrived, Officer Larry Diaz was already on the scene, directing traffic around a deep gouge in the southbound lane. The impact point was outlined in red chalk. Skid marks and tire impressions led off the parkway through the woods toward Rock Creek. Several sections of guardrail were missing where the vehicle had crashed through.

Down by the water, she could see searchlights and the amber strobes of a tow truck flashing.

Lowri surveyed the scene and the assembled officers. "Where's Graves?"

"Called in sick," Diaz replied.

"Wimp." She made a mental note to check on him later. "What happened?"

"Vehicle went into the creek."

"And the driver?"

"DOA. Drowned. Coroner removed the body ten minutes ago."

"Do we have identification?"

"Running the plates now. Registration should be in the vehicle."

Lowri cursed under her breath. A traffic fatality meant hours of paperwork. She would be here until at least four in the morning, then another hour back at the district completing reports. "What about the other vehicle?"

The gouge marks clearly indicated a collision.

"Hit and run. Looks like someone rear-ended the victim at high speed and sent him careening down the embankment."

"Careening?" Lowri raised an eyebrow. "What is this, one of those online courses you're taking? ABCmouse?"

Diaz worked third shift so he could attend Howard during the day. She knew he wanted to be a lawyer. While she admired his energy, she questioned his career choice.

"Actually, Sergeant, I'm currently enrolled in a literature course."

"I'm kidding. Now show me the car."

They followed the tire tracks through mud and grass until they reached the creek. A dark green BMW X7 lay on its driver's side, windows shattered, muddy water flowing through the passenger compartment.

"Victim was found face down," Diaz explained. "He probably lost consciousness from the impact before he went into the water."

"Dispatch said suspected DUI?"

"Take a look." The rear cargo area had burst open on impact, spilling dozens of empty Monkey 47 gin bottles across the creek bank. The smell of alcohol and juniper hung in the air.

Something felt off beyond the obvious. "So we have a drunk driver who happened to be the victim of a hit and run. That's supposed to be poetic justice?"

"Actually, it's tragic irony. Poetic justice requires that logic triumph over..."

"Shut up, Diaz." He was right, though. Logic definitely had not triumphed here.

Two other Park Police officers, Lieberman and Robinson, stood knee-deep in the creek with their pants rolled up, pulling items from the submerged vehicle and sealing them in evidence bags.

"Hey, Lieberman," Lowri called. "You got the registration?"

"Yeah, right here."

"Bring it over. I've stood in enough water this week."

Lieberman splashed through the creek and handed her the registration card. It was mostly dry, likely protected by the glove compartment.

Lowri tried to read the document using the glare from the portable floodlights, gave up, and switched on her flashlight.

Virginia registration. Diaz read over her shoulder: "Bernard David Clough, 4107 North Wellington Lane, Arlington, Virginia 22207. Never heard of him."

But Lowri had.

Dr. Suicide.

Chapter 31

Saville fell asleep on Cynthia's couch around 11:00 p.m. The next thing he knew, she was shaking him awake. He opened one eye. The mantel clock read 1:36 a.m.

"It's about time," Cynthia said, arms folded across her chest. She stood at the great room's Palladian window, her toe tapping against the Persian rug. "He's never been this late before."

Saville swung his legs to the floor and rubbed his eyes. Through the window, he saw headlights winding down the circular driveway. The lights swept across the garage doors and illuminated the front of the house.

Before he had dozed off, Saville had watched Cynthia dial her husband's number repeatedly without success. She had alternated between fury and genuine worry. One moment she was cursing Bernard's name, and the next she was voicing concern that something terrible had happened to him. The last word Saville remembered before sleep took him was "asshole."

He had no opinion either way. He felt rested, and now he would finally get his interview with Bernard Clough.

"I'm going to read him the riot act," Cynthia muttered.

Saville hoped she would wait until after he questioned the man. He joined her at the window and pulled back the curtain for a better view.

"Oh, my God!" Cynthia gasped. "That's not Bernie!"

A police cruiser sat quietly in the driveway, its engine running but no emergency lights flashing. Late-night police visits were never about good news. Saville took a deep breath as Cynthia pressed her face against his shoulder.

His interview with Bernard Clough had not just been postponed; it would never happen at all.

***

Lowri despised these calls. They were worse than traffic stops on dark highways, worse than domestic disturbances where violence could explode with a single word, and even worse than dealing with crack addicts who would do anything for their next fix.

Death notifications were the hardest part of police work. She had done them nearly a dozen times, and it never got easier.

Standard procedure called for two officers, but Joel Graves was her usual partner and had called in sick. She would have to handle this alone. She planned to give Joel hell about his timing when her shift ended.

The only positive was that she had been able to leave the accident scene early. Once they identified Clough, Lieutenant Fuentes had arrived personally and dispatched her to notify the family.

"You're the best we have at death notifications," Fuentes had told her. "You have the right temperament. The right amount of compassion."

Lowri tried to model herself after the officer who had informed her of her father's death years ago. His calm professionalism had helped her through the worst moment of her life. She had memorized the department manual on death notifications: Use plain language with warmth and compassion. Avoid police jargon and graphic details. Use the deceased's name. Never say "remains," "corpse," or "the body."

That part was simple. Just act human.

The manual also advised officers to imagine themselves in the recipient's position and deliver the news gradually, avoiding blunt disclosure through careful word selection.

Sometimes that backfired. Twice she had been verbally attacked for dragging out the revelation. People knew a police officer at their door meant trouble. Someone was hurt or dead.

The manual emphasized allowing time to process the news: there may be silence as the next of kin tries to grasp the information. Allow them time to absorb it. Once they begin to speak, listen without interrupting.

Lowri was not looking forward to knocking on that door, but she had a job to do. Even the family of a corrupt, incompetent doctor like Bernard Clough deserved kindness and respect at a time like this. Everyone was loved by someone.

Even Dr. Suicide.

***

Saville watched through the window as a young female officer exited the white-and-blue Park Police Dodge Durango and approached the house. Her movements were deliberate and professional.

"Oh my God, Bernie!" Cynthia cried, rushing toward the front door just as the officer climbed the porch steps and pressed the doorbell.

Saville followed Cynthia into the foyer. She flung the door open before the chime had fully sounded, tears streaming down her face.

"What happened to my Bernie?" she demanded, cutting the officer off before she could respond.

"Are you Mrs. Clough?" the officer asked, her gaze shifting to Saville, who stood behind Cynthia. He could see her assessing the situation: a distraught woman with an unfamiliar man in her house at two in the morning. Any officer would draw conclusions.

"What happened to my husband?" Cynthia's voice cracked.

The officer remained on the porch, looking at them through the screen door. Her nameplate read Sgt. L. Pritchard. She appeared younger than Saville had initially thought, perhaps in her early thirties, with intelligent blue eyes darting between him and Cynthia.

Saville stepped forward and opened the screen door. "Sergeant Pritchard, please come inside."

She entered and turned to face Cynthia directly. "I'm sorry, Mrs. Clough, but there's been an automobile accident."

"Those bastards murdered Bernie!" Cynthia's composure shattered completely. "First my son, now my husband!"

She dropped to one knee, hyperventilating. Saville instinctively knelt beside her and placed a steadying hand on her shoulder, imagining what Pritchard must be thinking.

The officer waited for the initial wave of grief to pass before speaking. "Please accept my condolences on behalf of the United States Park Police." Her tone sounded practiced. "Mrs. Clough, did you say you believe your husband was murdered?"

Saville stood and produced his FBI credentials. "Special Agent Mike Saville, Federal Bureau of Investigation." He extended his hand.

"Sergeant Lowri Pritchard." She studied his identification carefully before shaking his hand, her grip firm. "Agent Saville, can someone explain what's happening here?"

Cynthia looked up from the floor, tears still flowing but her hysteria subsiding. Saville helped her to her feet.

"Let's sit down," he said, guiding Cynthia toward the living room. "We all need to talk."

They settled in the spacious room. Pritchard chose the sofa while Saville took the leather recliner. Cynthia found tissues on the end table and worked to compose herself.

"Can I get anyone coffee?" she asked, crumpling the damp tissues.

"No, thank you," both Saville and Pritchard replied simultaneously.

"I hope you don't mind, but I need some." Cynthia headed toward the kitchen.

As her footsteps faded, Saville leaned forward. "Sergeant, you didn't seem surprised when Mrs. Clough mentioned murder."

"With respect, Agent Saville, neither did you."

The woman was sharp. "Was Dr. Clough murdered?"

"I should wait for Mrs. Clough to return."

"She's lost a son and now her husband in less than a week. Both deaths appear suspicious."

"I'm sorry about her son, but I never said Dr. Clough's death was suspicious."

"Her son's name was Davy. He was found dead in Kendall County, North Carolina, staged to look like suicide."

Pritchard's eyebrows rose slightly. "There's been a lot of that lately."

Something in her tone made Saville's pulse quicken. "What do you mean?"

"Victor Farnsworth."

Saville raised a hand. "What about Farnsworth?"

"I worked that crime scene. I had questions about the official findings."

"We need to talk privately. Away from here."

"Is this an official Bureau investigation, sir?"

Saville studied her face. The question was pointed and careful. "I should ask you the same about your presence here."

"I'm here officially to conduct a death notification."

"Cut the act, Sergeant. We both know there's more to this."

Her posture stiffened. "I'm just a patrol sergeant, Agent Saville. Detective Peter Sprague handles major investigations."

"Officially."

She looked away without responding.

"What do you know about the Farnsworth case?"

"You'd need to speak with Detective Sprague."

"I'm asking you."

"I really can't—"

"I'm here unofficially too," Saville interrupted. "But you already figured that out."

She nodded slowly. "It's two in the morning, sir. Most federal agents keep business hours."

It wasn't entirely accurate, but Saville didn't correct her. "There's a lot about the Bureau you don't know, Sergeant."

"May I speak freely, sir?"

"Please do."

Cynthia's footsteps on the carpet interrupted them. She returned carrying a steaming mug, her emotional state more controlled but still fragile.

Neither Saville nor Pritchard spoke, but Saville knew their conversation was far from finished. Something was very wrong with the Farnsworth investigation, and this young sergeant might hold the key to understanding what really happened.

Chapter 32

The bourbon or whatever Cynthia Clough had been fortifying her coffee with announced itself before she'd spoken three words. Saville recognized the sweet, medicinal edge beneath the alcohol, probably peppermint schnapps. He'd spotted the bottles earlier when she'd opened the liquor cabinet: Rumple Minze and Stoli Vanil. The earlier nap had helped, but now fatigue was creeping back, and the alcohol fumes weren't aiding his focus.

By the time they reached the Office of the Chief Medical Examiner on E Street Southwest, Cynthia had crossed the line from self-medicating to certifiably drunk. She alternated between silence and rambling about "poor Davy" and "poor Bernie," her words running together.

Saville understood the impulse. Burying a child violated the natural order. Add a murdered spouse to that equation before the first wound had begun to heal, and most people would lose their grip on reality. He'd seen enough grief in his career to know that sometimes the bottle was the only anesthesia strong enough.

Inside the morgue, he positioned himself near the door, allowing him to observe while giving Pritchard room to work. She handled the process with practiced compassion, guiding Cynthia by the elbow into the viewing room and maintaining physical contact as the identification unit technician pulled up the digital image on the monitor. At Cynthia's request, Saville stepped into the private viewing room, though he kept his distance, watching from the periphery. He blinked hard, forcing himself to stay alert.

The image on the screen bore little resemblance to any living person. Death and refrigeration had drained Bernard Clough of color and definition, leaving behind puffy, distorted features. Cynthia's nod of confirmation was barely perceptible.

The technician led them back through the corridors to a small desk where forms awaited signature. Saville knew this ritual: the bureaucracy of death reduced to checkboxes and signatures. During his years in law enforcement, he'd witnessed every variation of grief: wives collapsing, husbands frozen in denial, parents demanding explanations from God, and adult children barely concealing their impatience to collect inheritance.

When Cynthia finally spoke, requesting to be taken home, Saville recognized the exhaustion that came from too much death. Davy Clough, Victor Farnsworth, Van Romano, Dr. Bernard Clough, even Sheriff Helm. The body count kept climbing, and Saville suspected he wasn't seeing the full picture yet. How many more names would be added before it was over?

His earlier doubts about continuing the investigation evaporated. Walking away was no longer an option. The killer or killers were accelerating, and Cynthia herself might be next. The last surviving Clough, the final link to what? That was the piece he couldn't grasp.

He couldn't afford to eliminate her as a suspect, despite her losses. Her emotional volatility, swinging between detached indifference and calculated outrage, raised red flags, though he recognized this pattern in wealthy individuals accustomed to control. Her grief appeared genuine, but Saville had learned never to trust appearances. Statistics haunted him: approximately two hundred

American mothers kill their own children each year. Could Cynthia Clough be one of them? The possibility had to remain on the table.

A uniformed officer appeared in the hallway. Pritchard made the introduction: Officer Diaz would handle the transport.

Pritchard squeezed Cynthia's hand. "I hope you don't mind, Mrs. Clough, but I've asked Officer Diaz to drive you home."

"I was hoping you would stay with me." The abandonment in Cynthia's eyes was clear.

"I promise I'll stop by when my shift ends." Pritchard gently withdrew her hand, maintaining eye contact.

Cynthia nodded, but disappointment was evident.

"Is there anything else I can do before I go?" Pritchard asked.

"Yes." Cynthia's voice suddenly sharpened. "Find whoever murdered my husband."

"Count on it."

Saville leaned close to Pritchard's ear, keeping his voice low. "Someone needs to stay with her. With her husband and son dead, she could be next."

Pritchard absorbed this, then addressed both Diaz and Cynthia. "Officer Diaz will remain outside your door. If you need anythin g..."

"What could I possibly need?" Cynthia interrupted, carrying complete defeat. "Everyone I loved is gone. There's nothing left to lose."

The words lingered in the morgue corridor. Saville sensed he was entering dangerous territory, where grief and recklessness collided. People with nothing left to lose were unpredictable; they could easily become either victims or perpetrators.

He needed to act quickly.

***

"Okay, Sergeant Pritchard," Saville said, wrapping his hands around the coffee cup. The warmth felt good against his palms. "Let's get to the truth."

After leaving the morgue, she drove them to the Wawa on 19th Street Northwest. They claimed a booth in the convenience store's food service area, nodding at a pair of paramedics grabbing a meal between calls. The medics appeared as tired as Saville felt.

"First of all, call me Lowri," she said, biting into a lemon Danish, cream smearing on her upper lip. "Sorry." She laughed, wiping her mouth with a napkin.

"Okay, Lowri," Saville replied, keeping his voice steady. "I need to know about Victor Farnsworth."

She met his gaze directly. "How do I know I can trust you?"

The bluntness caught him off guard, but he respected it. She understood the stakes just as well as he did.

"For the same reason I know I can trust you," he said. "We're both working off the books, and we both stand to lose everything if this goes wrong."

"I'd be fired. Police work is all I know."

"Yet you're willing to take that risk." Saville understood the calculation. His best-case scenario would be a transfer to a remote outpost in Alaska; more likely, he'd be facing unemployment, assuming he could avoid federal charges. The Bureau had already given him too many second chances.

They studied each other across the laminated table. The terms of their partnership didn't need to be explicitly stated. They would work together out of mutual necessity. Two cops pursuing the truth while trying not to get burned. Trust was a luxury neither could afford, but neither could they work alone.

It suited Saville just fine.

"No secrets between us," Lowri said. "That's the deal."

"No secrets."

"I applied for a position with the Behavioral Science Unit," she added, pausing. "I want you to recommend me."

"The BS Unit, huh? I wouldn't have pegged you for a Mindhunter."

"Will you help me or not?"

"I'll do what I can," he replied. She had proven sharp enough to recognize his unofficial status within minutes of meeting him.

"Thank you. Where should I start?"

"Tell me about the Farnsworth investigation."

"I think he was murdered, but nobody's listening."

"I'm listening."

"Cynthia Clough's husband didn't. He performed the autopsy and ruled it a suicide."

"Same situation with their son, Davy. The ME in North Carolina had a legitimate excuse for missing the homicide; the body was embalmed before the autopsy, contaminating the toxicology results."

"Embalmed?" Her forehead creased. "Before the autopsy?"

"No conspiracy there," Saville clarified. "The funeral director had plans for the evening and didn't want to wait. He proceeded without authorization from the state or the family. I hope his date was worth losing his license and facing criminal charges."

"We call Bernard Clough 'Dr. Suicide' around the department. This is at least the second time he's ruled a probable homicide as suicide. The first was a software salesman named Todd Byers. The family raised hell until he amended the death certificate."

"Software salesman?" Saville's exhaustion evaporated. "Which company?"

"Symmetric Technical Solutions."

The pieces clicked into place. "Clough's involvement runs deeper than you know." Saville laid out the connection to the SAINTS program, linking Clough to his son, to Farnsworth, and potentially to Byers.

"There's more," she said. "The same detective handled both the Byers and Farnsworth cases. Peter Sprague. I have a photograph of him with Farnsworth."

Saville leaned forward. "Recent?"

"Desert Storm, 1991. There's a third person in the photo, but that section's been torn away. I'm still trying to identify him."

"Bernard Clough?"

"Doubtful. Different unit. I don't think Clough served at all."

"Where's this photo now?" Saville lifted his coffee, then set it back down. Stone cold.

"Locked in my apartment."

"I need to see it."

"We can go now." Lowri checked her watch. "You look dead on your feet. After I show you the photo, you can crash at my place while I finish my shift. I'm off at eight. We can pick this up then."

"Works for me." The mention of sleep made his eyelids heavier. He'd been running on fumes since his last nap, and his body was demanding payment.

They left money on the table and headed for the door. The paramedics had already gone, probably called to another emergency. Outside, the pre-dawn air carried a chill that helped clear Saville's head momentarily. He would need every bit of alertness he could muster. They were walking into something that had already claimed at least four lives, possibly five if Byers was connected.

And Bernard Clough, the medical examiner who had covered up at least two murders, was now a victim himself. Either the killer was cleaning house, or someone else had entered the game. Either way, Saville and his new partner were running out of time to find answers.

Chapter 33

The photograph had been a dead end, and Saville knew he'd disappointed her.

She had produced the Desert Storm photo as if it were evidence in court. Three soldiers in DCUs stood against a backdrop of sand and military vehicles. He recognized none of them. The image was thirty-four years old, faded and creased. Even Farnsworth took him a moment to identify, younger and leaner in his desert camouflage. Sprague was a complete stranger. The third figure existed only as a fragment: a nose with an unusual continuous slope from bridge to tip. Not enough to determine even gender.

Lowri had made coffee without comment, her frustration evident in every movement. She left for work without saying much, the door closing with more force than necessary.

Now Saville jerked awake on her couch to the sound of his watch alarm. 7:20 a.m. He'd managed four hours of sleep. Enough to function but not enough to feel human. He found Lowri's phone on the kitchen wall and dialed Jack Mayfield's direct line in Greenville.

"Where the hell have you been?" Mayfield's voice carried an edge that meant Saville was skating on thin ice. "I'm about thirty seconds from pulling you back."

"Ken Burton," Saville said, cutting through the preamble. "You were supposed to compile a profile."

"You've got balls, I'll give you that."

"I'm close, Jack. Burton might be the key to this whole thing."

"That's not an update. I need specifics, or you're on the next flight home."

"Bernard Clough was killed last night. Davy's father. He was in business with Burton. I need that profile."

The line went quiet. Saville heard papers rustling. "Have I ever let you down?" Mayfield finally said. "Got it right here. Should I go secure?"

"I'm on a landline. My cell's gone."

Saville knew the implications. Without both parties on STE-equipped phones with matching encryption keys, their conversation was vulnerable. His Bureau phone was probably in some Israeli evidence locker if Mond hadn't already destroyed it.

"Christ, Mike. When did you lose it?"

The question was loaded. Bureau phones contained enough metadata to compromise operations even with encrypted content. Call patterns, contact networks, location data. Protocol demanded immediate reporting for remote wipe activation. Saville had violated that protocol.

"Yesterday. Maybe the day before. It's been complicated."

"You're not exactly building confidence here."

Time to pivot. "The deaths are connected," Saville said. "Clough, his son, Farnsworth, probably others."

"Suspects?"

"Multiple."

"Burton among them?"

"Yes."

"Based on what?" Mayfield's exhale was audible through the phone. "His record's clean as a whistle."

"You'll have to trust my instincts."

"That's a big ask, given your recent history."

The barb found its mark. Saville's margin for error had evaporated months ago. Losing the phone without reporting it immediately had just made things worse. But if he was mistaken about this, better that the blowback hit him alone.

"We need to interview Burton," Saville said. "You should handle it yourself."

"You can do it."

"I can't come back yet. There's still—"

"He's in DC."

Saville's exhaustion vanished. "Say that again."

"Burton's in Washington for meetings. The Ritz-Carlton, Georgetown. I told his secretary you'd make contact."

Saville processed this gift. Burton coming to him saved time he didn't have.

"You're supposed to call his private line. Ready to copy?"

Saville spotted Lowri's notepad and pencil beside the phone, everything squared away with military precision. He wrote down the number Mayfield recited.

"Watch yourself, Mike. Burton's got serious juice."

"Understood. Who's he meeting with?"

"DOJ. He's exploring a lawsuit against the government. Apparently, someone pirated his software."

The SAINTS program. Burton was going after the government for stealing his code. This meant he might not know his software had become a weapon, or he was establishing plausible deniability.

"Mike, one more thing," Mayfield said. "If this goes sideways—"

"It won't come back on you, Jack."

"It better not. And Mike? Find your damn phone."

The line went dead. Saville stared at Burton's number. The man who might have engineered a series of murders was less than five miles away, likely enjoying room service eggs at one of DC's finest hotels.

He checked his watch: 7:35. Lowri would finish her shift in twenty-five minutes. He decided to wait for her before approaching Burton. She was his only backup now that he was operating off the books. Two officers were better than one, especially when one had lost his phone, his credibility, and possibly his mind.

But first, coffee. He would have to settle for Lowri's instant powder. He needed to be sharp for Ken Burton. The man hadn't built a software empire by being foolish, and if he was connected to these murders, he was also dangerous.

Saville glanced at the torn photograph on Lowri's coffee table. Three soldiers, one face missing. How many more faces would be erased before this was over?

***

The calls began Monday afternoon, starting with *Clay & Buck*, followed by *Hannity*. By evening, White House Press Secretary Amelia Sylvester's phone system was overwhelmed.

The conservative media's initial attack was predictable: the President was having an affair with Molly Farnsworth, Victor Farnsworth had discovered this, and now Victor was dead. Draw your own conclusions. Sylvester handled it by the book, instructing her staff to issue the standard "no comment" that right-wing outlets always received.

But when CNN called, furious about being scooped by Fox, she realized the containment strategy was already faltering. The networks demanded answers. NBC, ABC, and CBS all wanted to know what was true, what wasn't, and who had leaked the story. Even MSNBC called, though their inquiries were gentler, apologetic. Sylvester knew their relationship with the administration was symbiotic enough that they would hold back until instructed otherwise.

The print media moved faster than anticipated. By Monday evening. *The New York Post*, *The Washington Times*, *The Wall Street Journal*, and *The Daily Telegraph* had all published online articles questioning the official narrative. Tuesday morning brought the real issue: *The New York Times* and *The Washington Post* ran stories in their print editions. When the friendly press turned skeptical, damage control became triage.

Then Mason Avery weighed in from his New Beacon Collective megachurch, calling for a special counsel to investigate what he termed the President's "un-Christian behavior." When the evangelicals mobilized, the midterms were suddenly in jeopardy.

Sylvester's initial response had been textbook: dismiss the allegations as partisan mudslinging aimed at influencing the elections. It bought them twenty-four hours. Now the networks wanted the President on camera to address the allegations directly.

They also wanted Molly Farnsworth. The widow had supposedly fled to North Carolina immediately after Victor's death. In reality, Sylvester knew she and her children were sequestered at an undisclosed location, her attorney issuing generic statements about grief and privacy. The woman was radioactive, and keeping her off camera was essential.

Calvin Gates had overruled Sylvester's recommendation to remain silent. The Chief of Staff had scheduled the President for five-minute segments on all three morning shows, reserving the eight o'clock slot for *Good Morning America*. GMA had the ratings, and their chief political correspondent had served in the previous Democratic administration. He'd throw softballs while maintaining a serious demeanor.

Gates made her skin crawl. With Farnsworth dead, he'd become the President's primary advisor, and Carney treated his word as gospel. Staff members who challenged Gates tended to vanish from the West Wing. His temper was legendary, and his management style was autocratic.

The rumors about his background were deliberately vague. Special Forces, then CIA, specializing in wet work. She couldn't determine what was true and what was a cultivated mystique. Regardless, she kept her distance. She had her MSNBC contract waiting and a book deal her agent promised would clear six figures once Carney's second term ended. She wasn't going to jeopardize that by clashing with Calvin Gates.

If the term ended on schedule. The way things were trending, that timeline might accelerate.

She stepped aside as Gates entered the Oval Office. The President sat behind the Resolute Desk while a technician adjusted his lavalier mic. Carney was laughing, projecting an air of confidence he might or might not feel. Politicians learned early to perform regardless of their internal state.

The technician gave a thumbs-up. Gates moved to stand beside her, and Sylvester's shoulders tensed involuntarily.

"Thirty seconds, Mr. President," Raymond Snow announced. The White House videographer had been counting down these moments for three administrations.

"He's not focused," Gates said quietly, close enough that she could smell his coffee breath. "Not thinking clearly."

"He looks fine to me."

"Twenty-seven, twenty-six, twenty-five. . . ."

"This is Hellen's doing. She's got him twisted up."

"Then why put him on camera?"

"Seventeen, sixteen, fifteen. . . ."

"He's not responsible for his actions right now," Gates said.

The phrasing made Sylvester's stomach tighten. "What actions?"

"Twelve, eleven, ten. . . ."

"Hellen's affair with Victor pushed him over the edge." Gates's voice was barely audible, almost as if he couldn't believe what he was saying. "Victor got what he deserved."

"What are you saying?"

"Seven, six, five. . . ."

"You're right. This was a mistake."

"Three, two, one. Quiet. Mr. President, you're on."

Sylvester watched Graham Stone deliver his prepared questions with the reliability of a batting practice pitcher. The President connected with each one, his charm dialed to maximum wattage. By the end of the interview, Stone was actually apologizing for his "tough" questions.

When the cameras stopped, Sylvester exhaled slowly. The immediate crisis had passed. But Gates's words gnawed at her.

As the crew packed up their equipment, she turned to him. "The interview went fine. What were you trying to tell me?"

"You really don't see it." Gates's contempt was unmistakable. "The President's going down, and he's taking the rest of us with him. Better update that résumé."

He yanked open the east door and strode into the Rose Garden, disappearing among the crabapples and lindens that bordered the formal hedges.

Sylvester remained in the Oval Office, processing what Gates had just revealed. Victor got what he deserved. Was the Chief of Staff confessing or expressing a terrible suspicion about the President? With Gates's rumored background, either possibility was conceivable. He looked shaken, but that could mean anything.

She glanced at President Carney, who was unclipping his microphone and chatting with Snow about camera angles. He seemed utterly normal, completely in control. But Gates knew him better than anyone, and Gates was scared.

If Gates was right, if the President had crossed that line, then the scandal about to break would make Watergate look like a parking violation. And everyone in this building would be tainted by proximity.

Her MSNBC deal suddenly felt very distant.

Chapter 34

"Can you believe that?" Hellen threw her hands up. "Graham Stone should be ashamed. So obsequious. So fawning. Why didn't he just drop to his knees?"

"Stone's a journalistic lightweight, but he's easy on the eyes," Cecelia Leehan replied. "I wouldn't mind if he dropped to his knees for me." She flashed the wicked smile that Hellen had come to appreciate these past few days. There was much to admire about Cecelia: her warmth, humor, blind ambition, and eagerness to be seduced by proximity to power.

"I trust you'll be tougher with Woody at this afternoon's press conference." Hellen moved across the bed and kissed Cecelia's cheek. "A little hardball never hurt anyone."

"I'll roast him alive." Cecelia took Hellen's hand. "The press corps can pick over the carcass."

After the President's morning interview, Press Secretary Sylvester announced he would appear at the two o'clock briefing. It was perfect timing for Hellen and Cecelia to advance their campaign. As the self-appointed queen bee of the White House press corps, Cecelia always got the first question. Today's would be devastating. They had crafted it together, word by word.

The question would be: "Mr. President, you stated on Good Morning America that rumors of an affair with Molly Farnsworth are partisan attacks designed to influence the midterms. If that's your position, how do you explain the inconsistencies in the autopsy report, the truncated police investigation, and the fact that any cover-up would require authorization from the highest levels of government, possibly the White House itself?"

Hellen anticipated Woody's reaction with something approaching excitement. Would he maintain his trademark composure, that smug confidence the media found so charming? Or would the mask slip, revealing the rage she'd witnessed so many times in private?

Having an ultra-liberal like Cecelia deliver the blow made it perfect. Her progressive colleagues in the press room would have to take it seriously. Cecelia had championed the administration for six years. Why would she ask such a damaging question without proof?

The anticipation of the upcoming spectacle sent a thrill through parts of Hellen that she preferred not to scrutinize too closely. She kissed Cecelia on the mouth, closed her eyes, and envisioned herself on the Senate floor. The Vice President would administer the oath. Her name would be added to the roll. She would sign the Senate Oath Book.

Senator Hellen Carney. After years of being a supportive spouse, she would finally wield power in her own right. Real power, not just the reflected glow of being First Lady.

Soon now. Very soon.

***

Eight unanswered calls in two hours. Seven had gone to voicemail, and the eighth informed her that the mailbox was full.

Lowri stared at her phone, calculating the odds. Joel Graves was either too sick to reach for his phone or he wasn't sick at all. The latter possibility gnawed at her more than it should have. Maybe he was with someone else right now, some Fairfax County divorcée with time and money to burn.

She had no claim on him. They were colleagues who occasionally ended up in bed together. No promises had been made, and none were expected; that was their unspoken agreement. Joel could do whatever he wanted, with whomever he wanted. Perhaps he was with someone else right now, such as that attractive firefighter from Engine 7, Serrano, who worked out of the Tenleytown station. He had asked her to dinner three times and coffee twice. She had declined each invitation, Joel's face materializing every time she considered saying yes. Soon, Serrano would stop asking. Maybe he already had.

Did Joel extend her the same courtesy? Doubtful.

Not that it mattered. A relationship between them was impossible anyway. U.S. Park Police regulations were clear: while personal relationships weren't forbidden, any fraternization that affected the chain of command was prohibited. She was Joel's sergeant, his direct supervisor. One of them would have to transfer out of Central District for anything legitimate to happen between them, and that wasn't happening unless the FBI accepted her application.

She tried Joel's number once more from the Central District station. Nothing. She checked her personal email on her phone. Ben Manning hadn't responded. Maybe he'd called her apartment instead.

Her shift ended at 8:30. She had already changed out of her uniform and was heading to her car when she called Saville from her cell.

"Any calls?" she asked.

"Your phone hasn't made a sound."

"No messages?"

"Nothing," Saville replied. "Expecting someone?"

She told him about Manning, keeping their no-secrets agreement intact.

"I'll pick up if anyone calls," Saville said. "When will you be back? I've got an interview in Georgetown with Ken Burton, the software CEO. It could be the break we need."

Under normal circumstances, news of Burton would have commanded her full attention. A CEO connected to SAINTS in D.C., willing to talk. But Joel occupied too much of her mental space at the moment.

"I need to make a stop first," she said. "If I'm not back in time, take an Uber."

"I'd prefer not to."

"Then wait."

She disconnected and headed southwest toward Merrifield. The drive from the Central District station on Ohio Drive to Joel's apartment complex near the Dunn Loring-Merrifield Metro usually took twenty minutes. Tonight, traffic on 395 South crawled, adding another ten. Each passing minute tightened her anxiety.

She had also promised to check on Cynthia Clough. The widow was alone now, possibly in danger, definitely unstable. But that visit would have to wait; her concern for Joel overrode protocol, common sense, and professional obligations.

The parking lot of Joel's complex was well lit, with security cameras mounted at regular intervals. His black Tundra sat in its assigned space, its Virginia plates dusty from lack of recent driving. She pulled her Honda into the adjacent visitor slot and turned off the engine.

Two scenarios played out in her mind. Behind door number one: Joel was genuinely ill and possibly needed medical attention, and she'd been an ass for doubting him. Behind door number two: Joel was perfectly healthy, thoroughly occupied with company, and she was about to humiliate herself.

The building's entry system required a code or buzzer access. She knew Joel's apartment number—314, third floor. She'd been there before, though not often; their encounters usually defaulted to her place, maintaining some illusion of control on her part. Now, she stood outside his building like a jealous girlfriend, about to buzz his apartment and do what, exactly? Demand to know if he was really sick? Check his temperature? Search for evidence of another woman?

Her phone buzzed. Saville.

"Burton moved up our meeting. I really need that ride."

"I'll be there," she said, though her finger hovered over Joel's buzzer.

Whatever was happening in apartment 314, she either trusted him or she didn't. Showing up unannounced at his door would answer that question in the worst possible way.

She pressed the buzzer anyway.

Chapter 35

"Thanks for agreeing to see me," Saville said. "I know you're busy."

Ken Burton crossed his legs in the Louis XIV armchair. "I'm curious to hear your theories about Davy Clough's death. And now Bernard, my business partner, is dead as well. Quite the coincidence."

The software mogul had taken the Ambassador Suite at the Ritz-Carlton Georgetown. The living room where they sat could have swallowed Saville's entire apartment. Between them was a glass-and-marble coffee table that probably cost more than his annual salary, a salary he might not be collecting much longer.

Saville's irritation from the Uber ride still simmered. Lowri had failed to show, forcing him to use the ride service despite his reluctance to leave digital breadcrumbs. After this interview, he'd need to rent a car. Another trail, another risk.

Marshall Kelsey occupied the leather sofa to Burton's right, reading documents through designer glasses. Saville knew the attorney by reputation: the East Coast's answer to Johnnie Cochran, defender of billionaires and political dynasties. His presence sent a clear message: Burton wasn't just wealthy; he was connected.

"Mr. Kelsey is here to protect my interests," Burton said.

"It's your right to have an attorney present," Saville acknowledged.

"I'll be monitoring this conversation closely," Kelsey said, looking over his reading glasses. "My client is extending you a courtesy. Against my advice."

Saville focused on Burton. The man's calm demeanor bothered him more than hostility would have. "The SAINTS case brought you to D.C.?"

"We're filing suit against Homeland Security under the Digital Millennium Copyright Act. We're also pursuing criminal charges against the individuals responsible. We want to ensure all guilty parties receive the punishment they deserve."

"Did Victor Farnsworth receive the punishment he deserved?"

"Agent Saville," Kelsey warned.

Burton raised a hand. "It's fine, Marshall. Agent Saville knows Victor Farnsworth killed himself."

"The suicide determination was made by your business partner," Saville said. "Dr. Clough had a reputation for mistaking homicides for self-harm. They called him 'Dr. Suicide' at Park Police."

"I'm aware of the nicknames. Unfortunately, Bernard's surgical abilities were beyond my scope of knowledge. His administrative and analytical skills, however, were first-rate when it came to medicine. Perhaps he was in the wrong field."

"Tell me about Todd Byers."

"A former employee—"

"Whose death Clough also ruled a suicide. Later changed to homicide after the family protested. How did Clough happen to be the ME on two cases involving your company?"

"You're suggesting Mr. Burton controls the medical examiner's office?" Kelsey interjected.

"I'm suggesting Mr. Burton's influence extends to many places."

"Ken, we should end this."

"Let him ask his questions," Burton said. He seemed to be en-joying himself, which only deepened Saville's irritation. "Todd Byers was a tragedy. Bernard was devastated by his error. He apologized extensively."

"What was Byers's role at Symmetric?"

"Route salesman. His territory covered D.C., Northern Vir-ginia, and most of Maryland. He sold our products to hospitals and clinics."

"Including SAINTS?"

"Our flagship product, yes. Until he started embezzling funds and stealing proprietary documents. That's what got him killed. Greed is dangerous, Agent Saville."

"Who would kill him over that?"

"He obviously crossed the wrong people. I told the police the same thing at the time."

Saville shifted tactics. "Your wife performed the autopsy on Davy Clough. Another suicide that wasn't."

"My understanding is that Davy was investigating the theft of his father's software. My software. A forensic pathologist at East Carolina confirmed my wife's findings."

"After the body was embalmed. The results were compro-mised."

"You're grasping."

"Your wife handled Davy Clough. Your business partner han-dled Farnsworth and Byers. Everything connects to you."

"Careful, Agent," Kelsey said.

"I'm stating facts. Is your wife infallible, Mr. Burton?"

"I trust Samantha completely. She's an expert in her field, and she's convinced Davy Clough took his own life. Apparently, he was troubled."

Burton's composure never cracked. The man sat there in his ex-pensive suit, unfazed by accusations that would make most people sweat. Saville had interrogated enough suspects to know the difference between innocence and arrogance. He couldn't tell which one Burton was displaying.

"How did you learn about the SAINTS modifications?" Saville asked.

"What DHS did was a bastardization of my life's work."

"That must have made you angry. How long did it take to develop SAINTS?"

"Ten years of my life."

"That's a strong motive for murder."

"Ken, enough," Kelsey interjected.

Burton ignored him. "Many murderers feel wronged by their victims. It's human nature to seek protection."

"Is that a confession?"

Burton smiled. "Did DHS really think they could steal from me without consequences? My revenge will come in a courtroom, Agent Saville. Legal and public."

"To ensure the guilty are punished?"

"Precisely."

"I ask again: Did Farnsworth get what he deserved?"

"Guilt is powerful. Despite his crimes, Farnsworth had enough of a conscience to take his own life."

"And Davy Clough?"

"Karma handled him too."

"How exactly?"

"You asked how I learned about SAINTS? Davy Clough tried to extort me."

Saville leaned forward. "Explain."

"Initially, he offered help. He wanted to expose DHS in exchange for an exclusive story to sell to the media."

"Initially?"

"When I refused, preferring to handle things legally, he changed tactics. He threatened to claim my company authorized the modifications and that we were responsible for the privacy violations. He wanted ten million dollars."

"Blackmail. Another motive."

"Either charge my client or leave," Kelsey said. "The attorney general arrives soon."

That detail registered with Saville. The AG was coming to Burton's hotel suite, not the other way around. Power like that didn't come from money alone.

"What was your relationship with Sheriff Helm?" Saville asked.

"None. My wife despised him. She called him incompetent and chauvinistic. I never met the man."

"Sources in Kendall County say you kept him on payroll."

"Absurd." Burton's voice rose slightly, the first crack in his composure. "I don't pay people like Helm. I don't need to."

"Because you have other ways of getting what you want?"

"Because I operate within the law, unlike certain government agencies."

Kelsey shifted on the sofa. "Agent Saville, these insinuations—"

"Five bodies now, counting Helm. Did karma get him too?"

"His autoerotic lifestyle probably played a larger role." Burton's smile returned, cold and knowing.

Saville studied Burton's face. He knew details about Helm's death that hadn't been released to the public. Either he had exceptional sources or direct knowledge. Saville filed that away.

"Helm was running when he died. From what? Who financed his escape?"

"How could Mr. Burton possibly know?" Kelsey interjected.

"Your client seems remarkably well-informed about a sheriff he claims never to have met."

Burton shrugged. "Small-town gossip travels. Samantha keeps me informed about Kendall County's colorful characters."

Too smooth, Saville thought. Too ready with an explanation.

"Helm also concealed evidence in the Clough case. He removed items from the scene and altered reports."

"Are you suggesting Helm murdered Davy?" Burton asked.

"No. Helm wasn't capable of that level of execution. Too sloppy. But someone paid him to cover it up. I'll find out who wrote the check."

"Good luck with that investigation," Burton said, checking his Patek Philippe watch. "Though I suspect you'll find Sheriff Helm's corruption was strictly small-time. Speeding tickets, minor drug busts. Not murder conspiracies."

The dismissal came too quickly. Burton knew more than he was admitting. The question nagging at Saville was whether Burton was protecting himself or someone else.

"You know, Mr. Burton, for someone with no connection to these deaths, you seem remarkably unsurprised by them."

"I'm a businessman, Agent Saville. Risk assessment is what I do. When someone like Davy Clough tries to extort ten million dollars, when someone like Todd Byers embezzles from his employer, when someone like Victor Farnsworth steals intellectual property worth hundreds of millions. These are high-risk behaviors. High-risk behaviors lead to predictable outcomes."

"Death being a predictable outcome?"

"In certain circles, yes."

"Your circles?"

Burton stood, smoothing his tie. "We're done here, Agent Saville. The attorney general will want the suite prepared for our meeting."

As Saville left, his mind processed what he'd learned. Burton had admitted to multiple motives: the theft of his software, Davy's extortion attempt, and connections to every victim through his wife or business partner. The man was either supremely confident in his innocence or certain he'd covered his tracks perfectly.

Either way, Burton had just painted a target on his own back. The question rattling around Saville's exhausted brain was whether Burton had done it intentionally.

***

Samantha found Ken at the glass desk in their suite at the Ritz-Carlton Georgetown, staring at his laptop. Marshall Kelsey had left an hour ago, after the attorney general's visit. Saville before that. She had stayed in the bedroom during all three meetings, but now they were alone.

"You gave Saville just enough to keep him distracted."

Ken's fingers hovered over the keyboard. "He's a dog chasing his tail. Better he wastes his energy on scraps."

"Are you sure there's nothing left for him to discover?"

Ken met her gaze. "There's always something to discover if you look hard enough. But SAINTS didn't just appear by chance. Someone built it."

Her anger flared. "I believed we were building oversight and accountability. Not secret black budgets and deaths disguised as accidents."

"You know why I did this. Our sons. I couldn't let them grow up unprotected, vulnerable to the same threats we faced. That promise drove every choice."

"At what cost? How many bodies are buried in the shadows?"

He laughed bitterly. "You think I don't carry that weight? Every morning I wake up with a ghost on my chest."

Silence filled the suite.

She looked away. Part of her stayed quiet because of what she'd built. The mansions, the luxury, the influence. Risking it all meant losing more than money. It meant losing herself. She couldn't destroy what they had, no matter how rotten the foundation.

"You could have walked away."

He shook his head. "The moment that first off-the-books order came, we were trapped."

She bit her lip. She hated how much she understood him. Hated that part of her agreed.

"You lost your soul, Ken."

He turned toward the window. "Maybe. But I kept us safe."

"What about the law? What if we go to jail?"

Ken chuckled. "Relax. We covered every angle. Our tracks are spotless."

She frowned.

"We're going to sue the federal government for stealing our SAINTS software. Saville thinks he's sniffing out a scandal, but we hold the cards. Not only do we avoid prison, but we come out smelling like roses." He smiled. "Financially, this will be one hell of a payday."

Relief and complicity twisted in her chest. The money, the power, the certainty of their invulnerability bound her tighter than any chain. But the cost of keeping silent grew heavier by the day.

Chapter 36

No response. Lowri pressed the buzzer again, holding it longer this time. Still nothing.

She tried once more, then tested the door handle. It turned freely. The door swung inward.

Wrong. Everything about this was wrong. Joel Graves was paranoid about security. He owned a Lionel train collection worth six figures and kept it locked in his attic like gold bars in a vault. The man who triple-checked his locks would never leave his door open.

Lowri drew her Glock 22, the polymer grip familiar against her palm. She crossed the threshold, weapon at low ready. The apartment was dark except for a strip of morning light filtering through half-closed curtains. She'd hung those curtains herself three months ago, tired of Joel's bare windows.

She moved through the entry, scanning corners. The living room was empty. No signs of struggle. Joel's recliner faced the television, a half-empty beer bottle on the side table, yesterday's judging by the condensation ring beneath it. No Joel.

A sound from the back of the apartment. Faint but distinct. Wet, struggling.

Her training said to call for backup, establish a perimeter, and wait for additional units. Her instincts said Joel didn't have that kind of time. She keyed her radio to silent and moved toward the hallway.

The corridor stretched ahead, narrow and exposed. Joel's bedroom was on the right at the end, the guest room on the left, and the kitchen beyond. Both bedroom doors were closed. There was no cover between here and there. The hallway was a fatal funnel, every tactical instructor's nightmare scenario. One way in, no way out if someone was waiting.

She could circle the building and try the kitchen's rear entrance. But if it was locked, she'd lose critical seconds. Joel might not have that long. The sound came again, weaker now. Definitely human. Definitely distressed.

Lowri moved down the hallway, shoulder against the wall, muzzle tracking her sight line. The photos she'd bought at Target watched her progress. Joel's apartment when she'd first seen it had been institutional, with blank walls and borrowed furniture. She'd tried to give it warmth. Now, those same pictures felt like witnesses to whatever was happening here.

First door: the guest room. She pushed it open with her left hand and swept the interior. Boxes, exercise equipment Joel never used, an empty closet. Clear.

Second door: Joel's bedroom. The bed where they'd spent too many mornings pretending this was just casual. Focus. She cleared it systematically. Closet, bathroom, under the bed. Nothing.

Another sound from the kitchen. Wet, labored. A gurgling that made her stomach drop.

"Joel!" Training evaporated. She rushed forward.

He was on the kitchen floor, back against the center island. His hands pressed against his throat, blood pulsing between his fingers. Carotid artery. The blood was bright red, spurting with each heartbeat. A kitchen knife lay three feet away, its blade dark with blood.

Lowri dropped to her knees beside him, holstered her weapon, and keyed her radio.

"Dispatch, 10-33, officer down! Sergeant Pritchard, Gallows Road Apartments, unit 314. Officer Graves has a severed carotid, conscious but critical. I need EMS and backup immediately. Suspect not on scene."

She pressed her hands over Joel's, adding pressure. His eyes found hers. Brown eyes that usually held confidence and humor now showed only fear. He tried to speak, but only blood came out.

"Stay with me, Joel. An ambulance is coming. Two minutes out."

Blood soaked through their combined grip. Joel's breathing became ragged and wet. He was drowning in his own blood. She needed to control the bleeding better. Direct pressure wasn't enough with an arterial bleed this severe.

Lowri stripped off her duty belt, yanked off her boots and socks. She tied the socks together, pressed the knot against the wound, and looped the ends under his opposite armpit to anchor the pressure without cutting off his airway. The makeshift dressing was saturated instantly.

Inova Fairfax was five minutes away. Where was the ambulance? She should be hearing sirens by now.

Joel's pupils were dilating. His breathing was shallow. He was going into shock. His skin had gone gray, lips blue. Classic signs of exsanguination. He was bleeding out faster than his body could compensate.

"I don't think he's going to make it, Dollface."

The voice came from behind her. Peter Sprague.

She reached for her weapon. Too slow. The muzzle of his Glock pressed against the base of her skull.

"Should have minded your own business, Dollface."

"Backup's thirty seconds out." A lie, but worth trying.

"No, they're not." Sprague's voice had a hint of amusement. "Right after your call, I got on the radio. I told dispatch that I was FBI Agent Mike Saville, already on scene running a joint task force operation with Officer Graves. I said the situation was under control, that you'd stumbled into an undercover operation and compromised it. I instructed them to cancel all units; we'd handle it internally through federal channels."

Her stomach dropped. Using Saville's name was brilliant. It would explain everything, create confusion, and leave a trail pointing away from Sprague.

"They bought it?" she asked, though she already knew the answer.

"Why wouldn't they? An FBI operation gone secret, a local cop stumbling in and nearly blowing it? Happens more than you'd think. Dispatch won't touch it now. Too much jurisdictional complexity. No one's coming, Lowri. And when they find your boyfriend here, guess whose name will be all over the logs?"

She'd followed procedure perfectly, but Sprague had exploited the system against her. The bitter irony. All those years of trusting the badge and the brotherhood, and now that same system would let Joel bleed out on his kitchen floor.

"You killed Farnsworth," she said, keeping her voice steady to buy time and look for an opening.

"Farnsworth was necessary. Like Helm. Like your boyfriend here."

"He's a cop. You're a cop."

"He was a liability. He started asking questions about Byers, about the Desert Storm photo. Some stones shouldn't be turned."

Joel's breathing had slowed to almost nothing. His eyes still tracked her, still aware, but fading. She watched the life draining from him, unable to stop it.

"What's in that photo?" she asked. Keep him talking. Buy seconds. "What's worth all this killing?"

"You really don't know?" Sprague sounded almost amused. "All that digging, and you never figured it out. You and I have some issues to work out in private."

She felt him shift behind her, the muzzle leaving her skull. She tried to spin, to go for her weapon. She'd probably die trying. But Joel was dying anyway, and she'd rather die fighting than be taken by Sprague.

His arm clamped around her throat before she could move. A carotid restraint. Hard and precise. She clawed at his sleeve, tried to drop her weight to break the hold, but Sprague had leverage and experience. He'd done this before.

The kitchen tilted. Her vision narrowed to a tunnel, edges turning gray.

"Should've stayed out of it, Lowri."

She fought to stay conscious, to keep her eyes on Joel. He was still breathing, barely. Still alive. Still looking at her, trying to speak. If she could just hold on, maybe someone had heard the original call before Sprague canceled it. Maybe someone would check anyway. Maybe...

The darkness was winning. Her muscles went slack. The room spun. Through the fading light, she saw Sprague step around her, his weapon raised. Joel's eyes widened, finding hers one last time.

"No witnesses," Sprague said.

The gunshot was impossibly loud in the small kitchen. Joel's face disappeared in a spray of blood and bone.

Then, nothing.

Chapter 37

"If this were Vegas," Saville said into the burner phone, "my money would be on Ken Burton."

"Then you'd lose everything." Mayfield's tone left no room for interpretation. He wasn't joking.

Saville sat on the edge of the motel bed in Arlington. The place smelled of cigarettes and industrial disinfectant. After leaving the Ritz-Carlton, he'd walked to the Budget rental on Wisconsin Avenue, signed for a Hyundai Elantra, and then found this cash-only motel. He missed his Greenville apartment, his desk, and his computer with direct access to NCIC, ViCAP, and the dozen other databases that made investigations possible. Here, he had nothing but instinct and whatever Mayfield could feed him without leaving digital fingerprints.

He was operating like the ghost squads Hoover had run decades ago, before congressional oversight and FISA courts, agents who didn't exist, running investigations that never happened. The difference was that those squads had institutional support, even if it was off the books. Saville had only Jack Mayfield, and that lifeline was fraying.

"Burton's dirty," Saville said. "Run his finances. Find the connection to Sheriff Helm."

"Businessmen buy influence, Mike. It's not illegal; it's lobbying."

"Helm covered up Davy Clough's murder. Burton paid him for it."

"You think Burton killed Clough personally?"

"Or had it done. Helm wasn't capable of that kind of precision."

"Why would Burton risk everything?"

Saville laid it out: Davy's ten-million-dollar extortion attempt, the stolen SAINTS software, Burton's decade of work bastardized by Homeland Security. "He's testing us, Jack. Seeing how far money and connections can protect him."

"I need evidence, not theories."

"Give me time—"

"We don't have time. Headquarters is asking questions."

Saville's stomach tightened. "What kind of questions?"

"Your leave timing. They know you're in D.C."

"One more week—"

"Forty-eight hours," Mayfield said. "That's all I can cover."

Two days. Saville had no leverage to negotiate. Jack had already risked too much.

"Your call," Saville said. "But I need something from you."

"I'm out of favors."

"Not a favor. Information. What do you know about Samantha Burton?"

"Leave the wife alone, Mike."

"She made the preliminary determination on Davy Clough. Called it suicide when it was murder."

"She's in D.C. with her husband. Stay away from her."

"Funny. Ken never mentioned she was here."

"Why would he?"

Because innocent people don't hide things, Saville thought but didn't say. His grip on the case was slipping. Without evidence, his instincts meant nothing.

"What's your next move?" Mayfield asked.

"I need to talk to Samantha Burton."

"I just told you—"

"She knows something, Jack."

"You're going to make powerful enemies. Not just the Burtons."

"I'll be careful."

"No, you won't."

Mayfield hung up.

Saville set the phone on the nightstand and lay back on the bed. The ceiling had water stains that looked like continents drifting apart. Forty-eight hours to prove Ken Burton was a killer or watch his career finally and definitively end.

He thought about the interview he needed to arrange with Samantha Burton. But first, he should check in with Lowri. She'd been radio silent since this morning, and they were supposed to be working together. Partners, or whatever they were calling themselves.

The exhaustion hit him then, the accumulated weight of too many hours without real sleep. He closed his eyes just for a moment. Tomorrow would bring whatever it brought. Now, he just needed to rest.

***

The Park Police cruiser locked onto Saville's bumper halfway across Key Bridge.

He checked his speed. Twenty-five, right at the limit. The Elantra's speedometer might be off by a mile or two, but nothing worth this level of attention. When he cleared the bridge onto M Street Northwest, the cruiser hit its lights and siren.

Saville pulled over at the first safe spot, hands visible on the wheel before the officers reached his window. Twenty years in law enforcement had taught him the choreography of traffic stops from both sides. Keep your hands visible. Move slowly. Don't give them a reason.

Two officers approached in textbook formation: the primary on the driver's side, the secondary on the passenger side. Both male, one clean-shaven, the other with a mustache. Their hands rested on their weapons.

Two more Park Police units screamed in from the opposite direction, crossed the median, and boxed in his Elantra. Four officers emerged with weapons drawn.

"Engine off. Step out of the vehicle. Hands where we can see them."

This wasn't a traffic stop. This was a felony takedown.

Saville opened the door slowly. The moment his foot touched the asphalt, hands grabbed his shoulders and slammed him face-first onto the pavement. The taste of blood and grit filled his mouth.

"Where is she?" The primary officer's knee pressed into Saville's kidney.

"There's been a mistake. I'm FBI—"

"We know who you are. Where's Lowri Pritchard?"

Lowri was missing? Saville tried to process this. "She was supposed to be at work—"

The knee drove deeper. Someone wrenched his arms back, snapping cuffs onto his wrists. The metal bit into the bandages from the Israeli safe house, reopening wounds that hadn't fully healed.

"Check the trunk!"

Footsteps. Keys jangling. The trunk popping open, slamming shut.

"Not here."

Someone grabbed Saville's hair, yanking his head back. "She called in a 10-33. Officer down. Found another officer dead at the scene. Joel Graves. Throat cut, shot in the face. You canceled her backup call, told dispatch it was a federal operation. What did you do with her, you bastard?"

The pieces clicked into place with horrible clarity. A dead officer. Lowri missing. Someone had used his name to cancel her emergency call. Now her colleagues thought he was responsible for a cop killing and Lowri's disappearance.

The name Graves meant nothing to him, but the implications were clear. A dead cop, a missing cop, and his name on the canceled backup call made him suspect number one.

"I never made that call. Someone's setting me up—"

"Bullshit!" The primary officer's fist connected with Saville's side. "Where is she, motherfucker?"

They hauled him upright and threw him into the back of a cruiser. The door slammed before he could finish explaining.

As the vehicle drove away, Saville spotted his abandoned rental car surrounded by police units, officers already rummaging through its interior. Whatever had happened to Lowri, and whoever had used his name at dispatch, had done a masterful job. He was in deep trouble.

The cruiser turned onto Rock Creek Parkway, heading south. Or was it east? Saville struggled to orient himself, but the route was confusing. They passed the Kennedy Center and then the Lincoln Memorial.

"Where are we going?" he asked.

No answer came from the front seat.

"I have a right to know where you're taking me."

Silence. The primary officer's knuckles were white on the steering wheel, while the secondary kept glancing in the rearview mirror, watching Saville as if he might somehow disappear from the locked cage.

Constitution Avenue flashed by. They weren't heading toward any police station Saville recognized. His mouth went dry. Cops who hurt other cops sometimes didn't make it to booking; sometimes, they faced a different kind of justice first.

"Listen," Saville tried again. "I was at a motel in Arlington when that emergency call came in. Check the records. Someone impersonated me—"

"Shut up." The primary officer's voice was flat, menacing.

The secondary officer finally spoke, but not to Saville. "How much longer?"

"Ten minutes."

Ten minutes to where? Saville tested the cuffs again. The bandages underneath were soaked with blood, and his wrists throbbed from the pressure. His face hurt where they'd pressed it into the pavement.

They thought he had hurt Lowri. Maybe even killed her. In their minds, he had canceled backup for an officer in distress, making him the worst kind of criminal: a cop who betrayed another cop.

The cruiser turned again onto another street Saville couldn't identify from his angle in the back seat. They were deliberately keeping him disoriented, ignoring his questions, not following any procedure he recognized.

Outside the window, D.C. rolled by. Normal people living normal lives while he sat cuffed in the back of a police car, framed for something he didn't do, heading toward an uncertain fate that might not involve due process.

"She's my partner," Saville said, knowing they wouldn't believe him. "We were working a case together. Whoever used my name—"

"I said shut up." The primary officer's hand moved toward his baton.

The secondary officer checked his watch. "Seven minutes."

Seven minutes until what? Saville's mind raced through the possibilities, none of them good: an abandoned warehouse, a parking garage. Somewhere without cameras or witnesses.

He thought about Lowri, wherever she was, and if she was still alive. Someone had used his name to cancel her distress call, meaning they wanted her vulnerable and isolated. The same person who was now using him as the fall guy.

The cruiser slowed for a red light. Saville could see pedestrians on the sidewalk, close enough to hear if he screamed. But what would that accomplish? He was a suspected cop killer in the back of a police car; no one would help him.

"Five minutes," the secondary officer said.

They crossed back over Rock Creek, but not on any main road. The cruiser turned onto a narrow access road running parallel to the parkway. Trees closed in on both sides. No buildings. No witnesses.

Saville's throat constricted. They were taking him somewhere isolated.

The road narrowed further. Through gaps in the trees, he glimpsed the Potomac below. They were near the C&O Canal towpath, the wooded area between the river and the parkway. Perfect place for something off the books.

"Two minutes," the secondary officer said.

The cruiser turned onto what looked like a maintenance road, barely wide enough for the vehicle. Gravel crunched under the tires. The trees blocked any view from the parkway.

The cruiser stopped in a small clearing.

"Out," the primary officer commanded.

They dragged him from the vehicle. The secondary officer grabbed his left arm, while the primary took his right. They began walking him toward the treeline.

Into the woods. They were taking him into the woods.

Saville's mind cataloged the possibilities: a beating for answers, an "accident" while attempting to escape, or perhaps they wouldn't bother with a cover story. To them, he had hurt one of their own.

The trees enveloped them. Dead leaves crunched underfoot. Traffic sounds faded, replaced by the wind rustling through branches.

Someone was waiting deeper in these woods. Someone who had orchestrated all of this. But who? And what did they want that couldn't be done at a station?

The cuffs bit into his wrists. No give. Whatever was coming, he'd face it defenseless.

They continued walking deeper into the shadows.

Chapter 38

Consciousness returned like a sickness. Lowri's head throbbed, and her mouth tasted of chemicals. Chloroform. The memory hit. Sprague. Joel's face disappearing in blood and bone.

Total darkness enveloped her. Something covered her eyes. She tried to reach for it, but her wrists were bound. Her ankles too. Duct tape sealed her mouth. Testing the restraints, she felt they were zip ties. Police-grade, the kind they had both carried in their duty bags.

Where had Sprague taken her?

She forced herself to focus on sounds, smells, and movement. A gentle rocking. The creak of wood. Diesel fumes mixed with river water. A boat. It had to be. The faint slap of waves against a hull confirmed it.

The image wouldn't leave her mind: Joel's eyes finding hers in that last moment before Sprague pulled the trigger. She had failed him, doubted him when he needed her, thinking he was with another woman when he was dying on his kitchen floor. Now he was dead because she had been too slow, too late, too suspicious to trust the one person who had always had her back.

"Welcome back, Dollface."

Sprague's voice made her skin crawl. She felt him grip her under the arms, hauling her to her feet. His hands were cold against her shirt.

He ripped the tape from her mouth. Pain flared across her lips.

"Scream all you want," he said. "No one will hear you."

"Where am I?" Her voice came out raw. "And stop calling me Dollface."

His palm cracked across her left cheek. She tasted blood and spat it toward his voice, hearing him step back.

"Missed by a mile." Another slap sent her sprawling to the floor. "Your aim sucks."

She pushed herself against the wall, using it for leverage to stand despite the ankle restraints. This time, when she spat, she heard him grunt and swear.

"Better," Sprague said. "Direct hit. If you're lucky, I'll let you lick it off."

"I'll never be that lucky."

He grabbed her hair and dragged her across the floor. She bit down on the scream building in her throat. She wouldn't give him that satisfaction.

He threw her onto something soft. A mattress. Springs creaked. She bounced forward and hit her head on a wall.

"Oops." His laugh was wrong, broken. "You look like the type who likes it rough."

A bed. He'd thrown her on a bed. Her breathing quickened despite her efforts to control it.

"Stay still," he said, "or you'll end up like your boyfriend."

Cold metal pressed against her throat. A knife blade. The blindfold fell away.

Overhead lights pierced her retinas. When her vision cleared, Sprague stood there grinning. He folded the knife, shoved it into his pocket, then leaned in and kissed her mouth. She tried to turn away, but he held her face.

"Miss me?"

She stayed silent, conserving her energy. He held a Glock in his right hand. The same one he had used on Joel.

"Now you can see everything," he said, "everything I'm going to do to you. The pleasure and the pain."

"The only pleasure I'll get is watching you die."

"Sorry, Dollface. I'm not going anywhere."

Lowri scanned the room. Narrow bunk beds, cherry wood paneling, nautical decorations. A boat's master cabin. Sprague's boat. The Suwanee 47 he never shut up about at the station. She recognized the zebrawood nightstand he had described and the cherry panels he claimed had cost him a fortune to restore. The master stateroom where he had promised to "show her a good time" more than once.

"Why did you kill Joel?"

"Joel was worried about you. Thought you were in over your head. Wanted to talk to the veteran detective in that old photo." Sprague pulled a chair from the corner, turned it backward, and straddled it. "Called me yesterday morning. Said you'd been acting paranoid. Obsessed with some conspiracy above your pay grade. Asked if I could meet him."

Joel had died trying to protect her.

"Poor bastard let me right in. Even offered me coffee before I cut his throat. Kept asking what kind of trouble you'd gotten yourself into." Sprague's expression didn't change. "Then I waited. Knew you'd come running when he didn't show up for work."

Joel. Bleeding out on his kitchen floor while this man sat in the next room.

"I saw his evaluations. Poor judgment was a recurring theme."

"Why kill him if he thought I was crazy?"

"The photograph, obviously. But he didn't know where you'd hidden it. No matter how many cuts I made."

"You'd have killed him anyway."

"Probably right."

"Just like you killed everyone else: Farnsworth and the Cloughs."

"Farnsworth was weak. The Cloughs were idiots."

"Was Todd Byers weak?"

No surprise in his eyes. "You've been busy. I'm impressed."

"You're insane."

"Technically accurate. Cluster B personality disorder with narcissistic features, if we're being precise." He waved the gun casually. "That opens up interesting legal defenses: diminished capacity, irresistible impulse, the Brawner rule. Five years in a hospital, then back on the streets."

She recognized the terminology. Sprague wasn't just a killer; he was a malignant narcissist who'd studied his own pathology. The worst kind.

"Who hired you?" she asked.

"You have no idea what I'm capable of."

"Someone's paying you. Who?"

"Nice try, Dollface. Delay tactics won't work. We had the same interrogation training, remember? I just scored higher."

Keep him talking. Narcissists loved to hear themselves talk.

"You always wanted to show me your boat," she said, "just not like this."

"Oh, you're going to see everything. Right after you tell me what I need to know."

"Henry Gilmore, the aide from Indiana—"

"Not mine. That was an actual accident."

He turned to the nightstand, set his gun on top, and pulled something from the drawer: a black baton with copper terminals connected by wire to a control box.

"*Picana eléctrica*," he said, admiring it. "High voltage, low current. Allows for extended sessions without premature death."

Her mouth went dry.

"Fourteen thousand volts at minimal amperage. Less than a Taser, but precisely controllable. Dan Mitrione's favorite tool when he taught interrogation techniques in South America: 'Precise pain in precise places for precise effects.'"

He was enjoying this, building the anticipation.

"Picked this up in Uruguay years ago," he continued. "Former military intelligence contacts. This particular unit has quite a history from the Alvarez regime. The previous owner used it on political prisoners. Students mostly. Kids who thought they could change the world."

He moved closer, running his finger along the baton. "The beauty is in what I can control. I can make you feel pain you didn't know existed, in places you didn't know could hurt. But you won't die. Not for hours. Maybe days if I'm careful."

"I'm not telling you anything."

"Everyone says that at first."

"Is this what you used on Farnsworth? On the others?"

Sprague laughed. "No, Dollface. This is special. Just for you. I've been saving it for someone who really deserved the full experience. Farnsworth went quickly. Just the sound of the electrodes, and he pissed all over himself. Started singing like a songbird. He didn't suffer like you're going to suffer."

"Why? What makes me so special?"

"You couldn't leave things alone. Had to keep digging and asking questions. That photograph. The Desert Storm photo. You have no idea what you've stumbled into."

Sprague checked his watch. "Your FBI friend should be in custody by now. The Park Police probably aren't being gentle with him either. Cop killers don't get professional courtesy."

She tested the restraints again; the zip ties were cutting off circulation to her hands.

"We're anchored in a cove near Mount Vernon," Sprague said, noticing her struggle. "A private spot I've used before. No marinas nearby, no river traffic. By the time anyone thinks to check here, we'll be long gone. Maybe take a cruise down to the Carolinas. I hear

Beaufort is nice this time of year. You always wanted to travel, didn't you?"

"I'm not telling you anything," she repeated.

"You don't understand. With this, I can target specific nerve clusters. Destroy your ability to have children. Eliminate your senses one by one. You'll talk."

"Go to hell."

He twisted the rheostat dial. Blue electricity arced between the terminals with a high-pitched whine.

"Usually, you'd get rubber to bite on," he said. "Prevents tongue severance. But I seem to be fresh out."

He climbed onto the bed and brought the baton close to her face. She could feel the electricity in the air, making her skin prickle. She pressed back against the wall, but there was nowhere to go.

She spat in his face again. "You're not man enough."

He laughed and proved her wrong.

Chapter 39

"You may be FBI, but you've got a lot of explaining to do, Agent Saville."

The voice came from the front passenger seat. Captain Rufus Morrow, Central District Commander, U. S. Park Police. He had introduced himself after they'd marched Saville back to the cruiser. Polite and professional, but with the edge of a commander who'd lost two officers that morning.

The primary officer, Simpson, sat behind the wheel, watching Saville in the rearview mirror. The secondary officer stood guard outside.

They'd already confiscated Saville's burner phone and credentials and confirmed he was legitimate FBI. That wasn't the issue.

"I didn't make that call," Saville said. "I wasn't at Graves's apartment. I didn't cancel the 10-33."

"We know." Morrow turned slightly. "You were interviewing Kenneth Burton at the Ritz-Carlton, then rented the Hyundai from Budget on Wisconsin. But dispatch logged a call from Lowri's work phone to her home at 0832. Why would she call herself?"

"She called me. I stayed at her apartment last night while she worked." Saville knew how it sounded. "She wanted to know if she'd gotten any messages."

"What messages?"

"She didn't specify."

"How do you know Sergeant Pritchard?"

Time for the truth. The covert investigation was over. This was about finding Lowri alive.

Saville laid it out: their unofficial partnership, the Farnsworth investigation, and the connections to Clough, while keeping Mond and Romano out of it.

Morrow nodded slowly. "Sounds like Lowri. I told her to leave Farnsworth alone."

"She suspected Detective Sprague was dirty."

"Peter Sprague is one of our most decorated detectives." Morrow's tone hardened. "He and Lowri had issues, but that's a serious accusation."

"Could Sprague have made the call? Voice masking software?"

"We're checking." Morrow turned to Simpson. "Call dispatch. I want Sprague located immediately. If he doesn't answer, send units to his residence."

Simpson made the call while Saville felt the first flicker of hope. They were listening.

"Why Sprague?" Morrow asked. "What was Lowri's evidence?"

"His investigation of Farnsworth was compromised. And she had a photograph. Farnsworth and Sprague together during Desert Storm."

"Where's this photo?"

"Lowri took it with her last night. There was a third person in the image, but the face was torn away."

Morrow sighed. "Does the Bureau know you're here?"

"They think I'm on leave."

"Your supervisor?"

"Jack Mayfield. RAC in Greenville." Saville gave him the number.

Morrow was reaching for his phone when the black Nissan Armada came bouncing down the maintenance road.

"What the hell?" Simpson said.

"Wrong turn. Get rid of them."

Simpson got out and motioned to the secondary officer. They approached the Armada, which was slowing to a stop.

"Turn around," Simpson called, pointing to his badge. "Go back the way you came."

Both front doors of the Armada burst open. Two figures in tactical gear and balaclavas emerged, FN P90 submachine guns already raised. A third exited from the rear.

"On the ground!"

Simpson's hand moved toward his weapon, then stopped. He and the secondary officer dropped to their knees.

The third operator moved to Morrow's window, weapon aimed. "Don't move. Hands on the dash."

The voice. Saville recognized it.

"Cuffs," the operator called.

Two of them hauled Saville from the cruiser. Pain shot through his shoulders as they pulled him out and dropped him onto the gravel. He looked up to see the familiar-voiced operator draw an unusual pistol from his vest.

Two shots into Morrow's chest. Four more shots outside. Simpson and the secondary officer collapsed forward.

"Jesus Christ!"

They dragged Saville to the Armada and threw him in the back. One operator climbed in beside him. The others took the front.

"Go! Go! Go!" the familiar voice shouted from the passenger seat.

The Armada accelerated onto Rock Creek Parkway, then onto surface streets Saville didn't recognize. Ten minutes of hard driving, doubling back twice, before heading north. The operators stayed silent, weapons ready. Saville kept his head down, trying to process what he'd witnessed. Three cops down. Mond had executed them point-blank.

They made a hard left. Saville slid across the seat, his head hitting the window. He found the door handle with his cuffed hands and tried to work it.

The operator beside him noticed, punched him in the face, and yanked him back to center.

Twenty minutes after leaving the woods, the Armada pulled into an alley in Columbia Heights. Saville recognized the neighborhood despite his disorientation.

Then he saw it. The Israeli safe house.

The front passenger removed his balaclava. Hillel Mond.

"Get him loose," Mond said, wincing and touching his shoulder.

The rear operator produced a long-handled universal cuff key from his vest.

"You murdered those cops!" Saville said.

"Hurry." Mond avoided his eyes.

They pinned Saville against the Armada's hood. The operator yanked his wrists upward. Saville clenched his jaw, expecting a bullet to the back of the head.

Metal clicked against metal. Twice.

The cuffs fell away.

Saville rubbed his numb wrists, confused. Running wasn't an option. Not with three operators and nowhere to go.

"The helicopter is waiting," Mond said.

"What helicopter?"

"Ditch the Armada," Mond instructed one operator. "Take the Suburban."

"I'm not going anywhere until you explain why you just executed three cops."

"They're fine." Mond revealed the weapon he'd used earlier. "Tranquilizer gun. Concentrated ketamine blend. They'll wake up in two hours with headaches."

Saville stared at him. Tranq guns were real but rare outside wildlife management. Could Mond be telling the truth?

Mond reached into his vest again, pulling out Saville's Glock and his phone from their earlier visit.

"The policewoman. We know where she is. We thought you'd want to come when we retrieve her."

Saville took his weapons, his mind racing. Mond had just assaulted federal officers to free him. The Israelis were committing acts of war on U.S. soil.

But they knew where Lowri was.

"Where?" Saville asked.

"On a boat. Detective Sprague has her."

So it was Sprague. Saville had suspected it, but hearing it confirmed made his blood run cold. Lowri was alone with a psychopath.

"How do you know this?"

"We've been monitoring since Romano's death, tracking everyone connected to SAINTS." Mond opened the passenger door. "Sprague's been careful, but not careful enough. We intercepted his boat's GPS beacon."

The Suburban's engine was already running. Saville had seconds to decide: go with the Israelis who'd just committed multiple felonies, or lose his only lead to Lowri.

"If those cops die—"

"They won't. You have my word."

Mond's word. The same man who'd saved his life when Bashevis tried to garrote him. The man who'd just risked everything to free him.

Saville climbed into the Suburban. The operators took positions around him, weapons ready but not threatening. They were treating him as an asset now, not a prisoner.

"Let's go," Saville said.

The Suburban accelerated through empty streets, heading south. Every minute meant more time for Sprague to work on Lowri.

Saville knew what interrogation looked like when someone enjoyed it.

"The woman was getting close," Mond said. "That photograph she found means something. That's why Sprague took her."

"Where is Sprague's boat?"

"He's anchored near Mount Vernon," Mond said. "In a cove about two miles south of the estate. No marina access. No witnesses."

"Perfect isolation."

"Perfect for us too. No civilians to worry about."

They turned onto a service road. Through the windshield, Saville could see chain-link fencing ahead. A private airfield.

"Sprague won't expect an air assault," Mond said. "Police think tactically, not strategically. He'll be watching the water approaches, maybe the access roads, but not the sky."

The Suburban slowed as they approached a security gate. One of the operators produced credentials. The guard waved them through without inspection. Saville wondered what kind of reach the Israelis had.

"There." Mond pointed to a hangar. "Five minutes to wheels up."

Saville checked his Glock again: seventeen rounds in the magazine, one in the chamber. Against a desperate cop with a hostage on a boat designed for concealment.

"Does Sprague know we're coming?" Saville asked.

"Not yet. But he will soon. These things get noisy."

They pulled up beside the hangar. Through the open doors, Saville could see movement inside. Equipment being loaded, weapons checked.

"Remember," Mond said as they exited the vehicle. "Sprague needs her alive. Whatever he wants from her, he hasn't gotten it yet."

"And if he has?"

Mond didn't answer. He didn't need to.

They walked toward the hangar, the sound of turbines growing louder. As they entered, Saville saw the assault team making final preparations: black tactical gear, communications equipment, medical supplies. Professional soldiers preparing for war.

A figure emerged from behind the aircraft, checking a tablet. The woman looked up, saw Saville, and stopped dead.

Major Ilana Zahavy.

The same woman who'd argued for Saville's execution at the safe house. Who'd called him a liability that needed to be eliminated. She'd only been overruled by Mond's intervention.

Zahavy's expression was unreadable behind her tactical sunglasses. She handed the tablet to another operator and walked toward them.

"Agent Saville." Her voice was neutral and professional. "I understand you'll be joining us."

Saville looked at Mond, then back at Zahavy. "Last time we met, you wanted me dead."

"Last time we met, you were a liability." Zahavy removed her sunglasses. Her eyes were cold. "Now you're an asset. The policewoman is being held by the same people who killed our targets. Our interests align."

"That's it? That's all the explanation I get?"

"That's all the explanation you need." Zahavy turned to Mond. "Five minutes to departure. The boat hasn't moved from its anchor point. No activity visible on thermal imaging for the past hour."

Mond nodded. Zahavy walked back toward the aircraft without another glance at Saville.

"She still wants me dead?" Saville asked.

"Probably," Mond said. "But not until after we get your friend back." He smiled. "A joke, Agent Saville. The major will follow orders."

They were coming for Lowri. But Saville would watch his back the entire way.

Chapter 40

He touched the picana to her lips.

Current coursed through her nervous system. She stiffened, her entire body locking up. Her tongue went rigid against her teeth. The taste of copper filled her mouth. Blood. She'd bitten through tissue.

"Where's the photograph?" Sprague pulled the device back.

She tried to speak. Nothing. Her mouth wouldn't obey. Neurons misfiring, synapses scrambled from the voltage.

He lowered the baton toward her torso, letting it hover. "You know what electrical burns do to nerve endings? Permanent damage. Depending on where I apply this, you'll never feel anything there again."

Her vision blurred. She could process his words and understand the threat, but her body had disconnected from conscious control. The electricity had disrupted the signals between her brain and muscles.

He slapped her. The sharp pain cut through the fog. "The photograph. Where?"

She managed to turn her head. Tried to form words. Only produced a low sound.

"Not good enough." He pressed the picana against her mouth again. Held it.

Her body convulsed. Bile rose in her throat. When he pulled the device away, she vomited, aspirating some of it. Choking.

"Pathetic." Sprague stepped back, disgusted.

She rolled sideways, trying to clear her airway. Fell off the narrow bunk. Her head struck the deck. The impact sent white light through her vision.

Then darkness closed in from the edges.

The last thing she heard was Sprague's voice, distant now: "We're not done, Dollface. Not even close."

***

The pain receded into something else. Memory.

She was seventeen again, standing outside Ballou High with Megan and Crystal. The April sun felt warm on her face. Megan had a bottle of vodka in her backpack, stolen from her mother's liquor cabinet. They were supposed to go to Crystal's house. Her parents worked until six.

"Come on, Lowri," Megan said. "Just for an hour."

She checked her phone. Three-thirty. She needed to be at the store by four. Her father would be waiting. He'd been talking about the eisteddfod all week, practicing his Welsh pronunciation while restocking shelves. The St. David's Welsh-American Society of Washington, D.C. was hosting it tonight. Seven o'clock start. He'd bought his ticket weeks ago.

"My dad needs me at the store. He's going to that Welsh thing."

"He can miss it for once," Crystal said. "When's the last time you did anything fun?"

"I can't. I'm supposed to cover for him."

"So he'll go late. Big deal."

The vodka tasted like rubbing alcohol. She should have known better. Should have remembered what alcohol did. Her mother had died when she was three. Cirrhosis. Her father never said the word alcoholic, but she'd figured it out eventually. The lack of pictures from her mother's last years. The way relatives went quiet when her name came up. The absence of wine at dinner, beer in the refrigerator. Her father had built a sober house for his daughter, a safe space free from the thing that had killed his wife.

And here she was, seventeen and drunk on stolen vodka.

By four-fifteen she'd stopped checking her phone. By five, she couldn't stand without swaying.

Something about a photograph. Crystal was showing them pictures on her phone. Or was that Sprague? The memories tangled, present bleeding into past.

No. There had been a photograph that day too. Her father had shown it to her that morning. Something he'd found while cleaning out the storage room. Her mother from the early days, before the drinking got bad. Standing in front of the store's grand opening banner.

"This was a good day," he'd said. "One of the last good days."

She'd barely looked at it. Late for school. Always late for something. She didn't remember much about her mother anyway. Just fragments. The smell of something sweet on her breath. Stumbling in the hallway. Her father carrying her to bed again.

The memory shifted. Fragmented.

Blue lights in Crystal's driveway. Two officers at the door. The taller one had kind eyes. He asked if she was Lowri Pritchard.

"There's been an incident at your father's store."

The words didn't make sense. Not at first. Then the floor tilted. Crystal's mother was home somehow, holding her shoulders, saying something about the hospital. But the officer was shaking his head.

"I'm sorry. He didn't make it."

The convenience store felt wrong with yellow tape across the door. Although someone had cleaned the blood from the linoleum, she could still picture where it had been, behind the counter near the cigarette display. The security footage captured everything: two men with guns, her father reaching under the register. The assailants assumed he was going for a weapon.

Three shots. Center mass.

One hundred seventy-two dollars. That was what they took, the detective told her at the station after they processed her for underage drinking. Her father had died for one hundred seventy-two dollars. The cost of a decent pair of shoes, a week's worth of groceries. Nothing.

The suspects were never caught. The surveillance footage showed only baseball caps and sunglasses. They could have been anyone. They were anyone. They were still out there somewhere, living their lives, unaware or uncaring that they had killed a widowed father for the contents of a Friday afternoon till.

Her father had been alone since three-thirty, waiting for her. He must have checked his watch, seeing the clock tick past four, four-thirty, then five. The eisteddfod was set to start at seven. He had already missed the opening reception at six.

The customer who found him at six-fifteen said he had still been breathing, trying to say something. A word the man couldn't understand.

She knew what it was. The same thing he had said every night when he tucked her in, even when she was too old for it: *Cariad.* Welsh for darling. Love.

Sprague's voice cut through the memory: "Where's the photograph?"

Different photograph. Different time. But her scrambled thoughts couldn't separate them. The image Sprague wanted, something that could destroy him, merged with the memory of her father reaching under that register into one impossible thing.

"I don't know," she heard herself say. Or had said. Or was saying. Time had collapsed.

The ticket was still in his shirt pocket when they found him: Seat G-14, Washington Chapter, Annual Eisteddfod. He had circled the poetry reading on the program. It was the first eisteddfod he had planned to attend since her mother died. Fifteen years of putting his life on hold, raising a daughter alone, never touching a drop of alcohol, never bringing anyone home. Fifteen years of being both parents, filling the void her mother's addiction had carved into their lives.

The memorial service was small. The Society sent flowers with a card in Welsh that she couldn't read. Someone spoke about how much her father had looked forward to finally joining them, how he talked about her, how proud he was.

She sat in the front row, reeking of alcohol, the drunk daughter of an alcoholic mother and a murdered father. The irony cut deeper than grief. He had spent fourteen years keeping her from her mother's fate, and she celebrated by getting wasted while he bled out for one hundred seventy-two dollars.

The dream shifted. She was in an evidence locker. No, Sprague's yacht. No, her father's store. Photographs everywhere. Her mother, glass in hand, eyes unfocused. Her father, young and hopeful, before he understood what he had married. Crime scene photos. The empty register. The bloodstains.

A picture hidden behind another picture in a frame on the coffee table.

"The photograph," Sprague said again. "You know where it is."

Desert Storm. Kuwait. Not the store. She tried to hold onto that distinction, but it slipped away. Everything was slipping. Her father had protected her from one poison only to die while she embraced it. One hundred seventy-two dollars. The perpetrators who took it were still free. Still breathing. Still living the lives they had stolen from him.

She opened her eyes. The ceiling swam above her. Real or dream, she couldn't tell anymore. Sprague leaned over her, but his face kept shifting. The gunman they never caught, her father, her mother with a wine bottle, the detective who had told her.

"I was supposed to be there," she said. To Sprague. To her father. To Joel. To the ghost of her mother who had drunk herself to death when Lowri was too young to understand. "I was supposed to be there."

He had given her everything: every sober morning, every sacrificed opportunity, every moment he could have moved on and started over but didn't because she needed stability. And she repaid him with absence, with vodka on her breath while he died for pocket change.

The darkness pulled at her again. She saw him clearly now, not in the crime scene photos, but as he looked that last morning. Gray at the temples, tired around the eyes. Still making her breakfast even though she was seventeen. Still checking that she had lunch money. Still calling her *cariad*.

"Dad," she whispered, or thought she did. Her lips might not have moved. "Dad, I'm sorry. I'm so sorry."

But sorry was just a word. Five letters that couldn't bring him back, couldn't put her in that store at four o'clock, couldn't stop two men from taking his life for one hundred seventy-two dollars.

In the void, she heard his voice one last time, speaking Welsh she had never bothered to learn. Words he had spoken every morning, staying strong, staying sober, staying present for a daughter who would fail him when it mattered most.

The weight that never lifts. The weight that defines you. The weight of being sorry, always and forever, with no one left to forgive you.

***

Mond finished explaining the plan and raised his voice above the turbine whine of the MD 530's engine. "I can't help you. My government can't be directly involved. You understand?"

Saville understood perfectly. They were already involved, just not in any way that could be traced back to them. The Armada was untraceable by now, probably already stripped down and scattered across three countries. Mond and his operators had no official existence, which left him as the only witness who could place them at the scene. Either he would have to lie when this was over, or they would eliminate him the moment the operation concluded.

But then why rescue Lowri at all? Why go to such lengths to save her if they planned to kill him afterward?

The logic didn't track. Not yet.

Saville studied the helicopter's interior. The Little Bird had been configured for special operations with weapons pylons, a FLIR turret, and fast-rope bars. But someone had stripped it down and repainted it in civilian markings. Yet it was still loud. The twin-bladed rotor system wasn't designed for quiet infiltration. Their approach would be anything but covert.

That wasn't his only concern. His tactical training was dated, and he couldn't remember the last time he executed a dynamic entry or cleared a room under fire. This was work for HRT or Delta. But they couldn't be tasked. Not for this.

Mond sat beside him on the rear bench. Zahavy occupied the left seat up front, next to the pilot. Both were trained for exactly this type of direct action.

The original plan had called for Zahavy to lead the assault with him as number two. He had vetoed it. He wasn't exposing his back to an unknown operator, regardless of Mond's assurances about the major's professionalism.

"Your probability of success increases exponentially if Major Zahavy takes point," Mond said. "She's Sayeret Matkal trained."

"I'll pass." Saville press-checked his Glock and adjusted the retention on his drop-leg holster.

"*Tipesh*," Mond muttered. It didn't sound like a compliment.

"You're compromising the mission," Mond continued. "We'll maintain overwatch from the high ground. Major Zahavy qualified expert marksman at your Marine Corps Scout Sniper School. Distinguished graduate."

"I'll manage."

"I insist." Mond peeled two IR reflective squares from their backing and slapped them across Saville's plate carrier, then reached around and affixed two more between his shoulder blades.

"What's this?"

"IFF markers," Mond said. "So the major doesn't put a round through you by mistake."

Chapter 41

Maritime assault operations were typically conducted in darkness. There was no concealment on open water, no dead ground to exploit. It was now 1600 hours. The sun hung mercilessly in the southwestern sky, the temperature eighty-seven degrees, the heat index approaching triple digits; a standard August afternoon in the Potomac basin.

Sunset: 1957 hours. Nearly four hours away.

Lowri didn't have four hours.

The tactical disadvantages compounded with each passing second. Saville's fast-rope currency had expired years ago. The Little Bird's rotor signature would telegraph their approach from half a mile out. The gusty Potomac thermals would destabilize any hover. Factor in the possibility of blue-on-blue fire, whether negligent or deliberate, and the probability of mission success hovered somewhere between marginal and nonexistent.

But mathematics had ceased to matter. He owed Lowri more than calculations.

Saville studied the Suwannee 47's deck plan one final time. Generic schematics pulled from the manufacturer's website, worthless for identifying custom modifications or defensive preparations.

He was entering a fatal funnel with no tactical intelligence. But imperfect data beat blindness.

"This woman, this Sergeant Pritchard," Mond said. "She means something to you?"

Saville nodded. He was an only child. Lowri had become the sister he'd never had.

"Ready?"

Saville raised his thumb.

The helicopter approached from the southwest at a forty-five-degree angle, with the sun behind them at six o'clock. If Sprague emerged topside, he would be staring directly into the glare, risking temporary blindness. Perhaps three seconds for Zahavy to acquire and engage him. But Sprague was too experienced to make that mistake. More likely, he would use Lowri as a human shield or, worse, he might have already executed her and was waiting in ambush below.

As they descended to fifty feet above ground level, the pilot halted their forward momentum and transitioned to a hover. Through the hellhole, the yacht's aft deck appeared impossibly small, a postage stamp surrounded by water.

Mond verified the FRIES attachment and deployed the fast rope.

Saville didn't wait for clearance. He locked his gloved hands around the rope, positioned his boots in the doorway, and committed.

Fast-roping was controlled falling. No mechanical descender, no safety backup, just grip strength and friction. This technique required constant practice to maintain proficiency, a practice Saville hadn't had in three years.

The friction heat hit him immediately. Even through the Nomex gloves, his palms felt like they were gripping molten steel. Then came the rotor wash, hammering him into an uncontrolled pendulum motion. He attempted a leg lock to brake his descent.

But the lock failed. Twenty feet from impact, his grip gave out.

He hit the fiberglass deck hard, driving the air from his lungs. Momentum carried him into a tactical roll that ended against the stern rail, bruising his ribs.

Recovering to a kneeling position, he indexed his Glock and scanned for threats. The flybridge was empty, and the main deck was clear. The Little Bird had already moved southeast, the rotor noise fading but still audible.

Sprague should have responded by now. He should have investigated the noise, taken a defensive position. Something.

Unless he wasn't there. Or worse, unless Lowri was already dead.

Saville entered through the salon doors and cleared the galley, systematically working through the dining area and helm station. He employed textbook room-clearing techniques, modified for single-operator limitations. Every corner represented a potential fatal funnel. Sprague was Special Forces trained, an expert in unconventional warfare. He'd know exactly where to position himself for maximum advantage.

The forward stateroom was empty. Saville controlled his breathing as he approached the master cabin. Sprague would aim for a head shot to neutralize the ballistic vest and exploit the ten-ring. Two rounds, rapid fire, standard failure drill.

He was calculating angles of attack when the first round punched through the bulkhead six inches from his head, showering him with teak splinters. The second round followed a heartbeat later, destroying the veneer and revealing raw fiberglass beneath.

Saville dropped prone and identified the source. Through the doorway, he saw two figures in the master stateroom: Lowri, her face swollen beyond recognition, blood streaming from her nose, and Sprague behind her, his forearm locked across her carotid in a standing rear naked choke, a Browning Hi-Power in his right hand.

Saville low-crawled to the doorframe, using the bulkhead for cover.

"Agent Saville!" Sprague's voice carried a manic edge that made Saville's skin crawl. "Come out, come out wherever you are!"

Silence.

"Getting shy on me now?" The same unhinged singsong. "Don't make me provide additional motivation."

That's exactly what Saville wanted. He needed to draw Sprague out, create separation from Lowri. He press-checked his Glock. Seventeen rounds plus one, more than sufficient.

"Release her, Sprague. You're surrounded."

"One helicopter hardly constitutes a perimeter. The Israelis, obviously. You couldn't involve the Bureau, and Metro would come in heavy. How am I doing?"

Saville ground his teeth.

"MD 530 from the rotor signature," Sprague continued. "Single sniper platform. Not Mond since I turned his shoulder into ground beef. Should have finished the job. How's Colonel Romano, by the way? I heard he didn't make it."

Saville forced his breathing to remain steady. Sprague was baiting him, trying to trigger an emotional response.

"They'll vector in additional assets," Saville said, though the words rang hollow.

"Then we'd better resolve this quickly. Drop your weapon, or I'll demonstrate what a picana does to human tissue. Again."

Saville risked a quick look. Lowri was semiconscious, petechial hemorrhaging in both eyes, electrical burns visible on her neck and arms. On the nightstand was a picana with exposed copper electrodes, the control box showing wear from repeated use.

"I'm waiting." Sprague's tone had gone flat, clinical.

Saville edged closer and reassessed. Sprague had the Hi-Power pressed against Lowri's temporal lobe. Behind them, that obscene device waited like a coiled snake.

"Time's expired."

Sprague shifted his aim to Lowri's right shoulder and fired. The report was deafening in the confined space. The round tore through her deltoid and trapezius, blowing out a fist-sized exit wound. Blood splattered the bulkhead as Lowri's scream filled the cabin.

"Bastard!" Saville shouted.

The recoil and Lowri's collapse created separation. Sprague's eyes tracked downward, following her fall.

Saville rolled into the doorway, extending into a prone shooting position. Two shots, controlled pairs. The first round caught Sprague's radius and ulna just below the elbow, shattering both bones. The second punched through his left flank, destroying the kidney.

Sprague dropped hard, his skull bouncing off the nightstand with a wet crack. The Browning skittered across the deck.

Saville maintained his sight picture, advancing in a combat crouch. Lowri was moving, pressing her palm against the hemorrhaging wound. Sprague appeared unconscious, but Saville had seen too many supposedly dead men resurrect themselves.

He counted to three Mississippi and started forward.

Sprague's hand twitched, then his whole arm moved, reaching for the Browning.

Twenty feet. No time for hand-to-hand. Saville tracked with the Glock, front sight centered on Sprague's occipital bone.

Suddenly, Lowri lurched upward on one knee, directly in the line of fire. Saville's finger was already moving. He jerked the muzzle up, sending the round into the overhead fixture. Glass rained down like shrapnel.

Sprague's fingers found the Browning. He pivoted, dragging the heavy pistol across the deck, his shattered forearm buckling under the weight.

"You bastard!"

The words choked off as Lowri grabbed the picana and rammed it between his teeth.

She triggered the device.

Twenty thousand volts at minimal amperage coursed through Sprague's oral cavity. His mandible locked in a tetanic contraction, teeth clamping down on the copper electrodes. The picana was designed for torture, not execution. It delivered agony without immediate death.

Sprague's body went rigid. His eyes bulged with full consciousness, experiencing every second. Lowri, operating on pure adrenaline despite her injuries, held the trigger down.

The smell hit immediately, burning tissue mixed with ozone. Sprague's lips split and blackened at the contact points. The mucous membranes where the electrodes touched began to carbonize. Saville could hear the sizzling, like meat on a griddle. The prolonged contact was turning a torture device into an execution tool.

Sprague's eyes rolled back, burst capillaries painting the sclera red. Pink foam bubbled from his nose as his lung tissue began to fail. The electrical current was destroying the tissue at the contact points, creating deep burns that penetrated through his soft palate.

After ninety seconds, Sprague's respiratory center failed. His body continued to twitch from the electrical stimulation even as his brain began to die from hypoxia. The flesh around the electrode contact points had turned black and necrotic, peeling away to reveal charred muscle tissue beneath.

Finally, his heart went into ventricular fibrillation and stopped.

Lowri didn't stop until Saville gently placed his hand on her wrist and eased the device away. By then, Sprague's mouth was a blackened ruin where the electrodes had maintained contact, the surrounding tissue blistered and weeping.

Given what Sprague had done to her with that same device, Saville felt no compulsion to intervene sooner. Some deaths were earned.

Chapter 42

Lowri spent four days in the ICU and another week on the medical ward. The surgeons debrided necrotic tissue from her shoulder twice before declaring the wound clean enough to heal. Physical therapy began on day three, though she could barely lift her arm six inches without morphine. The electrical burns required daily dressing changes. The nurse explained that picana wounds often developed secondary infections because of the depth of tissue damage. Lowri never complained, but Saville noticed her swallow hard when they peeled away the gauze.

Saville visited every day except one. The day FBI Director Walter Shaffer summoned him to the Hoover Building's seventh floor.

The debriefing lasted nine hours. Shaffer had assembled a panel: OPR, Criminal Division, and even someone from the Inspector General's office taking notes on a yellow legal pad. Saville provided a carefully edited version of events that acknowledged five dead bodies while omitting any mention of Israelis, safe houses, or Little Birds. He claimed memory gaps from head trauma. Shaffer wasn't buying it, but Saville's story never wavered. Not through the polygraph, not through the voice stress analysis, not through the seventh retelling.

"You expect us to believe you tracked down a trained sniper all by yourself?" Shaffer asked during the sixth hour of questioning.

"I got lucky."

"Lucky," Shaffer replied, his tone clearly skeptical.

They presented him with satellite imagery of the Potomac, time-stamped from the day of Sprague's death. The resolution was insufficient to identify the helicopter. Saville studied the photos, confused, and suggested it might have been a news chopper. The IG representative made another note.

Shaffer placed him on unpaid administrative leave pending further investigation, confiscating his Glock, credentials, and Bureau phone. This was standard protocol for an agent-involved shooting, though everyone knew this situation was beyond the usual. A GS-5 from Personnel handed him a replacement device "in case we need to reach you." The message was clear: You're not fired yet, but don't leave town.

Saville assumed termination papers were being drafted when the media cycle intervened. Fox News ran extensive coverage, labeling him and Lowri "the heroes who saved taxpayers the cost of a show trial." MSNBC condemned their "vigilante justice" but acknowledged that Sprague's death simplified matters for the administration. The *Washington Post* editorial board managed to both criticize and praise them in the same column. CNN brought in a forensic psychiatrist to analyze whether Sprague's use of a picana indicated South American training, missing the truth by several continents.

Attorney General Judith Ramsey understood the optics. Firing the agents who had stopped a serial killer would not play well in swing districts with midterms approaching. She reversed Shaffer's suspension, authorizing full pay and benefits during the administrative review. Beltway gossips claimed the Oval Office had weighed in; specifically, Chief of Staff Bradley Morrison allegedly made three calls to Justice in one afternoon. Saville didn't care who made the call; he still had a paycheck.

The political machinery churned predictably. Republicans demanded a special counsel to investigate any White House connection to Farnsworth's death. Senator James Whitfield of Texas gave a floor speech invoking Watergate twice and Whitewater three times. Democrats were relieved that the nightmare was over. Both parties' leadership quietly agreed that a prolonged investigation served nobody's interests. Republicans would get their talking points for the midterms without the messiness of actual hearings, while Democrats could claim the system worked. Everyone won except the truth.

Hillel Mond's name never surfaced, nor did Major Zahavy's. Saville told investigators he had been grabbed by masked men and held at an unknown location. His escape remained conveniently vague on details. The boat insertion? He had paid cash to a recreational sailor whose name he never got. The Bureau had three agents checking every marina from Baltimore to Norfolk. They would find nothing because there was nothing to find. The Bureau was still chasing that ghost.

Jack Mayfield hadn't been as fortunate. OPR gave him two choices: early retirement with a partial pension or termination with cause. He took the deal and disappeared within forty-eight hours, his desk cleaned out after hours when no one would see him go. Rosena Wyatt wouldn't forward Saville's calls. She'd answer the phone, recognize his voice, and suddenly remember an urgent meeting. Mayfield's home phone rang unanswered. Saville tried his cell six times, leaving increasingly apologetic messages that went unreturned. He even called the Greenville field office's main line, pretending to be a reporter, but the receptionist saw through it immediately. Saville added this to his growing list of debts that couldn't be repaid.

The media circus performed its usual three-ring act. The *National Enquirer* ran a special edition dubbing the White House "Camelot meets *Peyton Place*." They somehow obtained a photo of Molly Farnsworth leaving a Georgetown restaurant six months ago, possibly with the President, though the image was too grainy for certainty. Amelia Sylvester worked eighteen-hour days in the Press Office, issuing denials that nobody believed. Her staff leaked to *Politico* that she had kept a bottle of Mylanta in her desk drawer. The First Lady gave exactly one interview denying any relationship with Farnsworth while conspicuously avoiding questions about her husband and Molly.

Cecelia Leehan wrote three columns for the *Post* suggesting Hellen Carney should become the first sitting First Lady to file for divorce. She floated trial balloons about a Senate run from Hellen's home state of North Carolina. The columns read like job applications for a future campaign. Leehan appeared on *Meet the Press* to discuss "the evolving role of First Ladies in modern politics," which everyone understood was code for measuring curtains in a Senate office.

Molly Farnsworth emerged from seclusion to thank law enforcement through her attorney. She scheduled a brief press conference for 3 p.m., to be handled through the White House Press Office, followed by an interview with the *Post's* Style section. The next day, she'd begin the morning television circuit. Her literary agent had reportedly negotiated a seven-figure book deal with Random House, though the announcement would wait three months out of respect for the dead.

Cynthia Clough played her part with similar calculation. She visited Lowri's hospital room with a photographer from the Examiner, delivered a prepared statement about justice being served, then departed for what her publicist called "a period of private mourning" in Saint Barts. The publicist accidentally copied a reporter on an email discussing appearance fees for future interviews.

Ken Burton's name surfaced briefly in connection with defense contracts influenced by Farnsworth. Symmetric Technical Solutions paid a half-million-dollar fine for procurement violations. Burton and Marshall Kelsey promptly sued DHS for a hundred million, claiming defamation and intellectual property theft. They settled for twenty-five million within six months. In Washington, even the penalties turned profits. Burton was already using the controversy to market Symmetric's services to foreign governments less concerned with procurement regulations.

The press speculated about an unidentified dinner companion who had met with Farnsworth and Davy Clough in North Carolina three weeks before the murders. Witnesses described a Mediterranean-looking man who paid cash and spoke accented English. One waitress recalled he ordered his steak well done and hadn't touched the wine. The FBI's Behavioral Analysis Unit classified it as a dead lead, but Saville knew better. Mond had been typically thorough in establishing his cover.

Park Police Chief Dewayne Pennington scheduled a ceremony on Interior's Grand Staircase to award Lowri the Citation of Valor. The medal would wait until she was able to stand for photographs. Pennington needed the positive coverage after one of his officers had turned serial killer. He had already commissioned an external review of hiring practices that would conclude the screening process needed minor adjustments. The consultants would bill six hundred thousand for that wisdom.

It was, Saville reflected, a typical Washington conclusion. The guilty were dead or departed, the innocent were damaged, and the system had already closed ranks. Five bodies had produced a hundred hours of cable news coverage and zero lasting consequences.

Except for the feeling that gnawed at him during his hospital visits, watching Lowri struggle through physical therapy. Sprague hadn't operated alone. Someone had provided intelligence, funding, and, most importantly, protection. That someone remained free, probably watching the media coverage with satisfaction.

The case was closed. The conspiracy wasn't.

Chapter 43

The attending physician delivered the verdict bluntly: maximum medical improvement. It was insurance terminology for "this is as good as it gets." The electrical burns had healed as much as they would, and the nerve damage was permanent. Physical therapy would continue, but recovery had plateaued.

They discussed only the physical injuries. The psychological trauma wasn't their department.

Saville helped Lowri pack while she sat in the wheelchair, hospital policy until she crossed the threshold. The room had accumulated three weeks' worth of deliveries: flowers from the Park Police union, teddy bears from citizens who had seen the news coverage, and cards from strangers, including two marriage proposals that Lowri dropped unread into the trash. A maintenance supervisor led them through the loading dock to avoid the reporters still camped at the main entrance.

The drive took forty minutes in silence. Lowri kept her face turned toward the passenger window, her right hand occasionally rising to touch the scarring around her mouth. The plastic surgeon had done what he could. The keloid tissue where the picana's electrodes had made contact would fade from purple to white over time, but the contracture scars at the corners of her mouth were permanent. She would need to massage them daily to maintain flexibility.

The deeper damage was invisible: second-degree burns to her torso and thighs where Sprague had applied the picana for maximum pain without leaving obvious marks. Classic torture technique. The nerve damage caused constant burning sensations that gabapentin only partially controlled. The gynecologist had been professionally vague about long-term effects, but Saville had overheard enough to understand.

The gunshot wound was healing surprisingly well. Clean and through-and-through, with no major vessels involved. The orthopedic surgeon had repaired the rotator cuff and anticipated near-full range of motion within six months.

Lowri navigated the steps of her apartment using one crutch, her right arm still immobilized in a sling. She declined Saville's assistance until he reached for the door, at which point she allowed him to hold it open.

Saville made three trips to the car. When he returned with her discharge paperwork, she sat on the couch, studying a photograph of her father in his Welsh Guards dress uniform: a scarlet tunic and bearskin cap. It was taken at Windsor Castle in 1982 during ceremonial guard duty. She had heard the story a dozen times. Her father, twenty-four years old, fresh from the Rhondda Valley, still believing he would make the SAS selection course. This was years before America, before her mother, before everything that came after.

"Where should I put the flowers?" he asked. "And all these stuffed animals? You could stock a nursery."

She didn't respond immediately. Then her shoulders began to shake. Tears came quietly at first, then turned into gasping sobs. Saville sat beside her and drew her against his chest. She buried her face in his shoulder, trembling.

After a moment, she pulled back and looked at him, a shift occurring in her expression. She had noticed that involuntary flicker of his eyes toward her scars.

"I'm sorry," he said, reaching for the tissue box. "I didn't mean—"

"It's okay." She took a tissue and turned away. "You should go. I need to be alone."

"You have that appointment tomorrow morning with the psychiatrist who specializes in trauma recovery. I can pick you up at nine."

"I'm not going."

"Lowri—"

"Please. Just go."

Saville recognized her tone; she had made her decision. But leaving her alone felt like abandonment or, worse, enablement. The Park Police had placed her on indefinite medical leave with full pay, but they had secured her service weapon at the hospital. Standard protocol. Still, there were other ways for someone determined enough.

He wrote his new cell number on her notepad. "Call me. Any time, any reason."

"I won't need it."

He left it on the counter anyway. At the door, he looked back. She was still holding her father's photograph, studying it as if it might provide answers.

Outside, Saville sat in his car for five minutes, watching her window. The clinical term was survivor's guilt compounded by disfigurement trauma. The real term was a friend drowning while he watched from the shore.

He needed to hear a voice that could make sense of the senseless, even if that voice belonged to someone too young to understand. He called Jennifer's house, bracing for another battle over visitation rights and backed-up child support.

"Daddy?" Emma answered on the second ring, sparing him from negotiating with Jennifer. "Are you coming to see me this weekend?"

"I'll try, sweetheart."

"Mommy says you always say that."

The innocent accusation hit harder than he expected. He heard Jennifer's voice in the background, asking who was calling. Emma's response was muffled, her hand likely over the receiver. Then she was back, speaking quickly, aware her time was limited.

"I made a painting of a rainbow. Mrs. Peterson put a gold star on it."

"That's wonderful, Em."

"Mommy's coming."

"Okay, sweetheart. I love you."

"Love you too, Daddy."

He listened to Emma's hurried description of her art project, then the muffled sounds of the phone changing hands, followed by the click of disconnection. Jennifer hadn't even bothered with accusations this time.

He sat there holding the dead phone. He had failed to protect Lowri, and her scars felt like his responsibility. Every time she looked in a mirror for the rest of her life, she would remember the price of his mistakes.

He watched Lowri's window and wondered if he was failing everyone who depended on him

***

She heard his car pull away and immediately regretted sending him off. From the window, she watched his taillights disappear around the curve leading out of the complex.

She had been cruel, aware of it even as the words left her mouth. Maybe she had imagined that flicker in his eyes, that involuntary glance at her scars. Perhaps she simply needed someone to punish, and Saville was the only one who had stayed close enough to hurt.

He had visited her daily, except when the FBI had him downtown. Others came out of obligation, signing cards with pre-printed sentiments before disappearing back into their intact lives. But Saville kept returning. Part of it was guilt. He blamed himself for her injuries, just as she blamed herself for Joel's death. She recognized the weight he carried because she carried it too.

The truth was, she knew almost nothing about Special Agent Michael Saville. Their acquaintance had been measured in days, not years; crisis, not conversation. Yet she knew what mattered: he had walked into Sprague's kill zone to save her. He had been willing to die for someone he barely knew.

And what had he saved? She caught her reflection in the dark television screen. The scarring pulled at the corners of her mouth. Beneath her clothes, the electrical burns formed a road map of her torture. She would never work patrol again, never feel comfortable in her own skin, never be anything more than a curiosity behind a desk, processing paperwork while real cops did real police work.

She thought about Joel, trying to summon the exact angle of his jaw, the specific shade of his eyes. The details were already fading. She whispered an apology to his memory, knowing it changed nothing. The guilt would return tomorrow, and the next day, and every day after that, an endless loop of self-recrimination she wasn't sure she could endure.

The Ruger SP101 sat in her nightstand drawer where she had left it before the hospital. Five shots, .357 Magnum. She had bought it as a backup piece, liking how it fit her small hands. Now, she retrieved it and returned to the couch, setting it on the coffee table beside her father's photograph.

She studied his young face in the Welsh Guards uniform, then remembered what lay hidden behind it. She opened the frame and extracted the second photograph: Farnsworth, Sprague, and the torn section where a third person should be. What did it matter now? Sprague was dead. Farnsworth was dead. The case was closed.

She placed the photo beside her laptop, its screen dark in sleep mode. The gun waited within reach. One pull of the trigger would end the pain, the memories, and the future of stares and whispered comments. She imagined Joel waiting somewhere beyond, then realized that even in death, he wouldn't want her. Not anymore, not looking like this.

Her fingers found the laptop's spacebar instead of the gun.

The screen illuminated, revealing her Gmail inbox. Among spam and promotional emails sat a message from Ben Manning dated six days ago: "24th MEU – Muster Roll."

She opened it. "Lowri, sorry it took me so long to get back to you. Hearing from you brought back some really great memories. Your name's been all over the news. You're a true American hero. Anyway, here's the list you wanted. I wish things had turned out differently. Just so you know, you were my first too. Must go. Love, Ben."

She almost smiled. Ben Manning, trying to rewrite history. The star athlete, who had bedded half the cheerleading squad, claiming she had been his first. Sweet lie or casual cruelty, she couldn't tell. It didn't matter; he had his perfect military wife now, and she had her scars.

The attachment opened as a Word document with names in alphabetical order. She found Farnsworth, Victor, under F. Found Sprague, Peter, under S. Methodically, she worked through the rest, her eyes growing heavy, knowing this was pointless yet needing to finish something, anything, before making her final decision.

She reached the T section. The fifth name stopped her cold.

Tennyson, Margaret Claire.

The monogrammed stationery at Molly's house flashed in her memory. Molly Tennyson Farnsworth. Tennyson, like the poet. And Molly was a common nickname for Margaret.

Her pulse quickened. She stood too fast, sending a sharp pain through her injuries, and limped to the kitchen counter where Saville had left his number. Her fingers shook as she dialed. For the first time since Sprague had started his torture, she felt something beyond guilt and self-pity.

She felt purpose.

Chapter 44

Saville had just ordered his first Sierra Nevada at City Tap House in Penn Quarter when his phone rang.

He almost didn't answer. Only four people had this number: the Bureau, Lowri, Jennifer, and Jack Mayfield. Jennifer and Jack had likely gotten it by text, if they had even saved it. He answered anyway.

"I know who the third person in the picture is," Lowri said.

The change in her voice was immediate. The deadness from an hour ago had been replaced by something sharp and focused.

"How?"

She told him about Manning's email and the muster roll. "Margaret Claire Tennyson. Molly's maiden name was Tennyson. She served in the same unit."

"You're certain?"

"Molly's holding a press conference at three o'clock in the White House Press Room. We need to be there."

"We don't have credentials."

"We're heroes, remember? They'll let us in."

Saville wasn't convinced. In Washington, today's heroes often became tomorrow's scapegoats.

He checked his watch: 1:33 p.m. The bartender set down a beer Saville no longer wanted. He had come here to drink himself numb, to stop thinking about Lowri's scars and his own failures. That would have to wait.

He dropped a twenty on the bar.

"I'm on my way."

***

Getting onto the White House grounds proved simpler than Saville had expected. They presented their credentials at the Northwest Gate, where the Uniformed Division officer was already checking their names against a printed list.

"You're both cleared," he said. "Someone will escort you to the West Wing."

"Heroes," Lowri said quietly. "Told you."

A junior staffer led them through security to Amelia Sylvester's office, adjacent to the Brady Briefing Room. The press secretary looked exhausted, her foundation barely concealing the dark circles under her eyes.

"Sergeant Pritchard, Agent Saville." She managed a professional smile. "I was hoping you'd come. How are you feeling?"

"Better," Lowri replied. "We're just here to observe."

"Not to participate? The press corps would love to hear from you both. Especially you, Agent Saville. Your story, unfiltered."

"I'm on administrative leave," Saville said. "Bureau policy prohibits media contact."

Sylvester's disappointment was palpable. "They'll be devastated. But I understand. Let me find you a discreet place to watch."

She led them to a small executive conference room equipped with a closed-circuit monitor. Two White House staffers Saville didn't recognize occupied chairs at the far end, while a Secret Service agent stood by the door and another near the window.

The press conference began six minutes late. All forty-nine seats in the briefing room were filled, cameras ready.

Sylvester made a brief introduction before yielding the podium to Molly Farnsworth. The widow wore black Armani, and a carefully crafted expression of grief. The Associated Press had first question privileges, and Cecelia Leehan didn't waste the opportunity.

"Mrs. Farnsworth, my condolences on your loss." Leehan paused. "How do you respond to allegations that your husband was killed to cover up your affair with President Carney?"

Molly's composure cracked. "That's beneath a response."

Sylvester leaned toward the microphone. "Cecelia, please. Show some decency."

"The American people deserve answers about whether their president was involved in a murder conspiracy."

The briefing room erupted. Reporters shouted questions, and photographers jostled for position. Sylvester let it run for ninety seconds before abruptly ending the conference, met with protests from the press corps.

"Quite a show," Saville observed.

Lowri actually smiled. It was the first genuine expression he'd seen from her since the hospital.

On the monitor, Sylvester whispered something to Molly before guiding her toward the exit.

"She's leaving," Lowri said. "We should intercept her."

They moved toward the door, but the Secret Service agent raised his hand. He pressed his earpiece and listened.

"Wait here," he said. "Mrs. Farnsworth wants to speak with you privately."

"Even better," Lowri said.

"You have the photograph?" Saville asked.

She touched her jacket pocket.

Saville wondered how Molly Farnsworth would react when confronted with evidence that she'd known her husband's killer for thirty-four years. In his experience, widows who scheduled press conferences just days after their husbands' murders rarely grieved as they pretended.

***

They waited fifteen minutes in the Red Room. Saville studied the Empire furniture and gilded mirrors while Lowri sat perfectly still beside him on the silk couch, the photograph in her jacket pocket. Above them, Dolley Madison gazed down from her portrait with nineteenth-century disapproval.

Molly Farnsworth entered through the State Dining Room, looking as if she'd been battered by a hostile press corps. She paused to sign the guest book, a performance of normalcy that fooled no one.

"Sorry to keep you waiting." She settled into a chair upholstered in red damask. "These reporters have no decency." She extended her hand to Saville, then turned to Lowri. The pause was a beat too long. "Sergeant Pritchard and I have already met."

"We have," Lowri said. "Or should I address you by your service name? Lance Corporal Margaret Claire Tennyson. Twenty-fourth MEU."

Molly's expression didn't change. "My military service is public record. I'm proud of it."

"Are you also proud of your relationship with Peter Sprague?"

"That monster murdered my husband."

"You served together during Desert Storm. You knew each other."

Molly crossed her arms defensively. "The Twenty-fourth MEU had over two thousand personnel. I was in logistics. Sprague was an infantryman. Different units, different areas. It's absurd to suggest I knew everyone who served."

Lowri produced the photograph. Molly reached for it, but Lowri pulled it back. Saville watched the interplay, noting how Lowri's injuries hadn't diminished her interrogation instincts.

"I'm sorry about what happened to you," Molly said. "The trauma you've endured. Perhaps Agent Saville could call someone to help you."

"You lied to me." Lowri handed over the photograph.

Molly studied it. "That's my husband."

"And Peter Sprague."

"The investigation already established that they knew each other." Molly's eyes welled with convenient tears. "This proves nothing new."

Saville had watched dozens of suspects manufacture grief. Molly's performance ranked among the least convincing; the tears appeared on command, but the underlying anger was genuine.

"You're in the photo too," Lowri said, pointing to the torn edge. "Right there."

The tears evaporated. "That could be anyone. There's barely anything visible."

"Look again."

"What's visible looks nothing like me. Did you suffer a head injury along with everything else?"

"It doesn't look like you because you've had work done. The facelift you mentioned. Rhinoplasty. To make yourself more photogenic for Victor's political career."

Saville took the photograph and examined it closely. The partial face didn't match Molly's current features exactly, but accounting for surgical alterations, the bone structure was consistent.

"Sergeant Pritchard's right," he said.

"What is wrong with you people?" Molly's composure cracked. "I asked for privacy so I could thank you, and you ambush me with conspiracy theories. You're as bad as that bitch Cecelia Leehan."

Lowri didn't flinch. "Are you denying an affair with President Carney?"

"I don't have to listen to this."

"You already told me your husband was sleeping with the First Lady."

"If you want to chase conspiracies, why don't you walk down the hall and interrogate the President yourself? I have an interview, then a flight to New York."

"Morning show circuit," Lowri said. "Wouldn't want to miss that."

"I pity you, Sergeant. I understand you're starting psychiatric treatment for your disfigurement."

Saville stepped between them. Molly was precise in her aim. "You're out of line, Mrs. Farnsworth."

"I'm not having an affair with anyone, and I won't be harassed further."

"That wasn't the question," Lowri said. "The question is whether you conspired with Peter Sprague to kill your husband."

"This is insane." Molly turned to Saville. "Am I under arrest?"

"No. We're conducting a follow-up interview."

"Then I'm leaving."

"Don't you want to know if Sprague had accomplices?"

"Of course, there were others. The President, the First Lady, probably both. But no one will touch them. They're bulletproof in this town."

"You have evidence?" Saville asked.

"She has nothing because there is nothing."

The voice came from the doorway. Hellen Carney stood flanked by two Secret Service agents, her presence filling the room. Saville had seen her on television hundreds of times. In person, she was smaller but more formidable.

Molly grabbed her purse. "Perfect. This day couldn't possibly get worse." She moved toward the door. "I'm not staying in the same room as that woman."

A Secret Service agent blocked her path with a raised hand.

"No one's leaving yet," he said.

Saville and Lowri exchanged glances. The interview had just turned into something else entirely.

Chapter 45

Molly sank back into the red silk chair. Saville and Lowri returned to the Empire couch, while Hellen Carney stood in the doorway, her Secret Service detail flanking her.

"What's the matter, Hellen?" Molly's voice dripped with old grievances. "No married senators waiting in the Lincoln Bedroom?"

The First Lady crossed the room with deliberate steps, her heels clicking against the parquet floor. She stopped directly in front of Lowri and produced a crumpled piece of photographic paper from her jacket pocket.

"I believe this belongs to you, Sergeant Pritchard."

Lowri took the fragment and held it against the torn edge of her photograph. The edges matched perfectly. The missing third of the image revealed a younger Molly Farnsworth, her arm linked through Sprague's, her face turned toward him in obvious intimacy.

"There we are," Lowri said quietly, holding both pieces together for Molly to see.

The widow's composure faltered. "That proves nothing. A photograph from thirty years ago."

"Military file photos will confirm it's you," Lowri insisted. "Before the rhinoplasty. Before the chin work. The bone structure doesn't lie."

Saville watched as Molly reassessed her stance.

"Even if it is me, it means nothing. People serve together. People take pictures," she insisted.

"It establishes a prior relationship with Sprague," Saville said. "That's enough for a grand jury."

"I didn't kill my husband." Her voice rose in pitch.

"No," Lowri said. "You had Sprague do it."

"Classic Molly," Hellen said from across the room. "Always getting men to do your dirty work. Maybe they'll let you run a honey trap operation from federal prison."

Molly sprang from her chair once more. "You sanctimonious bitch!"

She lunged at Hellen, but Saville moved to intervene. The nearest Secret Service agent shouldered him aside and drew his SIG Sauer. His partner seized Molly's arms and forced them behind her back.

"It's a federal crime to threaten a protectee," the first agent stated, producing handcuffs. "Title 18, Section 879."

He read her the Miranda rights while his partner secured the restraints. Molly's resistance faded as she grasped the reality of her situation.

"This is just the beginning," Lowri warned. "Conspiracy to commit murder. Murder for hire. Interstate commerce violations. You're looking at life without parole."

Molly began to cry again, but Hellen didn't relent.

"You always hated that I had him, didn't you?" The First Lady's voice remained steady. "Woody chose me over you in high school, so you settled for Victor. Then you couldn't even keep him."

"You poisoned Woody against me!" Molly shouted, tears mixing with rage. "He was taking me to prom until you told him those lies about the football team."

"They weren't lies. Everyone knew what you did under the bleachers."

"I wasn't born rich like you. My looks were all I had." Her sobs grew more intense. "Why else would Woody Carney notice me? I did what I had to do. It was working until you decided you wanted him."

"Victor was the better man. He deserved more than you."

"He was weak." She stopped crying. "All he did was complain about Washington and being surrounded by vipers. He wanted to go back to North Carolina. He couldn't understand that I was finally living the life I'd always wanted."

"He sacrificed everything for you and the children."

"He was about to sacrifice ten million dollars, plus residuals. The SAINTS commission would have set us up for generations."

Saville understood. "But Victor discovered that the software was stolen from Ken Burton."

"He wasn't just going to walk away," Molly said. "He was going to expose the whole operation. I tried to get Bernard Clough to reason with him. When that failed, I asked Peter to intervene."

"You mean you ordered Sprague to kill him," Hellen said.

"No! Peter was only supposed to scare him, make him think the Israelis would come after our family if he didn't complete the sale. But Peter went too far. He wasn't supposed to..." She stopped.

"What about the Cloughs?" Saville pressed.

"Bernard knew about Peter and me. He became a liability. And his son Davy was trying to blackmail everyone. Ken Burton, Victor, even his own father. Davy didn't care who he destroyed for his story."

"So you had them both killed."

"Peter made those decisions on his own."

"But you didn't stop him."

Molly said nothing.

"Colonel Romano? Joel Graves?" Lowri's voice was steady, but Saville heard the undertone. "They were just in the way?"

"Collateral damage," Molly whispered.

Saville studied her face. The woman who had entered this room fifteen minutes ago, playing the grieving widow, had disappeared. This was the real Molly Farnsworth: someone who could reduce five murders to military terminology. Someone who had served her country in Desert Storm and then spent thirty years climbing Washington's social ladder, willing to destroy anyone who threatened her ascent.

The room went silent except for the faint hum of climate control. Saville could hear tourist voices from the floor below, oblivious to the confession occurring above them.

"Agent Rutledge," the first Secret Service agent said into his sleeve microphone. "Coming out with a prisoner. Clear the press from the North Portico. We'll exit through the underground garage to East Executive."

"Rutledge, Control," came the response through his earpiece, audible in the quiet room. "Press pool is refusing to disperse. Recommend an alternate route through South Lawn to Treasury tunnel."

"Copy that. Request additional units for escort."

The second agent was already texting someone, likely the U.S. Attorney's office, alerting them to prepare federal charges.

They led Molly toward the door, her designer heels catching on the antique carpet. At the threshold, she turned back to Hellen.

"You think you've won? Wait until the special counsel starts digging into your husband's connections to all this. Woody knew about the SAINTS program. He knew about Burton's defense contracts. He knew everything."

Hellen's expression didn't change. "The difference between us, Molly, is that I didn't murder anyone to protect my secrets."

The Secret Service agents pulled Molly through the doorway. Saville could hear her sobbing as they descended the stairs, the sound echoing through the marble corridors until it faded.

Lowri stood slowly, favoring her injured side. She held the reconstructed photograph up to the light, studying the three faces from 1991. Desert Storm veterans who had become something else entirely.

"She'll claim diminished capacity," Saville said. "Crime of passion. Temporary insanity."

"She'll lose," Lowri replied. "This was planned over months. Calculated. She turned Sprague into a weapon and pointed him at anyone who threatened her comfortable life."

Hellen Carney remained by the window, looking out at the Rose Garden where tourists pressed against the fence, phones raised for photographs.

"There's one thing Molly was right about," the First Lady said finally. "This isn't over. There are more secrets buried in this administration than anyone wants to admit."

She turned to face them. "But that's tomorrow's problem. Today, you got justice for five good men."

Saville wasn't so sure. In Washington, you could cut out the visible cancer, but the disease always went deeper. Molly would take the fall while the real architects of SAINTS remained untouchable, protected by classification stamps and executive privilege.

But Lowri was already moving toward the door, the photograph still in her hand. She'd gotten her answers. For now, that would have to be enough.

Chapter 46

The late afternoon traffic on Constitution Avenue barely moved. Saville didn't mind. After the chaos of the last three weeks, sitting in gridlock felt almost peaceful. Beside him, Lowri held the reconstructed photograph in her lap, occasionally tilting it toward the window to catch the light.

"Burton walks away clean," she said, breaking the silence that had settled between them since leaving the White House. "Twenty-five million from his lawsuit, his company intact, and no charges."

"He was a victim," Saville said, though the word tasted wrong. "Technically."

"Technically." Lowri traced the torn edge where the pieces joined. "He knew what Victor was selling. Had to know it was his own stolen code."

"Knowing and proving are different animals in this town."

They inched past the National Archives. A tour group clustered on the steps, their guide pointing at the inscription carved into the base of the Heritage statue: "THE HERITAGE OF THE PAST IS THE SEED THAT BRINGS FORTH THE HARVEST OF THE FUTURE." Saville wondered what harvest would grow from the seeds they had planted today.

"What about Hellen?" Lowri asked. "She had that photograph piece. She knew about Molly and Sprague's connection all along."

"Maybe she found it in Victor's things after he died. Maybe she's been holding it as insurance." Saville changed lanes, earning a horn blast from a taxi. "Or maybe she's been orchestrating everything from the beginning."

"The grieving widow act was convincing."

"They all gave compelling performances. It's Washington. Everyone's performing all the time."

Lowri shifted in her seat, favoring her injured shoulder. The movement was less pronounced than it had been yesterday. She was healing, physically at least. The electrical burns would scar, but the human body was remarkably resilient.

"The President knew," she said. "About SAINTS, about Burton's contracts, about all of it. Molly said so."

"Molly said a lot of things. Some might even be true."

"You think we got the right person?"

Saville considered the question. "We got a person. Whether she's the only guilty party or just the one stupid enough to get caught..." He shrugged. "Above my pay grade."

"Someone's protecting someone else. They always do in this city."

"Always," he agreed.

They passed the Smithsonian, its red sandstone glowing in the afternoon sun. Saville had brought Emma here last year during his summer visitation. She had loved the butterfly pavilion, laughing as the insects landed on her outstretched hands. Simple joy. He wondered when he would see her again.

He glanced at Lowri, studying her profile as she watched the city pass by. The protective instinct he felt surprised him sometimes. He had never had siblings, but he imagined this was what it felt like to have a younger sister. Someone whose battles became your battles, whose pain you would take on yourself if you could.

"You did good work," he said. "The photograph, the muster roll, putting it together. Most people would have given up after what Sprague did to you."

"Most people didn't get Joel killed."

"That wasn't—"

"I know." She turned the photograph over, reading the faded inscription again. "But knowing and feeling are different animals too."

Saville recognized the deflection. He had used it enough himself. "You're tougher than you think. Always have been."

"My father used to say that. Said the Welsh were too stubborn to know when they were beaten."

"Smart man."

"He was." She smiled slightly, the scars pulling at the corner of her mouth. She didn't try to hide it. "Would have liked you, I think. Appreciated straight talkers."

Saville made a right turn onto 10th Street, heading north instead of south toward her apartment. Lowri noticed but didn't question it.

"Thing is," Saville said, "being tough isn't just about taking hits. It's about getting back up. Moving forward. Finding the next thing."

"Very philosophical, Agent Saville."

"I have my moments."

They drove past Ford's Theatre, where another conspiracy had played out over a century ago. Different players, same city, same game. Power, money, secrets, and the bodies they produced. Lincoln had gotten a monument. Romano and Graves wouldn't even get a plaque.

"Where are we going?" Lowri finally asked as they approached Pennsylvania Avenue.

"One quick stop. It won't take long."

The Hoover Building loomed ahead, brutalist and uncompromising. Saville had always hated the architecture, but today it looked almost welcoming. He pulled into the underground parking garage, showing his credentials to the guard, who waved them through despite his suspended status.

"Why are we here?"

Saville parked in a visitor space and turned off the engine. "Remember that application you submitted to the Bureau? Before all this started?"

"The BSU position. I never heard back. Figured that was their way of saying no."

"They've been holding off on it. Sometimes they do that with promising candidates, waiting to see how things unfold. But tracking down a serial killer and unraveling a multi-agency conspiracy definitely counts as progress." He pulled an envelope from his jacket pocket. "Conditional offer of employment. GS-12 to start. Behavioral Science Unit, Quantico. It's pending medical clearance and completion of onboarding."

Lowri stared at the envelope without reaching for it. "I can't. Just look at me."

"I am looking at you. I see someone who survived torture and kept fighting. Someone who uncovered a conspiracy that reached all the way to the White House."

"All I see are scars."

"The Bureau doesn't care about scars. Half the agents at Quantico have them, inside or out, sometimes both." He placed the envelope in her hands. "You have the instincts. You proved that. The BSU needs people who understand darkness because they've faced it."

"Saville—"

"Mike. We've been through enough to use first names."

"Mike." She held the envelope as if it might disappear. "Did you pull strings to make this happen?"

"I made a recommendation and highlighted your work on the case. Director Shaffer made the final decision. He values agents who deliver results, even if they bend a few rules."

"What about you? Are you still suspended?"

"Probably. But they'll need someone to testify at Molly's trial, and then there's the special counsel investigation that's sure to follow. I'll be kept busy."

Lowri opened the envelope and skimmed the offer letter. "When would I start?"

"As soon as you're medically cleared. Maybe in a month or two. The paperwork can begin today if you're interested."

She folded the letter carefully and looked directly at him. The garage lights illuminated her eyes, and for a moment, he saw the detective she had been before Sprague, the one she could become again.

"You feel guilty," she said. "You couldn't protect me from Sprague, so now you're trying to make it right with a job."

"Maybe. Or maybe I just recognize talent when I see it. The Bureau needs good people, and you're one of them, Lowri. Scars and all."

She was silent for a long moment. Outside, car engines echoed, and the distant sound of a siren reminded them of the city's relentless pace.

"Will they really not care about how I look?"

"You'll be analyzing crime scenes, not walking a runway. Besides, the BSU is full of quirky characters. You'll fit right in."

That earned him a genuine laugh, the first he'd heard from her since before the boat incident.

"Alright," she said. "Let's go do some paperwork."

They climbed out of the car and walked toward the elevator. Lowri moved with newfound confidence, her shoulders straighter and her stride longer. Not healed, not yet, but heading in the right direction.

"Mike," she said as they waited for the elevator. "Who do you think really ran SAINTS? Who's walking away free?"

"Probably someone we haven't even identified yet. Someone with clearance and connections, capable of making evidence disappear. This city is full of them."

"Will we ever find out?"

The elevator arrived with a soft chime. As they stepped inside, Saville contemplated the secrets hidden within Washington's marble halls, the conspiracies that would never be revealed, and the guilty parties who would die peacefully in their beds.

"Probably not," he said as the doors closed. "But that's tomorrow's problem. Today, we caught one of them. And you have a new beginning."

The elevator ascended to the fifth floor, toward Human Resources, forms, and the start of whatever lay ahead. Outside, Washington continued its age-old dance of power and deception. But inside this rising metal box, for just a moment, two damaged individuals who had found justice where they could were moving forward.

The sister he never had was going to be okay. That realization eased something in his chest he hadn't known was twisted.

This time, it would be enough.

Praise for the Novels Of Keith M. Spence

"A frenetic and engaging page-turner with an edgy protagonist." —*Kirkus Reviews*

"This action-packed thriller contains all the elements necessary to carry this genre, and Spence hit it right on the head." —*Jeff Pate, bestselling author of Winner Take All & Eye of the Beholder*

" A gripping story without a moment of marking time. Well researched, entertaining and absolutely consuming. Written in the legacy of that master of suspense Alistair MacLean; Keith Spence has inherited the magic." —*Alex Honeywell, Magicquill.com*

"Powered by a cat-and-mouse game of pursuit, attack, and ultimatums that change not just politics, but individual lives." —*Midwest Book Review*

About the author

Keith M. Spence is a business owner, freelance writer, and former legal investigator who brings an unusual blend of real-world grit to his mystery and thriller fiction. An English-Writing major turned auto repair shop owner, Keith draws on his investigative background and mechanical problem-solving skills to craft tightly plotted narratives that keep readers guessing. Inspired by the works of Alistair MacLean and Adam Hall, Keith writes because he loves it, even when his own characters refuse to cooperate. He lives in eastern North Carolina with his family, his cat Callie, and an ever-growing stack of books beside his favorite chair.

www.keithmspence.com

Also by Keith M. Spence

DEVIL'S BREW

AFTERSHOCK

THE BLACKEST DARKNESS (Coming 2027)